Blàs

of the Highlands

C. C. Hutton

Blàths is an imprint of

Dedication

To the best storyteller I know, my mum, Cathy Rossiter.

Foreword

Blàs is set in the spectacular Highlands of Scotland. There are many references to real places such as Inverness and Bonar Bridge, however, this book is a work of fiction. Both Blàs and Inbhirasgaidh are fictional as are all the characters. A crofters' fashion show did actually take place in Bonar Bridge. My thanks to all the committee – you inspired the one in Blàs.

It is impossible to live and work in the Highlands and not be inspired in one way or another. I travelled and worked within the Gaelic sector so naturally drew my inspiration from this world. Although the characters and organisations contained within these pages are all purely fictional, there are many real Scottish Gaelic organisations online that can help to further your knowledge if you are interested in the Gaelic culture and language.

The Screen Machine does exist but is not nearly so cumbersome as my imagination allowed it. Although when you see it on our narrow, wee roads, it certainly feels more like my imagined one.

There are a few other references to Scottish life and celebrations. Guisers are mentioned. The major difference between them and the trick-or-treaters in the USA is that guisers are expected to do something positive for any treats. The treat is payment for the song, story, joke or poem that they perform at the house they visit.

Chapter 1

Auntie Lottie was following in the footsteps of many a highlander. She was returning home. Her longing for the place of her birth had started not long after her fiftieth birthday. Not that she had really noticed it at first. Gradually, however, the short visits north had extended into weeks. Now, two years later, holidays were no longer enough. There was nothing else she could do. It was linked into her DNA, as true as a midge feeds on the blood.

She found herself swimming against the teenager exodus that infected our community. Bright lights and thriving cities pulled our young away. She herself had followed that same path in her younger days. Only, Auntie Lottie had carried on wandering the globe on foot, on motorbike and in old camper vans. All had been discarded, along with her numerous lovers, when she finally settled for city life.

Now she was ready to move again, and Blàs could celebrate the homecoming of one of its own, although not quite yet. There was one more important task to be carried out before her permanent return. This visit was more of an inspection trip. She was still wedded to her childhood church which had long since closed, a casualty of the growing decline in our population. Auntie Lottie needed to fill this gap in her life. She was here to judge which place of worship would best fit her expectations.

"You have to take her to the Sunday services. I can't. None of these damn ministers or priests have forgiven me yet. Though how they thought I could have persuaded Old Tam to have his cousin's funeral in one of their churches is beyond me. They know what he's like, a law unto himself, so he is." Ellen had been mum's best friend. This gave her that invisible power anyone attached to my parents had. "Lottie wants to try them out before she comes back. See which church feels right to her. She wants to know where she will be going on her first Sunday back. Don't worry, they won't convert you if that's what you're so fidgety about, just stay strong."

"And just how is Auntie Lottie going to mark these churches? I can just see her, 'the congregation with the best taste in hats wins my devotion'."

"Stroma, don't be facetious. She's a law unto herself as you very well know. Now, that's settled. Your parents wouldn't expect anything less."

There it was again, the ancestry wielded like a weapon. Arrow straight to the heart, Ellen knew it worked every time. The thing was, with my parents dying young, the community then sort of adopted me and my sister Iona. We weren't related to Ellen or any other member of the district nor, for that matter, was Auntie Lottie. We had no one else, so everyone seemed to think we somehow belonged to them. This allowed certain members of the neighbourhood to emotionally blackmail us in much the same way DNA-related relatives are prone to do. The thing was, I let them. Iona, my younger sister, on the other hand, had seen the writing on the wall and had skedaddled as soon as the education system and I allowed.

Ellen was the closest thing to a parent we had. She, mum, and Auntie Lottie had all gone through school together. Ellen was from a family whose blood and souls had been part of Blàs as far back as records went. She was still related to most of the inhabitants in some form. Auntie Lottie, on the other hand, like ourselves, had been born in the village but had no living relatives left in Blàs. All our generation referred to her as Auntie Lottie and none ever questioned it. Consequently, she commanded the respect and devotion given to any other blood relative of that age.

That was why I found myself once more in a church with Auntie Lottie squashed up against me on the pew. Her first pick on her quest to find the best Sunday service was underway. For some bizarre reason, it was not as cold as I have found it on many a wedding day, but then, on this occasion, I was dressed for a cold church, warm hat included. The volume of people helped too, generating their own self-powered, green energy to warm the place. I felt their body heat raising the temperature. The number of locals was quite respectable for early on a Sunday morning or, as some would consider it, early on the day after the night before. There was no church organ puffing its music out for the singers, nothing bar the voices of the congregation. Some would have considered this pure. Personally, I found it all a bit Wild West. Then again, ultimately, it was Auntie Lottie who was there to judge the style of worship not me.

The minister was presenting his sermon like an actor in a play. Children were mentioned, pulling them and their families into the story. He was a good orator. I felt sure that Auntie Lottie would mark this church high. After the preaching was finished, to add the icing on the cake, or biscuit in this case, coffee and tea were served, together with a dash of friendship and sip of warm hospitality.

"Stroma, hello, how lovely to see you. Your neighbours are just over there; I must get them to come and speak with you. It is so good to see you here." Our local doctor was genuinely happy and enthusiastic in his welcome. In fact, everyone appeared friendly and pleased to see us, or more precisely me. The minister came over to ask how we had enjoyed his sermon.

"Well," said Auntie Lottie, "you never said the Lord's Prayer. Why was that? Don't your sect believe in it?" I expected a thunderbolt to descend from the sky right about then.

"It's just my choice not to use it in my address. Nothing we as a church have decided. I could use it in my ministration, if I felt the need." The word church was emphasised to good effect I thought. "And what of yourself, Stroma? How did you find the service? We haven't seen you here before."

"I'm just the taxi driver today. Auntie Lottie is investigating which place of worship feels right for her. I mean, you are all very active in the parish, so I thought she should give you a try." Ellen had said to stay strong. She had been right; I was already starting to spout words that were not normally part of my everyday vocabulary. Seriously, I would need to try harder when visiting the other houses of prayer. Oh, for goodness sake, I was even starting to think in more biblical terms. Time I left before I started quoting from the Bible.

The minister had already summarily dismissed me with a nod of the head, and his immediate attention had switched back to the sinner who may well have been ready to repent and return to the true calling. But Auntie Lottie had got back into her stride again.

"And music. You don't just use the human voice all the time, do you? I couldn't see any musical instruments in your church?"

At least she had stopped calling them a sect. I moved away to speak to others in the community who it must be said looked a bit down-hearted when they realised I had not suddenly found a god that I didn't think I had lost in the first place. My neighbours were quite resigned to the fact that I had not found a calling and now greeted me with sad smiles.

"There will always be hope for you. We will continue to pray for your soul."

I smiled my thanks and went back to retrieve Auntie Lottie who was still engaged in a discussion that I could clearly see the minister was trying to get away from without much success.

As we left, Auntie Lottie said, "Thank you for bringing me along. I just can't understand how you can go into the Lord's house and not believe. How you can sit through a service and feel nothing?"

"Oh, I've often felt something during a sermon but, nothing that would lead me to believe in a god."

"Really, Stroma. He's not *a* god, He *is* God. Who's the next lot we are visiting then?"

I found out later that this was the congregation she found most friendly. But it was not to be for them. She chose the church that most closely resembled her old familiar place of worship. This, even though it was without a minister at that time and nobody had spoken to her at all when she went there. She didn't like the service the visiting minister had given, nor the hymns they had sung. It was very cold inside, she reported, and their members did not do much within the district outwith their own Sunday service. She also felt it was a little lacking in spiritual atmosphere. They did, however, she felt, have a nice arrangement of flowers, some lovely stained-glass windows, and of course, they housed the local parish organ. Whatever scorecard she was keeping, I couldn't fathom nor understand how they had come out on top. The first church we went to, I believe, was quite thankful that they had lost this one particular soul to their nearest rivals.

Now that her choice had been made, Auntie Lottie was much relieved. She left for the city with a big smile on her face, to continue packing for her return to Blàs.

Chapter 2

"Stroma, you're the only one who works from home; you've got the time."

Ellen, like many others, lived under the misapprehension that because I could be flexible with my working hours, it meant:

A) I either didn't actually work a proper job, or

B) I could just take four days off without any warning.

Okay, I admit, this did occasionally happen. But like many other organisations who offered time off for additional hours worked, GLADS (Gaelic and Language Development Schemes) expected development officers, like myself, to put in some of these hours unpaid. Even taking that into account, GLADS still owed me weeks of time off. The problem for me was I worked with volunteer committees who ran all sorts of events and courses that helped people reconnect with their Gaelic culture. I oversaw their work and helped manage the committees who, in turn, developed and ran their own local events. Together, we applied for grants and employed tutors and all sorts of other things their local areas wanted. But here was the rub – I got a wage; they didn't.

My boss argued the committees, communities and parents all got paid in kind with access to playgroups, courses, ceilidhs and community events that resulted directly from my work. Still, I felt obligated to work much more that the few extra hours expected and rarely took the time back as days off.

Here though was a chance to claw back some of that time and help Ellen out. Besides, it was easier than trying to persuade Ellen to ask someone else. Her mind was made up – I was to be the 'chosen one'. The honour of returning Auntie Lottie to the bosom of our community was being bestowed upon me. Whether I wanted it or not.

"Come on, Stroma, she has no blood relatives; we are the nearest to family she has. Besides, you did help her to find a suitable church. Here, I'll make you another tea." Ellen turned away while continuing to press home her point. "Mary and I have agreed to keep an eye on the workmen. We need to be sure her cottage is at least habitable for her return. Please, Stroma, it would help us so much." Ellen was looking a bit uneasy as she placed the mug in front of me again. Maybe organising Auntie Lottie's builders and move was becoming a bit much, even for her.

Ellen was the most capable person I knew. The first person most people thought of if the community needed movement on anything. It was Ellen leading again that had started and progressed the new hall project. But even Ellen must have her limits.

Perhaps, I wouldn't have misread why Ellen was so unsettled if I hadn't been so preoccupied with what she had just said. How had my helping Auntie Lottie, at Ellen's persistence, I might add, somehow made me responsible for bringing Auntie Lottie home? Ellen had missed her true vocation; she should have been a politician with her ability to manipulate and manoeuvre situations to her advantage.

Still, Auntie Lottie was relocating back to Blàs, and she needed help to do that. She had suffered bouts of flu, colds and sick bugs throughout the winter with no running off to warmer climates as in previous years. In fact, her fevered urgency to return home had almost become an illness in itself. Although well on the road to recovery, she was still very fragile and in need of someone to help relocate her and her eclectic belongings back to Blàs.

Now that the church worthy of her devotion had been selected, she was desperate to complete her transition north. The move was scheduled to take four days, accounting for the journey time. Much of Auntie Lottie's rented bungalow had been packed away already, so I was just going down to finish off and drive her back up.

Iona and I had often stayed with her for long weekends. Holidays in the big city had been full of fun, bright lights, meals out, visits to museums, play parks and pubs depending on the age we were at the time. Her home there would always hold a special place in our hearts. It was going to be sad not to see it again after the move. Unexpectedly and much to Iona's and my surprise, her bungalow, as it turned out, was not her home, just her dwelling-place. Her home was actually a rather dilapidated hovel in the village that now needed total renovation before anyone could live in it. Even wildlife would have found it difficult to find a warm, dry, sheltered spot.

Once the decision had been taken that Auntie Lottie was definitely returning to the village, an architect, roofers, joiners, electricians and plumbers had all been employed to recreate, remodel and regenerate what was left of the house into a modern, energy-efficient dwelling. The cottage was rising from the ruins, a monument to modern man's latest technology and building skills. I for one couldn't wait to see what it would look like with Auntie Lottie's eclectic furniture installed.

*

I arrived tired and happy to see her in her soon-to-be abandoned house. I failed to notice the early warning signs at first. There was hardly a box to be seen anywhere. I should have taken my cue from that. Where were the bubble-wrapped pictures and mirrors? Why was nothing in boxes?

"So, this move, are the removers going to be packing everything then?"

"Ach, no. I've got to do that. All they are doing is lifting the whole lot into their van."

"So, have you emptied the freezer and food cupboards at least?"

"Don't be fussing now, Stroma. I gave all the frozen food to old Mr Smith round the corner. I know he could use the extra. I didn't want to put anything else away in case we needed that for lunch or tea." It would have taken a very large town, perhaps even a city to have eaten their way through the contents of her cupboards.

"Surely, we don't need to leave out all these plates? We only need a couple of bowls, cups and cutlery to last us till Thursday."

"Ach, it will save on the washing up. I'm tired; do you mind if I just take a wee seat?" And there started four days of hard negotiations between what we could pack and what could be thrown out. By the third day, I had successfully disposed of most of the tinned and opened food. Anything that was visibly green or even slightly green automatically went in the rubbish without any sort of consultation, as did everything out of date. This meant that at least three quarters of the food cupboard was now away. The oldest tin was historic, years past its sell-by date.

The worst thing to endure, though, was the time spent in the living room. I was subjected to black-and-white cowboy films, soaps and old detective series booming out from the telly

9

as loudly as any rock music would from a teenager's room. There was no escape from this deluge of noise. I took to chanting inside my head in an attempt to block out the noise. "One more day, just one more day, hold fast, tomorrow is moving day, one more day." That was until the phone call.

"The sparky has fallen through the roof and broken his leg." And ... what does that mean? "So the cottage is not quite finished. Lottie can't stay there. The heating isn't finished, and the plumber can't finish until the sparky finishes and neither can the joiner." The poor joiner was just thrown in at the end like an afterthought.

"What about the decorator?" As the words left my mouth, I realised how stupid this was, but my mind had gone a little blank. "Never mind that. There can't be much left to do if it just happened today, surely." There was a slight pause.

"It happened two weeks ago, but you've been away on that course. We didn't want to worry you before you left. We were hoping something might have been sorted, but we can't find anyone else to carry on the work. Everyone is so busy."

There was no point in getting angry. This exasperating behaviour from them was totally normal and losing my temper would only result in me eventually feeling bad and apologising, this despite the fact they were in the wrong. Even so, I couldn't stop the sigh as I asked, "I take it we can drop off her stuff still tomorrow though?"

"Well, actually, obviously the carpets aren't down, and the work isn't finished, so there's no space to put anything. We have booked storage in Inverness though, so if you can pack some boxes of stuff she might need until the cottage is ready and take them with you, that would be grand. The rest can go into storage. Be careful how you present this to Lottie; I know she is still weak from being so ill."

Great, how to explain to a fragile lady she wouldn't be going home, and come to that, where *would* she be going? All her lovely possessions, the ones that I had so carefully packed, would not be coming with her right now. They would languish in some storage unit miles from her home. In the end, she took the whole thing better than I expected. She was emotional and rather tearful to begin with, but Auntie Lottie handled it like a trooper. That was until she started to talk about what she couldn't take with her and what she would have to put into storage. The longer the list of items going into storage grew, the shorter and faster her breathing became. She was sounding like a stream train.

"You'll be alright, nobody would see you without a roof over your head, and besides, it won't be for long. Might be fun to share and camp over at someone's, for a time. They can look after you until you are properly on your feet."

"You're right. Of course you're right. It will be fine. I'm still going home to Blàs; I'm still going home."

I could see she clearly didn't feel it would be fine. My heart went out to her. She wasn't used to sharing. Brief holidays when villagers came to stay was not like real sharing on a daily basis. This was just a tiny setback though; the move was still on.

The phone continued to ring off and on all day as city friends wished her well and good luck. I knew if this had been our village, everyone and their aunt would have followed this up with a quick 'pop-in just to say cheerio'. These 'pop-ins' could last a good few hours which was the last thing any mover wanted on what was probably their busiest day. Thankfully, in the city this was not going to happen. That was until Edie from next door just 'popped in to say goodbye'.

Three hours later, she was still there. The available subjects for discussion surely should have run out. Reversing, that's what they were talking about, reversing and how many times they had gone into a wall or a car. *Please, please just go*

HOME. There was so much I still needed to re-pack, accounting for Auntie Lottie's new circumstances. I couldn't keep breaking into what appeared to be important conversations to ask box, bin or pack for home? Unfortunately, there was not enough heading toward the bin.

Eventually, Edie left, leaving us re-organising and re-packing well into the night. Tired and exhausted, we finally found time for bed. Just as my eyes had closed, moving day dawned bright, sunny and bizarrely warm for January. By breakfast, my car was full to capacity with everything Auntie Lottie wanted to take with her for a few weeks. She assured me there was nothing left to fit in. Plants were carefully pressed up to the front seats. They had the most space of all. Through the jungle of leaves, I watched a white van screech to a halt outside the house, reverse and speed away. I had thought for a dreadful minute that it was the removal van. It would have been way too small to hold everything that lay within Auntie Lottie's bungalow. I watched as Auntie Lottie brought yet another unplanned-for, last-minute addition to the already heaving rainforest that used to be my car.

"That was the removal firm on the phone. Have you seen their van?"

Not the white van, please, I thought. That's all we needed. One of those notorious delivery drivers who screeches around recklessly, not caring what state their vans are in or how they drive, driving like the devil himself is after them. 'Get out of my way; I'm coming through' their mantra. They honk, hoot and claim the roads as if they are their own. I should have shouted my plea, maybe then some celestial entity might have heard me and intervened. Around the corner, at top speed, returned the van from earlier. This was the so-called removal van. Out jumped the jovial driver, lit fag hanging out of his smiling mouth. His silent and brooding sidekick slunk along behind him, hidden under his hoodie.

"Morning, lovely ladies, nice morning for a move, eh."

"I'll just put the kettle on; we didn't pack it yet. When does your bigger van arrive?" Auntie Lottie headed back into the house.

Luckily, she didn't notice the blank look from the removal man as he turned to me.

"We'll just get started thanks. We had a cuppa on the way down. Why does she think we have another van?"

"Maybe because there is no way you are going to get everything in that one," I said.

"Ach, you'd be surprised how much I can get in my van," was the reply. Yes, it was man with a van, packed full of his own self-confidence and little else besides. The lorry I had been led to expect by both Ellen and Mary, who had arranged it all, was not coming.

The van was barely big enough to carry the contents of a one-bedroom flat, let alone a large two-bedroom bungalow. Added to this was the fact that Auntie Lottie's house was not your normal two-bedroom affair. Oh no, it came complete with conservatory, large attic, larger garage, garden shed and, of course, green house. All originally filled to the brim with contents from Aunt Lottie's travels and other paraphernalia. Everything was supposed to fit in that white, rust-covered transit.

"Well, you're coming with me to tell her that you'll fit everything in."

Auntie Lottie listened to what he said but no amount of persuasion was going to work. Spatial awareness is not one of my many talents, but even I could see there was no way, despite what he said, that the much-loved contents of Auntie Lottie's home would fit into what was basically one step up from a people carrier. The shaking and breathlessness from before was returning at top speed. Even Joe, as his name turned out to be, was sending me worried looks as he watched Auntie Lottie descend into despair with tear-filled eyes. However, his confidence quickly reasserted itself. Obviously a practised hand – this must have happened to him many times.

"Come and sit you down, lass. We'll soon get started and pack all this stuff away. So, what is actually going?

"Everything," we both chirped together.

"Right, then, are you sure it is everything here?"

"Yes, and the garage stuff, garden tools, and summer-house furniture." Auntie Lottie gasped through her snatched breathing.

Fifteen minutes later, and they were back "You ever seen that TV programme about hoarders?" I could tell this was not going to end well. "You're a bit of one yourself right enough." And here came the punchline. "I don't think we are going to fit everything in, missus. We'll need another trip. Can't do it in the morning, other commitments, but could maybe fit you in in the afternoon."

"Ooh." Poor Auntie Lottie could hardly speak and was straining hard to breathe. "The keys have to be back by lunchtime. The other people are coming in then."

"So," I intervened, "that's not going to happen. You have to come back in the morning. Shift your other work; this job is not finished." My temper was rising as fast and hard as Auntie Lottie was sinking.

"Just let me make a few phone calls, and I'll see what I can do." Off he disappeared with his mate like a silent shadow two paces behind.

"What am I going to do? I need to get out of here."

"Not to worry. If we can get him to come down in the morning, the cleaner will still have time to do her bit. We'll get the remover to give her the key to hand back. We're leaving today."

Auntie Lottie had to get out of there, living surrounded by boxes and crates was not the best remedy for someone recuperating from continual bouts of flu and chest infections. I also had to return home as e-mails and phone calls from work would have been mounting up since I'd left. No time to dwell on that – I had to focus on getting Auntie Lottie home to Blàs as quickly as possible.

Despite my reservations, it was agreed that Joe would return the next day. After dropping off Auntie Lottie's things at the storage unit, he would meet us at Ellen's to pick up the key. He would head south again the next morning to collect her remaining furniture. Surely, even he could manage that without too much difficulty.

I decided to play safe and walked him around the area again and pointed out everything that would still have to come. "And don't forget the magnolia tree in this pot. She would be really upset if she lost that."

Finally, we set off, stopping a short distance up the road to get some lunch. It was a long road home. Traffic lights and roadworks slowed us down even more as we steadily headed north.

"I don't feel well. You'll need to stop." Auntie Lottie was turning a horrible shade of green. We managed to pull over and open the door to let more fresh air in.

"I've eaten something that doesn't like me." She ran over to a bush. I phoned Ellen after twenty minutes.

"We've still got the key to Auntie Lottie's house. Joe, the removal man, is expecting to pick it up from your house tonight. He'll need it to unlock her house again, so he can pick up the rest of the stuff. We thought we'd be at yours ages before him. Only Auntie Lottie is behind a bush being sick again." I just hoped that's all she was doing. "Phone Joe, tell him he will need to swing by in the morning for the key. As early as he wants; it doesn't matter, but I can't say when we will be back tonight." We kangarooed up the road, stopping and starting where we could and probably in some places we shouldn't have.

Mobile signal had returned for just long enough for Ellen to get in touch.

"The remover phoned from Inverness."

"Okay. When will he pick up the key in the morning?"

"You don't understand. The remover is stuck in Inverness. They say no storage unit has been booked. What can I do?"

Well, probably more than me. I was stuck in a car with a sick passenger and a fluctuating mobile signal.

"Well, you booked the storage. Phone them and find out what's going on. Then phone back the remover. He has to empty the van so he can go down again in the morning." As the phone call was piped through the car Auntie Lottie began to moan. Her breathing again became rapid. "I'm going to be sick again."

"Can you remember where I put the storage firm's number? What do we do if they say we can't have the storage?" Ellen sounded distracted. Where was the normally cool, organised person I was used to dealing with?

"What! Just find the number I'm—" Thankfully the phone cut out, or I don't know what I would have said, and a very old friendship could well have hit the dust.

Drumnadrochit loomed. After negotiating around a tourist who pulled straight onto the road from the castle, we made it safely into the car park in the middle of the village.

Sitting quietly for a few seconds afforded me the chance to consider our options and who might be able to help. Who would have the space to take Auntie Lottie's things? There was really only one name that came to mind – Paul of the Sheds. Where other people may well have owned old, new or used cars, Paul owned old, new and various sizes of sheds. He was bound to have some space in one of them for an emergency such as this. I felt sure, if we explained, he would be willing to help.

My phone still didn't have a signal. Auntie Lottie was dozing in the passenger seat, so I jumped out of the car and dashed to the phone box which promptly ate my first £1 coin.

"Ellen, try Paul of the Sheds; he may let you put Auntie Lottie's stuff in one of them. I'm running out of money. If you can't sort out the storage, try him." Click and the phone cut out. Back at the car, my passenger had gone walkabout.

For the love of God, where was she? Auntie Lottie was in no fit state to be out on her own. I was surprised she even managed to get out of the car. I hurried into the nearest shop.

"Have you seen—?"

"What were you thinking leaving her alone in your car when this lady is obviously ill? She shouldn't be out on her own." Auntie Lottie was sitting in a chair drinking some water out of a bottle.

"Well, I was just—"

"We bought her a bottle of water and packet of biscuits. You really should take better care of her." I looked over at Auntie Lottie; she did look dreadful.

"We can sort this all out, Auntie Lottie. Don't worry. Just let me know when you are able to come back to the car."

We stayed about ten minutes while customers and staff fussed over her, and I received rather stern looks. I didn't care by then; the need to get her home to bed and no longer my responsibility had become paramount.

"I've taken my anti-sickness tablets now." *What?* My mind screamed in disbelief. She had anti-sickness tablets, and she hadn't taken them? Why had she waited until most of the journey had passed? Worse, why had she not taken one before we started? *Don't say it out loud, don't say it, just breathe, breathe, breathe,* my mind screamed.

The roads we travelled after Drum were safely within my comfort zone. Normally, I would have dodged the traffic and towns by nipping over the familiar minor tracks in the area. It was not to be for that journey though; sightseers had obviously heard these roads existed. German tourist buses littered the route, crawling along at thirty miles an hour around narrow lanes with double bends not designed for vehicles like theirs.

I found myself dreaming of what I would do to whoever had come up with the notion of marketing our Highland roads in line with the USA classic Route 66. Our North Coast 500 is 500 miles of breathtaking beauty skimming around the northern tip of the Highlands. Almost overnight, we had turned into a must-do holiday destination. My route home was now cluttered with buses and tourists creeping along in fright at the single lanes, blind summits and adverse cambers.

Eventually, tired and weary, we reached home. I eased my locked fingers from the steering wheel and started to unwind. My shoulders slipped down from somewhere around my ears the same time as my concentration. The next thing I knew I had come to a stop by bumping into the back of a car parked outside Ellen's house.

"Bugger, bugger, bugger." Miles and miles of trunk roads, narrow roads and double bends, then at the last gasp, I totally misjudged it and rammed straight into the back of a stranger's car. Auntie Lottie had finally defeated me. I was now a total mess, a shattered, stressed-out mass slowly sinking into the ground. To top it all off, I still had to face the other driver.

I didn't recognise the car as local which made it worse somehow. It turned out the car belonged to Scott.

"It was so lovely when I opened the door, and there he was. Totally unexpected. You remember, Scott, my nephew, don't you, Lottie? So, Lottie dear, you will have to stay with Stroma. Good news is Scott has agreed to go down with the remover to pick up the rest of your stuff tomorrow. Good news on the storage front too. After a little heated debate, the storage firm finally agreed they had made a mistake, and all your possessions are safely in the unit."

I was past caring. A hot shower and bed were calling me. First though, I had to grovel to Scott who I hadn't seen for years. Considering he had done nothing wrong but had still ended up with a dent in his car, he took it fairly well. He probably saw that I was a little deranged in both appearance and manner by that time. Auntie Lottie, however, was fairing much better. After showering, she was given a warmed nightie, a hot-water bottle and tucked up safely in bed.

The nightmare removal had not finished with us yet though. The next day, Scott was as good as his word and went down in the van with the removers. He kept us informed on developments as Joe was staying well away from his phone. He knew he would be in trouble, if we could get hold of him. Scott phoned off and on, all morning. Our conversations went something like this.

Scott: "Joe is asking if we can leave the base of the bed? Can you persuade Auntie Lottie? It just won't fit in?"

Me: "But I checked with him yesterday. He said it would all fit in."

Scott: "Yes, but it won't."

After some gentle persuasion and pointing out that it was only a two-bedroomed cottage she was moving into. We did the maths for her.

"You already have two complete single beds in storage and a complete double. Where are you going to put another double bed?" She wasn't happy but agreed reluctantly to leave the other double behind.

"But you see, it's still my bed. The one I sleep in." Auntie Lottie wasn't going to give up without a fight.

"Yes, dear, but you don't need it." Thankfully, we were all installed in Ellen's kitchen, so she was on hand to help with Auntie Lottie.

Half an hour later, the phone went again.

"Can we leave the wardrobes in the main bedroom? They're falling apart." Scott once more. I relayed the message to Auntie Lottie.

"But I've had them for thirty years. They were given to me by an ex-lover who I was very fond of." Auntie Lottie was not happy, and Ellen's reply to her didn't help.

"They're not worth anything, dear. You could buy something much better and nicer."

"But they're worth something to me." Another debate ensued with a rather tearful agreement from Auntie Lottie to leave the wardrobes.

The phone went again. This time Scott sounded quite relieved.

"That's everything packed. We're leaving the wardrobes, the bed, the plant—"

"What! You tell that remover if he doesn't find room for that plant I will personally come down and stick it right up ..." The room had gone deathly quiet. I had finally had enough. Poor Auntie Lottie was fast falling back to the state she had been in the day before – stressed, tearful and fragile. I could hear Scott's voice.

"Okay then. The plant comes. Would you like me to hire a van tomorrow and come down and get the rest?"

"What do you mean the rest? I thought you said you were all packed?" I could hear my voice barking at him. Poor Scott, he was only trying to help.

"Well, yes, sort of. We were going to leave the contents of the garden shed, like the lawnmower, wooden table and chairs, you know that sort of stuff, but I could bring them up with me tomorrow, if I'm getting a van anyway."

"And the plant," I added just in case he had forgotten.

"Yes, of course, and the plant."

Thankfully, a firm that had a van of a suitable size for hire the next day was located by Ellen. It was a local holiday, otherwise the chances of hiring a van at twenty-four hours' notice would have been very low.

The final outcome was an extra unplanned-for two-day trip to collect the remaining contents of Auntie Lottie's home. What was supposed to have been a reasonably priced flit to the Highlands had cost double, plus the hire of a van and extra petrol. The largest outlay however was not a financial one nor even the time spent. It was, without doubt, the astronomical emotional damage.

I made the arrangements for moving all her stuff when her cottage was finally ready for her. It was a lot less stressful for me that way.

Chapter 3

"What do you mean three months?" Ellen's hot buttered scones, normally so tasty, had lost all their comfort for me.

"If you had been listening more carefully, Stroma" — Ellen held my gaze — "I said about twelve weeks not three months."

Maureen spluttered and choked on her tea. We were feeding her more than just cake. I knew she was greedily devouring and storing away this exchange between Ellen and me to regurgitate it again to anyone who cared to listen.

Maureen was the nearest person we had to a town crier. Well versed in what family belonged to where and who was related either through blood or marriage, she could have doubled as the local historian if it weren't for Angus. His wife, Mary, the fourth member of our little group, was once more sitting quietly in the background, sipping her tea.

On first acquaintance, you would be forgiven for thinking here was a lovely, elderly lady, soft in speech and thoughtful in nature. But Mary of the sweet nature and often silent disposition had a wild spark warming her soul. People who did not know the couple thought it was Angus with his loud stories and various exploits who lived life to the full. What they couldn't know was that it was Mary who instigated many of their little exploits. She was not the one holding Angus back from the edge, on the contrary, she was often the one who had led him there. Those pale blue eyes were not as demure as they seemed. That glint they held was more of a warning light – beware, this one will lead you astray.

Ellen threw Maureen a cloth as well as a look that would have frozen a rabbit on the spot. Normally, this would not have affected Maureen in the slightest, but she knew not to undermine Ellen when she was in full flow. At least I knew I had Maureen's sympathy.

Ellen continued. "The builders have to prioritise our new housing development. They still have the foundations to put in and that will take a few weeks to dry. Lottie is not that much of a burden, surely?"

She wasn't really, but I was used to my own space. Auntie Lottie had surprised me with how easily she had fitted around my routine. She spent a lot of time out and about doing goodness knows what, so she had not been quite the intrusion that I had expected. In fact, we had developed our own little living rhythm that suited us well. But that couldn't last. What had started out as a few weeks' stay was growing longer by the day.

"Besides, you are the one who has been complaining that we need new houses for the young. So, look on this as your contribution." Here was Ellen again, using her most formidable life skill. She had this gift of finding your soft spot then pulling the scab off leaving your nerves jangling until you agreed to whatever she had suggested.

Housing or rather the lack of it for young families and the elderly was one of my topical moans. Locals couldn't afford the prices being asked and received for buying holiday homes in the area. Wages paid here were not high enough. We were used to the older teens and students leaving the area for work and university. Many, however, returned once they were ready to set up home and have children.

Things had changed though. Those who had never left and returning families were finding it increasingly difficult to compete with the prices being asked for accommodation. Some could inherit a croft, but there was not enough of them to fulfil the need. We were haemorrhaging young families as they had to look elsewhere to set up home.

The elderly had their own challenges, spirited away to live in nursing homes or with relatives when they were deemed unable to look after themselves. Our whole population structure was becoming unbalanced.

For years, the private sector had pushed the idea of buying a home and living in a retirement village where no nosy children could be found, no drunken youths enjoying high jinks could be heard and definitely no balls bouncing off walls could be felt. If this was what people aspired to and wanted, that was all well and good. But those who lived and worked in Blàs didn't want that. We wanted to keep our diversity. We wanted young, old and every age in-between represented and living here, not to be forced into becoming a village full of able-bodied, childless twenty-five to fifty-year-olds.

We wanted a community that was as varied as the flowers that grew on the machair, to see the children heading to school and watch them grow up and have children of their own, to see our village thrive and flourish with its people. For me, it was more basic even than that. I wanted more people my own age to live here and socialise with. I needed the local school to thrive and not be in constant jeopardy of closure due to a fall in numbers. Again, for selfish reasons. My best friend, Karen, was the schoolteacher … when she wasn't on what appeared to be constant maternity leave.

My development job involved working closely with parents and pre-school children. It was mostly them who wanted the language classes, childcare groups and ceilidhs. More importantly, my work was part of my culture; it was part of me. All my development work involved keeping and returning my native language to its home. To lose the school would not only mean mine and Karen's job going but would also mean a further loss of Gaelic speakers from an already fragile native community.

Ellen, Maureen, Mary and I all had our own reasons for wanting the community to survive. We had talked about how to do this around Ellen's kitchen table through our long, hard winters. Ellen being the catalyst she was had then gone about setting up a development trust. She targeted our populace and, one by one, zeroed in on all their weak spots, until they succumbed and agreed to her terms. Basically, that meant they were on the committee needed to run said development trust.

We had found ourselves applying for various funding packages resulting in acquiring a piece of land with some old buildings. The foundations for a variety of new houses suitable for families, the old and infirm were just about to be laid. The timetable for this first important step in regenerating Blàs now lay firmly at my feet. Ellen knew all these considerations were tumbling around in my head. She was looking directly into my eyes. I tried not to flinch. Maureen hid behind her mug of tea, refusing to meet my gaze. Mary watched and sat quietly, a soft smile on her lips. She knew what was happening.

"Okay, okay, she can stay. But *you* have to tell her that she needs to release the builders to start the houses. I'm not doing it." Of course, it had to be the same building firm working on renovating Auntie Lottie's cottage and the new housing project. The direct outcome of which was that Auntie Lottie was now having to stay with me for a further three months ... sorry, twelve weeks.

"Consider it done."

I didn't doubt Ellen for a moment.

Chapter 4

Newton's law states that for every great accommodation there is an equally and oppositely challenging one, or something like that. I think, maybe, Auntie Lottie and I were in one of the more challenging ones. This thought was being reinforced as Auntie Lottie pulled her weekend case up on a bed that wouldn't have looked out of place in *The Princess and the Pea*. Mattresses appeared to tower over her like layers of lumpy candy floss.

"I was never much into science. You didn't meet Mr McKay, did you? If you had, you would understand why. His voice waves could have cracked a greenhouse. Any blossoming bud in my brain shrivelled back to earth. The only sort of interaction of molecules or any other form of energy was his hair crudely orbiting round his bald patch as his spittle rained down on my poor unsuspecting classmates who had made the mistake of sitting at the front." I was trying to distract Auntie Lottie from our crash pad for the night.

Normally, when she lectured for us, our abodes would be pretty good. We were, however, piloting a winter course in February. This meant we had to take what we could find in terms of bed and breakfasts. The views, of course, were probably the best that could be found on this planet. Being winter, however, they didn't last long, and we were left considering our old Victorian hotel and its rather perplexing 'improvements' carried out by the multitude of owners over the decades.

I had hoped that the views from most of the windows would take her mind out of its present surroundings and into the exterior beauty. Large, golden sandy bays surrounded by craggy cliffs with enormous, rolling, white-tipped waves breaking onto their sparkling, deserted beaches were laid out just in front of the hotel. The absolutely stunning scenery should have distracted her had we been able to see it through the dark, deep, windy night.

"Let's try out the food." That's what we needed to cheer ourselves up, something nice and hot to eat. When we entered the bar where the meals were served, we could have been forgiven for thinking we had emerged into the Wild West in another era. All conversation stopped as the locals turned to stare at who had entered their watering hole.

As highlanders, this didn't faze us one little bit. We knew they were just wondering what kind of lunatic was holidaying in the area in the middle of a very dark and dismal February. The other reason for the silence and staring was they knew everyone who lived within ten miles of the place and were wondering which other local desperado had ventured forth who they could possibly cadge a lift home with as it was now freezing outside.

After supper, which was both hot and delicious, Auntie Lottie headed upstairs.

"I'll see you in the morning, sharp for breakfast. Are you sure you don't want me to help you set up tonight?"

"No, it shouldn't take long. You sleep well. I'll see you in the morning," I replied.

On my return to the hotel, I was cold, wet and freezing from trudging that short walk back through a north wind and biting rain. I dripped my way upstairs to my bedroom knowing that a warm and comfy bed awaited.

Like so many old Victorian hotel rooms, mine had also undergone some remodelling to provide an en suite of sorts. The toilet was located in a thin cupboard within the room, which I thought was rather unique. However, I don't think they had thought it through very well as a concept. The slatted louvre doors didn't exactly give much privacy, if I had been sharing with someone else. To add to which, if I had been even a little bigger, I doubt whether even sitting in a sideways position I could have fitted in. The etiquette of how you would use this type of tiny marvel if said conditions applied, I was totally unsure about. However, the towels were big, dry and fluffy, so I could forgive the rather novel toilet.

Looking up, it was easy to see that the original room must have been quite large but had been divided to make two rooms. The renovations had only gone so far though as the ceiling light hung about as far to the right as it could without being the other side of the dividing wall. The bulb was perched high on the totally opposite side of the room from the bed, but it did give you that old-fashioned feel of dangling lights and deepening shadows. At the time, I couldn't have cared less. I was so cold and tired; I just wanted to hibernate till spring.

Each room appeared to have its own idiosyncrasies. Apart from the strange toilet, my bed was really different to that of Auntie Lottie's. Picture one your great-granny would have been proud of. High, definitely single and so soft. The only real problem came if you were vertically challenged. I had not actually taken note of how high the bed was until I found myself pulling my body up onto it then crawling up toward the top. I flopped down, ready to drift off to dreamland but just kept going, down, down, until I was totally cocooned in the mattress. Small walls seemed to have sprouted on either side of me. Thankfully, having no trouble with claustrophobia, I drifted off on warm, comfy waves of slumber.

It wasn't until morning, on waking, I realised my real dilemma was how on earth I was going to get out of this mattress. I tried to sit up … nope, that wasn't going to work as my feet shot up in the air the moment I tried to lift my shoulders. Lifting my feet only pushed me even further into my marshmallow-like abode. Rolling from side to side did absolutely nothing as the mattress had compressed around me while I slept. During the night, without my knowledge, I had been captured by an enormous, immoveable, cushy monster.

Frustrated and tired from my struggle, the need to evacuate my bed was becoming more desperate as the whispered plea from my waking bladder was building to a roar. I was marooned in an ocean of softness, but I had no intention of remaining a stranded whale. I could just see the headlines: 'Death by Divan, Woman Swallowed Whole'.

One more extra effort was needed. With walrus-like wriggles, I rippled myself round until one side of me was engulfed in the smothering folds. Throwing my free arm and leg up, I grabbed the side of the mattress and clung on with my knee then pulled with all my might. Like a melted toffee breaking free, I surged up and flopped out of the side of the bed to land with a thud on the threadbare carpet. Goodness knows what any unsuspecting guest below thought was going on. By now, the cold was seeping into me, and I was tired from my struggle. I looked at the monster inviting me back with its enticing smile and decided the effort required to escape its clutches again was definitely not worth it.

I showered and dressed and finally saw the view from the window as daylight spread. It was as breathtaking as I had imagined in the dark. A fine flurry of snow had fallen during the night and gently covered the countryside in a delicate white shawl. I hurried downstairs to find Auntie Lottie already at breakfast, drinking hot tea. She took one look at me and immediately accused me of sleeping better than her.

"Guilty. I was swamped in a mattress and fell straight to sleep."

"I couldn't get the window shut. It was stuck open. I like my fresh air, but this was more like an icy blast blowing straight off the firth and in through my open window. I didn't notice it when we dropped off our bags. But when I got back from our meal, on opening the door, I was hit by a gust of sub-zero air. It felt like walking into a cold furnace."

Auntie Lottie went on to explain that a busload of tourists had arrived after us, and the hotel was full, so no other room had been available. After much huffing and struggling with the open casement, it had been decided that a portable heater would be brought in to counteract the wind howling through the now almost-closed gap.

"'Only a little open, mostly closed; how about a heater? That should work?' That's what the manager said. The keyword here is should! A fan heater, for goodness sake. You'd be lucky if it heated anything past a few centimetres. It was really noisy and didn't keep me or the room warm." Auntie Lottie was not impressed.

From previous experiences of trying to find accommodation in winter, it could have been assumed that I might have suggested to Auntie Lottie that she bring thermal pyjamas, an empty hot-water bottle and maybe a wee nip to keep her warm. But being an eternal optimist, I, of course, had not asked her to bring any of these things. I knew in my heart that each bad experience I had of boarding houses in winter was just a one-off.

It's not that us optimists don't learn for our mistakes; it's just that we are optimistic and therefore don't see the need to plan for failure that won't happen. Pessimists are the planners of the world who are also probably never found cold and shivering in a hotel as they have the hot-water bottle, pyjamas and wee nip. A new rule for the traveller: for survival reasons, always find a pessimist to share with.

Auntie Lottie went on to say that the gale I had slept through had been howling and screaming into her room through the 'almost-closed gap'. At one point during the night, she must have fallen asleep and had woken up to the sound of hailstones battering against the window.

"It went on for hours," she said. "I can't believe you didn't hear it. Anyway, I dropped off again and woke up with my nose stone cold and seeing my breath in the air. There was a white covering on the carpet near the window. Snow on the carpet, would you believe it? Snow. It soon shifted though." She went on to say that she would be moved to a different room that night once some of that day's guests had checked out.

"Perhaps we should stay at a cottage next time."

"Have you forgotten what happened last time?"

I had of course. Finding worms in the bath had been bad enough, but there had also been no sheets or towels and then the electric fire had started to melt. At least with hotels there was always someone there to try and sort it out. Well, I suppose

31

Auntie Lottie would argue that that depends on your definition of actually sorting the problem out. In her case, I suppose, she would have had a point.

Chapter 5

"Come on, you're needed. Angus and Mary sent me, *thugainn!*" No greeting, no 'how are you doing?' No 'and have you heard about?' No preamble at all. So unlike Maureen when I had answered the door to her tapping. The tapping was unusual in itself; most people I knew just knocked or yelled and walked in. But for Maureen, it was easier to rap with her stick on my door than try and negotiate her wheelchair into my kitchen.

"When would you like me to come?" I wondered why I was being summoned so early in the day.

"As soon as you can. I'll get them to pop the kettle on. It will be ready in a few minutes. *Greas ort.*" Maureen smiled; she still loved the fact that you could get a cup of hot water so quickly and at the touch of a button. I pulled on my boots and contemplated again why she had been dispatched to summon me. Mary and Angus usually came for me themselves. If not them, it would usually be Ellen, and now Auntie Lottie was in the mix as well.

As soon as I entered their kitchen and saw who was assembled there, I knew something was up. All eyes zoomed in. The kitchen had always been the real meeting place in most homes around the district. From farmhouses and cottages to grand mansions and small crofts, they all tended to have that same warm, friendly, cosy atmosphere. It made no difference whether I was greeted at the back door or front; we almost always made our way to that communal room wherever it was situated within the building. Maybe it was due to the weather conditions we got. There had to be a place where you could defrost, dry off and disrobe if necessary. It really didn't matter whether it was a large or small space so long as it was dominated by a source of heat. This fire could be ancient or modern and was generally fed by solid fuel, oil or liquid petroleum gas. The important thing was that it blasted out sweltering hot air.

Often as not, sitting in the two comfy chairs on either side of this source of heat were sleeping animals. The cats were never to be disturbed by the owners and visitors of the house. These felines were generally allowed to sleep on. Dogs, however, almost without exception, could be removed from the second chair and consigned to either their mat or bed. An overhead clothes horse attached to the ceiling for drying clothes and a small table with at least two hard chairs were all characteristics of most homes.

Croft houses usually also had the remnants of a dog bed, often made up of lots of large blankets close to the stove. In lambing season, this could double up for any orphan lambs that needed a little extra loving-care and warmth. Strangely, the light always appeared to be dimmed or low, even in relatively new houses. But in retrospect, this could, of course, have been due to the washing that dried on the clothes horse attached to the celling.

As I made my way to Angus and Mary's, I noticed the workmen in yet another holiday let. The warm, homely atmosphere was fast being ripped out of the kitchen to allow an easy-clean, bright holiday environment to take over. This was fast becoming one of the many differences growing between the static population, whose homes were lived and worked in, and those cottages and houses that catered for short-term lets.

My eyes automatically flicked over to where the foundations lay for our new housing development. A visual framework to attach our fragile hopes for the future of our community. They were difficult to make out, but I knew they were down. I wondered again: would the new houses still be able to capture the homeliness of our older cottages? Was losing some of the character worth it for new, clean heating systems and staying warmer in winter?

A blast of cold wind and rain brought back reality. On reflection, staying cosy and dry would be worth the changes. Hopefully, when the families moved into their new permanent accommodation, they would find their own modern twist on our Highland homes.

Mary had made the tea with leaves not bags. She had set out her best white china teapot with its red flower pattern. The matching side plates were edged with gold. These never saw the light of day, not unless someone had died.

Homemade baking was piled on top of a large matching plate. Milk in a tiny jug sat alongside a delicate sugar bowl. Cups waited patiently on wafer-thin saucers, all with the same pattern to complete an age-old look. Whoever had died, they must have been important to the community. The silence could almost be felt, broken only by the soft clink of bone china. Tea balanced in one hand, with homebaking in the other, I was silently going through a list in my head of who could have possibly died. The fact that I had been summoned here meant that their passing would matter to me. I knew Iona was fine, and those I was most close to were all there, sipping tea out of china cups, so I wasn't too worried. The chairs had been placed rather strangely though. Lined up, side by side, meaning we were all staring toward the sink rather than around the table.

"Almost ready," Mary said as she seated herself next to me, tea in hand, placing her cake on the small table beside her.

"Okay, everyone seated comfortably? Fine then. Go ahead, Angus, switch on."

Angus solemnly walked up to the amazing, brilliant white device in front of us. I had failed to notice its significance at first. He pressed a button on the front. Almost at once, the noise started, and the machine filled up with water. This was the wonder of wonders, an automatic washing machine that washed your clothes while you sat by and drank tea in china cups and had the time to eat homemade cakes and talk and laugh about frivolous things.

Our eyes held fast as the clothes went round and round. Mary, who all her life had hand-washed and eventually twin-tubbed her way through family life, had succumbed to modern technology at the grand old age of eighty. An automatic machine, deemed a necessity by my generation, had seemed to her, until now, a needless expensive accessory. Age had forced her into this purchase, her hands and arms not as strong as they once were. Her joy, however, as she watched that astounding piece of machinery complete her once tedious tasks, was infectious and well worth my plod through the February mud. Better still, the only death was that of her old, redundant twin-tub.

Chapter 6

A soft spring morning, ablaze with purple croci, sunshine daffodils and the heady coconut smell of the yellow gorse contradicted the sadness of the day. Nature's brilliance was triumphant, invalidating the bereaved family's dark clothing. His friends and their fellow mourners' colours, however, clashed and competed between themselves. Ranging from the traditional black right through to bright fuchsia pink.

"He was a cussed old sod, right enough." Archie shook his head slowly from side to side as he recalled the cutting remarks that the 'lovingly departed' had used on a daily basis; they passed as pleasantries in these parts.

"Ach away with you, man, he was a bad-tempered old git who wouldn't have given you the time of day without cutting your nose off." Although this did pretty much sum up the deceased's nature, it was taken as fact that all who attended thought well of the embittered man who lay beneath the Saltire-covered coffin.

"Well, thank God, she didnae get that minister to pray over him, or I'd be expecting Jock to rise right up and throttle the old bugger."

"Archie, will you watch your goddamn language. It's a funeral for Christ's sake."

I heard a sharp intake of breath coming from the sister who had fought tooth and nail to get Jock buried decently, as she saw it. A service should have been held in the church, but bolts of lightning could well have rained down on that rabble if they had to set foot in such a place. Thankfully, Jock's partner, who had faithfully helped him home from the pub for the last twenty years, had had the last say. Jock, in his very cussed and defiant manner, had made sure everything was in writing, including who got what and how his last stand, so to speak, was going to go.

So, there we all stood, in the clearing, between his beloved pub and the ancient graveyard. Jock and his coffin the most important elements there, closely followed in importance not by his family and friends but by three other essential individuals required at all the best funerals. A lone piper (as nothing notable in life happens here without one) to play a lament, a poet who stood right next to a piper in importance and someone to take care of the funeral service itself. Jock had also requested a guitarist to help serenade his departure. Essentially though, this was a funeral of two communities, made up of the embittered family on one side and his partner, friends and neighbours on the other. It was held together by that third most important person, in this case, a humanist who would take the service.

The birds continued the musical accompaniment as the last note of the piper's lament faded into the sky.

"I quite envied Jock, you know," said Archie.

"Why? Coz he has a good turnout? You daft old bat."

"Ach, no, but how many men do you know would have got away with moving in with their lover every Friday night and moving out again on a Monday morning? I suggested to the wife we could sleep separately, you know, just on Friday nights like, and she nearly killed me"

"Not surprised. Why would you want to do that then? You've not got a woman on the side that I know of. Ha, who else would have you?"

"Aye, aye, very funny, but my missus keeps moaning about me disturbing her when I'm getting up early for my fishing. I suggested one of us could sleep in the shed."

"What, so you were going to sleep in the shed at the bottom of your garden every Friday night? Do you not think it could get a bit cold?"

"Don't be so daft. I suggested she did. That way, I wouldn't disturb her when I got up so early. The shed is at the back of the house, see, so she wouldn't be woken up with the car starting."

"Oh, man, I'm surprised it's not you in that coffin."

"Aye, well, she did say something similar to me."

This was the second funeral in less than a month to hit the village. Unsurprisingly, Maureen had been the harbinger of doom on the first occasion. Iona, my younger sister, had just arrived home for one of her duty visits.

"At least offer her a cup of tea. I've got to work. I'm getting a video call."

Iona was not best pleased. Maureen, however, was more than happy to have Iona all to herself. Tea gave her plenty of time to interrogate Iona: an opportunity to extract new information to pass around the district about any developments in Iona's life in the big city. Iona struggled to keep her lifestyle and news to herself under expert questioning. She came out of their tea party a little fazed and with very few facts about who had actually died.

"Maureen said that one of the neighbours had died." Iona relayed to me.

"Oh, that's bad, and which one would that be?" I was not being callous here, just checking my facts. Neighbours here can live right next door or half a mile away. So, in a roundabout way, everyone in the village could, at some point, be regarded as your neighbour.

"For goodness sake, he lives around the corner; Maureen says you speak to him and his wife all the time." Yes, that was probably true. I did speak to a lot of people, especially those who lived nearby, but it didn't help me remember their names any better. I could be friendly with people for ages and still not have a clue what their real names were.

The Highlands were full of people who had at least two names. One they used all the time, more than likely representing how they looked, a habit or even a saying they used, such as Wee Wallace, who could be either small or, conversely, very tall. Wallace may not even be their given name either. Joiner John, Peter the Polis and Laura Law were all self-explanatory as long as you didn't make the assumption that John, Peter or Laura were actually their given names.

It got really complicated if their everyday names came from what their great-auntie, grandad or other distant relative had done at some point in history. These names obviously had no connection with their official birth names or job or anything related to them on a day-to-day basis. But it would be the name the local populous knew them by. The sudden use of their birth name at the time of their death rounded it all off but didn't really help anyone looking for, say, a Mr Charles Macleod when he was only known in the district as Pibroch Paddy.

"It was William MacKay. I'm sure that's who she said. So that would be Wullie the Lum, right?" Iona didn't seem totally convinced.

"Well, it could be." I said. "He has been poorly lately. But I seem to remember that William MacKay is Billy the Shake's real name too."

"Nope, nope, I'm sure she said William MacKay meaning Wullie the Lum. It's a shame, but what does it matter to me? You'll be going to the funeral," Iona said hopefully.

"Not this time. I'm sorry, but you will have to go. I'm busy all week. In fact, I'm not even here for most of it." I was off up north, and there was no way I could cancel.

"Me! Are you mad? Who would want me at their funeral?" Iona was pleading with me, but on this occasion, she would have to go in my place.

"Look, Iona, you're only here for a few days. You offered to help me out. Well, this is helping me out. I simply can't go. I'm working." I didn't like putting Iona in that position, but I had no choice. Someone had to go to represent our family. It would have been frowned upon by the community if one of us didn't show up.

On the day of the funeral, Iona returned looking pale and fragile. Ever since our parents' death she had avoided as many funerals as possible.

"God, his wife looks awful. I didn't even recognise her, poor woman; she was so upset. I didn't go for the tea. Auntie Lottie tried to make me, but I just couldn't."

"Not to worry, you went, and that's the main thing. I really appreciate it, you know. Was there anyone else from around here?"

"Not as many as I would have thought, but the usual professional mourners were there." They weren't really paid of course, at least not in monetary terms. Mostly, they consisted of a few worthies; worthies were recognised throughout Blàs. This title was bestowed on anyone who could be considered a little quirky in deed (such as never walking on the left) or nature (extra shy or, conversely, extra loud) and were recognised as such throughout the district. There were others like Angus who were so well known and loved in the area that they were regarded as being 'worthies' without the need for quirks or deeds. Not all professional mourners were labelled worthies. The professional mourners tended to come from old local families who knew almost everyone in the district and, as such, felt the need to go to nearly all the funerals. The reward for them came afterwards where they could participate in a friendly chat, nice hot cup of tea, some sandwiches and, if they were lucky, a few whiskys thrown in. You were nobody in this world if you didn't have either a professional mourner or a local worthy at your passing.

Two days later, a very white-faced Iona raced through the door.

"Oh my God, I've just seen a ghost."

Having gone through Iona's teenage years as her guardian, door slamming and wild stories rarely had me rattled – just part of a normal day, in fact.

"Really, and where would that be?" Keeping calm was a must, I had always found.

"At the top of the road. And I got such a fright that I nearly killed him."

"You can't do that if he is already dead." Which I felt was a fair point.

"I could. I could have! He's not, is he? Dead, I mean. My God, I nearly hit him. I rounded the corner and saw his pale face staring straight at me. I jumped, screamed, slammed my foot on the accelerator and nearly goddamn killed him, again."

"Firstly, you didn't kill him the first time. Secondly, by your own admission, he is not dead. And thirdly, it can't be him."

"It was him. It was Wullie the Lum. His wife came up behind, smiled at me through the window and said, 'That was close.' Then the pair of then walked off together."

"Ok, so …"

"Wullie the Lum is not dead then, is he?"

"Obviously not. Which leaves us with just one question. Whose funeral did you go to?" I asked

"It was William MacKay. It was. I heard the minister say his name. To be honest, I wasn't really listening to what he said about him. Although, come to think of it, I don't remember the minister saying anything about him being a chimney sweep," Iona said.

"Well, if it was mostly our neighbours at the funeral, and it was definitely a William MacKay, maybe it was Billy the Shakes who died," I mused. "On the bright side, at least we now know why you didn't recognise Wullie the Lum's wife as the grieving widow."

Iona looked at me in disgust before throwing her arms around my neck, and we laughed together until tears streamed down our faces.

Chapter 7

"Just follow the road past the church and keep going; you can't miss us." Oh, but you could. As directions went, they were not unusual in their vagueness. Of course, since I resisted using any form of GPS, it was inevitable that I often got lost. It didn't really bother me – I quite liked not knowing where I was. Auntie Lottie, unfortunately, was not of the same ilk. She wasn't happy that the road we had to take forked just past the church.

"So, what do you think? Is the left fork the correct way, or is the right fork the main road?" By main road, do not be fooled. Both ways were single-track after leaving the main road, and by main road, I mean a two-lane road and not one of those expansive dual carriageways.

Auntie Lottie pondered the question for a second. "I think … I will leave it up to you. You are the driver after all."

Great. I opted for the left fork, given I'm left-handed and not by some homing device in my brain. Anyway, most signs said keep left. On reflection though, that may not have been the right basis for the choice. How long to keep going? Five minutes? Ten minutes? Thirty minutes later, and we were still going, albeit a bit slower. The road was getting narrower by the minute; we hadn't seen any other cars, sheep, people or even deer for miles.

"Can't you call someone?" Auntie Lottie asked.

"Are you forgetting where we are? We're not down south now, you know. There is no chance of a mobile signal up here." To demonstrate the point, I passed her my phone.

"Oh, well, we will just have to ask the first person we meet." I decided no response was better than any at that point, besides which, I had more important things to think about. Was that really a blade of grass I had spied earlier growing up the middle of the road? Yes, there were some more wicked green shoots, cheekily sprouting up through the increasingly broken grey surface of what could be laughingly classed as a road. In reality, it resembled an ancient track more suited for those with hooves or a quadbike. We kept going. Then it appeared, like a mirage: the ubiquitous fishing shack complete with three large black cars squeezed into the parking area.

"Look, look a man! Is that Lachie's son? Yes, yes, it is. Stop!" Auntie Lottie was gesturing wildly.

Donald John, or DJ as he was better known, stood beside one of the cars, his collie, Jess, attached to his heel. I pulled over.

"Oh, it's yourself, then," said DJ as he stuck his head in the window. Not to be outdone, Jess appeared beside him. Old Shep stuck his nose out in greeting. Auntie Lottie had agreed to look after him while Old Tam was at a hospital appointment. "They caught you then. They didn't think they would be in time. Just as well; it's a hell of a long way back to get to the other side. You'd have totally missed the meeting. I think they're all there waiting now; you're the last car up the glen. Just follow the road for another five minutes. The house you're looking for is on the right. I just dropped Helga off for a visit there and noticed a nice pile of homebaking waiting for you. I'd best be off; I've got some clients to entertain."

"Ach, I didn't get a chance to ask how his dad was," Auntie Lottie moaned.

45

It turned out that I *had* taken a wrong turning at the beginning of the road, a left instead of a right. However, the meeting had been moved to the neighbour's house which we were was just five minutes from. If we had taken the correct road, we would have landed up on the opposite side of the river entirely. Then the only chance we would have had of making it to any of the meeting was if I had left my car there then walked across the moor and a very rickety bridge. No one was surprised to see us there; they all took it for granted that someone would have told me, forgetting that I wouldn't just bump into one of them in the local library, hall or during the school run.

Auntie Lottie knew a few of the women who sat snuggled in the warm kitchen. I spotted DJ's wife, Helga, helping our host, Jane, with teas and coffees. I had forgotten they were friendly. It felt a bit strange seeing her there. Previously, we had mostly met up at meetings involving Blàs and the Development Trust. I wasn't sure if Auntie Lottie and Helga had ever met as DJ and Helga lived slightly out of Blàs.

"You must be DJ's wife. We just met him on our way up the glen. So like his father, Lachie." Auntie Lottie had made her way across to Helga's side.

"I hope you don't mind, Jane, but I have old Shep with me. I did bring along Auntie Lottie too. She's willing to help out at any fundraising events you may have planned," I said.

"Oh, no, that's fine. Shep can hoover up all the crumbs we drop, and we are always happy to have an extra pair of hands to help." Jane beamed a smile across at Auntie Lottie.

"Yes, I've heard about you from DJ." Helga turned toward Auntie Lottie and regarded her closely. "Tea or coffee?"

"Tea is fine," followed quickly by, "and how is your father-in-law, Lachie, these days? I haven't seen him since my return."

Helga visibly blinked and paused for a moment. There was a strange atmosphere brewing. Helga and Auntie Lottie were holding their own private communications. Eventually, Helga replied. "I expect you haven't. Shall we get on with the meeting then?"

I nodded and looked across at Auntie Lottie who simply shrugged and sat down. The journey back would allow me the chance to find out the story behind this strange exchange between her and Helga.

*

We finally managed to drag old Shep away from all the treats and crumbs he had scrounged long enough to help him back into the car. Auntie Lottie turned and looked straight at Helga. "Now, you will give my best to Lachie, won't you? Hopefully, I will see him around and about." Before Helga could answer, Auntie Lottie had settled herself into the car and closed the door.

Driving away, I saw Helga standing in the doorway, staring after the car. Auntie Lottie was anxious to control any information she would give me. "And before you ask, there is little to tell. Just a misunderstanding. Lachie's wife was always the jealous sort. Nothing happened between me and Lachie. But you wouldn't think that if you listened to his silly wife. I mean, it wasn't my fault we got stuck in the hall together all night. That's all I am saying on the subject, so just keep your eyes on the road and your conversation on something else."

Never mind how much I tried, she remained closed on the subject. Maybe Ellen or Mary would be a bit more forthcoming on the incident. If not, I was sure Maureen would have her own version that she would willingly share with me.

"Since we are in the vicinity, why don't we pay a visit to Croft Cosy?" Auntie Lottie suggested as we approached the main road again. "I'm sure Shep would enjoy the extra trip in the car."

I didn't think Shep would have counted more time spent in a car as one of his most desirable things to do. A stroll along the beach would have been more preferable to him, I was sure, but I wasn't about to argue. I knew it would be a waste of time, and anyway, I liked having the old dog nearby.

"Okay, so how do we get there?" I asked. The directions Auntie Lottie gave, of course, were pretty vague.

"You turn off this road somewhere near here and keep going, just follow the signs after that. You can't miss them, apparently."

Sausage hunting; we were going sausage hunting for what we had been told were the finest ones you'd ever eat, at least according to Old Tam.

We were somewhere in a glen near a loch when I spotted it coming straight for us, a great snaking monster of a vehicle, rocking its slow inevitable way toward us. My bemused companion was holding a map upside down and hadn't noticed. *Breathe, breathe, don't panic,* I told myself. I knew the driver wouldn't apply his brakes. Once that thing got moving it would take a tank to stop it. If he did brake, the stopping motion would cascade down the vehicle like a centipede before bringing it to a juddering stop, normally about half a mile from where the brakes were first applied.

That machine was one of the main reasons that Auntie Lottie rarely drove around by herself. She had spent so long city-driving that she found the narrow roads and accepted norms up here difficult to grasp. She understood, however, that if a road was actually blocked, then a whole new set of rules applied. She could get out of her car, chill out and maybe catch up with any of the locals who were already stuck there too.

The 'beast' was still swaying its slow hypnotic way toward us. Like an everlasting gobstopper, it just kept on going. The road, of course, was at one of its narrowest points. The nearest passing place long gone some distance behind with the next one nowhere in sight.

He won't really just drive over us, will he? I wondered. Driving into the loch was becoming a real possibility. While I considered this as a relevant option, a small draw-in beside the loch came into view. I heard the 'beast' gasp, creak and groan as I slammed my foot on the accelerator and raced toward the passing place.

Auntie Lottie finally looked up from the map. "Oh dear, that's a bit big for the road."

I squeezed my car into the welcome passing place. My already small vehicle seemed to shrivel to fit inside the safety zone. The monster trundled past without inflicting the slightest bump or scratch as the driver of the 'beast' waved cheerily and bounced along on his way, dragging the heaving monster behind him. It was like an optical illusion, way too large for the road. The 'beast' just shouldn't have fitted, but it did.

The 'beast', or to give it its formal name, The Screen Machine, is our mobile theatre that takes films around the rural areas of Scotland. It is used by the many who don't have access to a local cinema. Complete with films, pull-out seats and all the other paraphernalia needed to screen the latest blockbuster. All folded and tucked inside its own transporter. Much loved, unless, of course, you happen to meet it on a single-track road.

At last, a signpost appeared, helpfully at a crossroads. It was a bit worrying though – it mentioned the name of the road to the right, the road to the left but didn't actually point or name the one we'd just come along. After a few minutes pondering, we once more decided on the left. The right looked like it ran out after a few hundred yards at what could have been the ruins of an old croft house.

If we had had any sense at all, we should have left the car where it was, stuck a lead on the dog and let him sniff our way there. It would have been way more helpful than any sort of directional aid we had. Anyway, 'Always stay with your car,' was good advice that I tended to follow.

Needless to say, the left road ran out after about a mile. No signs, no explanation, no paths, no humans, no animals if it came to that. A view, of course; there are always views in the Highlands, but more importantly, no turning space.

"Why would you just stop a road here, then?" asked Auntie Lottie.

Why indeed? Road end does not mean end of journey; it means end of the road.

The dry-stone dyke and drainage ditch that ran along either side of the track left little room for manoeuvring. No chance of a fifty-three-point turn, let alone a three-point turn. I got out of the car to stretch my legs and have a wee think. I watched the tips of two horns begin a slow rise over the stone dyke. Eventually, a large, hairy, ginger head appeared. A Highland cow with its shaggy coat, peered at me leisurely from its fringed brown eyes while it chewed the cud.

"I don't suppose you know where this master sausage-maker is then?" The Highland cow continued to stare back. "I would settle for a turning space; know of any hereabouts?" Still no response from the bonnie beast.

"Stroma, for goodness sake, will you stop talking to that cow, and just get us out of here." Auntie Lottie was getting fractious. I leant forward and scratched the cow on its forehead.

"I've got to go. No putting this off any longer. Goodbye, beautiful." Finally, a response as the Highland beastie blew down his nose. I climbed back into the car and began the slow, painful, reverse back along the way we had come. My four-legged hairy friend watched impassively as we disappeared from view.

We eventually found our prey. What had looked like an old, ruined croft on the right, turned out to be where the sausage-maker lived. Well, not the actual ruin. Once we had parked outside the old buildings, we could just see the side of a lovely new modern house. It was set back into the hillside where it got shelter from the winter winds.

We bought our sausages and some extra for Old Tam. The smell drove Shep mad all the way home. The old dog suddenly took on a new lease of life. He looked half-dead most of the time, but there was nothing wrong with his sense of smell. "Don't you worry, Shep, you'll get your share from Tam – we all know that."

"Here, Stroma, you take him home. I wanted to make you something special for your tea as a thank you for putting up with me, and these sausages should be just the thing."

Opening the door after dropping Shep back home, I was surrounded by the enticing smell of hot sausages wafting around. It wasn't only Shep who enjoyed their dinner that night. Both Auntie Lottie and I agreed that these were definitely the most delicious sausages we had ever tasted.

*

The next day, I had a fairly short journey of little over an hour. I was heading to Inverness. "You want to come to the big city then, Auntie Lottie?"

"No, dear, I think one trip with you this week it quite enough. Besides, I want to take a look at my cottage. I'm hoping I can move in soon."

Off I went, confident in finding my way to and around most of the Highland capital. However, I wasn't entirely familiar with the area in Inverness where Highland Grant Givers, the organisation I was visiting, was located, so I decided the time was right to, finally, use the GPS system in the car.

'Ping, take the next turning on your left.'

'Ping, your left.'

'Ping, no, your left, your other left.' I'm sure I heard it mumbling 'for goodness sake what kind of idiot am I dealing with.' It did nothing for my confidence. When it finally droned in its patronising voice 're-calculating route,' I'm sure I heard it whispering, 'fool.' I remembered why I kept the GPS off. It took the sense of adventure and relaxation out of a journey. It was a lot nicer way to travel without it. All I needed was to have a rough idea of where my destination was then, once I got near it, ask someone. That way, I got to meet the locals, or if I was unlucky, someone who had about as much local knowledge as me. Thank goodness for posties and little local shops. It mostly worked, and I got to talk to real human beings.

The condescending voice continued disdainfully, 'Take the next right.'

'At the lights, take the next left.'

The lights were at red. I had to fight the compulsion to do what I was told. I stopped, but I could actually feel my pulse rate increasing as the haughty voice continued to second-guess my actions. Just as I was thinking, *Where am I?* I was informed that I had reached my destination, top of the class. *Really? I have reached my destination, and where would that be precisely?* I was surrounded by suburbia. Highland Grant Givers used to be situated in the middle of the city. Easy to find, park near and travel to, be it by car, train, bus or air. It was an organisation much like the one I worked for in that it was basically a charity with a board of directors.

What they must be saving on having an out-of-town location would be lost in expenses as their directors charged them for their taxi fares to and from places like the airport. The main difference between Highland Grant Givers and GLADS, though, was they had money to hand out, while we were desperate to receive any money we could get.

That aside, my recent dictator of a machine had fallen disconcertingly quiet. Just when I needed it the most, it had gone into sleep mode, because as far as it was concerned, I was there. I suppose, in a philosophical sense, it was true. I was indeed there, but in a more directional sense, the there I was at, was not the there where I actually needed to be.

Back to basics then. Only, of course, there was no one in sight to ask. There was only one way to go then, onwards and upwards, or, in other words, push on further. Hopefully, I wouldn't get to the stage where grass started to grow up the middle of the road. I could make exceptions for that up a quiet glen, but on the outskirts of our one and only city in the Highlands, well, how unsophisticated would that have been?

Eventually, just as the road began to snake back toward the city, I spied my destination. A conglomerate of buildings you couldn't really have missed. Well, I possibly could have, if my trip up the glen was anything to go by. My contact at Highland Grant Givers had said this new building was more environmentally friendly than their last one and blended into its surroundings. Really? Blend was maybe not the word I would have used. Dominated, I believe would be more appropriate. I knew that it was the right building, because it was so noticeable. It hardly lived up to what I had been expecting.

Our new housing development in Blàs was supposed to be greener, more efficient and built to 'harmonise with the surrounding countryside'. I promised myself that as soon as I got back, I would take another look at our plans, just to be on the safe side.

Chapter 8

"No, mam! No." The terrified look on little Fergus' face as he pulled in the opposite direction from his mum, Karen, could only mean one thing: time for using the dreaded cludgie.

Our hall was vintage – sounds so much nicer than dilapidated. It was cold, smelly and dust-covered, with mice-ridden cupboards. The heating system sounded like someone's stomach after a hot curry. It did not have toilets; these were reserved solely for the modern, grant-built wonders – warm, inviting, usable. We had a cludgie instead.

It had been attached to the hall as an afterthought. Situated in a sort of lean-to, it was old and so cold the chill felt like a presence all of its own. You were at risk of frostbite if you were rash enough to sit down on the loo seat. The flush water inside was always a dirty brown as it was piped directly from a rather sad-looking stream. A bulb dangled from a wire that came out of a hole in the roof and gave out next to no light.

The cludgie was one of the reasons so many of our pre-school children were unable to use the toilet without some adult protection near at hand. Potty-training youngsters didn't have the luxury of avoiding the cludgie.

Avoidance, even for myself, was difficult when doing a workshop with parents. Ah, parents of all different shapes, sizes, political persuasion, eating habits, parenting abilities and styles ... and their bewildered children. If it weren't for the fact that I had been responsible for my teenage sister when I first started my job, I doubted that any parents would have listened to an unmarried, non-mother like me.

*

The region was full of characters, old and new. In Blàs the family affectionately known as The Odd Couple were just that – one was 6'6''while his partner was a good foot and a half smaller and older by at least ten years. They had a large family (which was great for numbers in a rural community) and not a care in the world. Nothing bothered them. Time was a thing used by others of a more worldly nature to mark the grinding of events. They drifted in and out of group sessions like summer butterflies, sometimes early and in full flight, other times you wouldn't see them for weeks then get a glimpse as they arrived for ten minutes at the end of a session. This, the group was informed, was so their children could see everyone and have a runabout. Their children seemed to thrive in their unconventional lifestyle, and they certainly got around, walking everywhere.

I heard tell that they had taken pity on an elderly lady just outside our village and invited her to their house for supper. They duly arrived on or close to the correct time but three days late to pick her up. Thankfully, the old biddy hadn't reached her great age without some backup planning. She had made some soup (the staple diet of all true Scots), just in case. The family, on the other hand, couldn't understand why she had supper on the table and were heard to exclaim, "But you knew we were coming to get you!"

One time, I was in the hall to run the second of two planned Gaelic movement and song workshops for families in the area. These workshops were designed to encourage parents to use the Gaelic they learnt in a fun way at home. It required the use of simple Gaelic songs, music and puppets to enhance their understanding.

The first workshop had seen the mum and dad, together with their youngest, Erin, arriving right on time to take part – an unexpected occurrence given their history. Puffing and panting my way through some of the movements, I noticed that Erin's mum was also doing the same thing, but a bit more obviously. In fact, worryingly obviously for someone who was so far on in her pregnancy. I tried to make my way over unobtrusively, keeping in time with the music, hoping that no one else would notice. This should not have been too difficult to achieve. However, I had told the parents to watch and just follow what I was doing. So, rather than keeping everything low key and off to one side, as I drew nearer to Erin's mum, so did the rest of the group while moving on tiptoes, making strange hand signals and puffing heavily. By the time I got to the expectant mother, she was leaning on the wall, blowing out and holding up her bump. More worryingly, she was watching the clock. It was the latter that got me really concerned. She never noticed time, never mind checked the time, so that could only mean one thing. Our mother of many previous bairns was on her way to becoming a mum again.

"How are you doing?" I asked, not really wanting to hear the answer.

"Fine, fine. Alex is just away off to get the use of a van from Archie, and then I'll be away home." I hadn't even noticed he'd gone. I thought he was in the kitchen helping put the snack together. That was better news than I had anticipated. I was afraid she'd say, "My waters have broken."

"Aren't you going to Inverness then?"

"Ach, no. They wanted me to, but last time I nearly gave birth in the ambulance, and I'm not doing that again. Archie just lives up the road, if necessary, but hopefully, the midwife will make it, if she's not in Inbhirasgaidh."

Archie was a local crofter and their friend and neighbour. He did raise his own sheep, but I wasn't sure how happy the midwife would be having her skills measured against those of one of the crofters. Although, we'd had a few midwifes at our groups, and they all seemed pretty laid-back about most things. They were in charge of all the local births for miles around without any major help or hospitals nearby. A calm disposition had to be part of their nature.

While I had been attending to the soon-to-be mum, parents had been on their phones, tracking down any known midwifes on or off duty near at hand. Plans had also been put in place for a delivery on the floor if necessary. Thankfully, the aforementioned Archie, together with Alex burst through the doors at that point and gently started to manoeuvre our mum-to-be out to the van.

"The midwife is on her way. She's just finishing up in the next village and will meet us at the house." We heard this as the two men almost bodily lifted her into the van. For one horrible minute, I thought they were going to put her in the back on a mattress and drive off, but thankfully that didn't happen, not that time! Alex, with his wife in front, revved his way off, leaving Archie discarded at the hall with no transport.

"Do you think he realised he left you?"

"Probably not; he's got enough to deal with I'm thinking," Archie replied. "I won't say no to a cup of tea and some cake before I hike back, like."

I had already decided to abandon that workshop; tea and cakes seemed the next logical step. Archie was inundated with offers of lifts home. Personally, I think it was the chance of finding out any news of the new baby rather than Archie's great charm. As for my workshops, from then on, parents-in-waiting were going to be informed that, if they were near their time, they were not to use the workshop as a way of bringing on labour.

*

Fergus running thankfully back into the hall brought me back from my ruminating. It was great to be on my own patch. Not so great was that I had to visit the dreaded cludgie before we started in earnest. Perhaps, if it hadn't been a cludgie but a smart, warm toilet, I would have taken my time, and then I wouldn't have had to live with the embarrassment I caused myself.

In my hurry to get back to the warmth and out of the freezing cold and semi-dark, I rushed pulling up my clothes. An easy enough task, after all I'd been doing it all my life. That time, however, was different. I don't know what exactly I did wrong, but just as I went to pull my breeks up – ping, a searing hot pain went right through my hand. Like most people in pain, I danced around as much as the wee room would let me and looked down at my hand while trying to pull up my clothes with my other, not very successfully. What was going on? Why wasn't my hand doing what I asked?

At first glance, everything looked quite normal until my eyes came to rest on the last joint on my third finger. The tip just dangled down. My finger looked like a sideways L. I tried pushing the tip back into place, which was extremely painful, but it just flopped down again. The end of my finger just wouldn't stay up. It wasn't broken, that much I knew, but it definitely wasn't working the way it should have.

Not to be undone, I tried again to get the end of my finger back to its rightful place. I drew my breath in through clenched teeth and jumped around on the spot in pain while I pushed the end joint back up. My joint was swelling up along with the tears in my eyes. Stop, stop, I had to stop; it was just too sore. I looked at my hand. It just looked silly. A wee thing, a little thing not quite right. Not enough to evoke much sympathy from the parents; it looked idiotic.

No matter how much I tried to make my finger work, it wouldn't. I found out later that it is commonly known as mallet or baseball finger. The tendon snaps at the end of your finger, and the tip drops down. Apparently, according to NHS UK, mallet finger is a common sports injury. Great! I suppose, pulling up my knickers could be regarded as a sport! That bit of information I have kept to myself.

I was contemplating what to do about it next when I heard banging on the door.

"Yes, yes, just coming." It was a complete lie, but what was I to do? Jump out with my dangling finger and say, "Actually, can you pull up my breeches, please, and while you are at it, my knickers as well."

"Umm, the parents are waiting. Is everything alright in there?" Which I knew was code for, "The bairns are getting fed up, and the hall is about to descend into numerous paddies and tantrums, and that's just the adults."

There comes a point in everyone's life when they know they will just have to suck it up and ask for help, never mind the consequences. After a further few minutes of trying to negotiate with a pair of undies that had grown a life of their own, I knew my moment of embarrassment had arrived. This was going to be prolonged as, of course, I had sent away my Good Samaritan.

Hobbling and shuffling my way out the door, I passed what some would optimistically have described as the washing basin area. Some more realistic individuals had kindly supplied antibacterial wipes for use. I was waving my sore hand in the air, while my other hand gripped like grim death to my angled undies and trousers. Both had become twisted and bound together like rope, making them impossible to pull up one-handed. Determined that some of my dignity would remain intact, I just needed to catch Karen's attention.

The door flew open to reveal two very determined individuals who, whatever the cause of my tarried appearance, were going to get to the bottom of it and sort it out. Thankfully, Karen was one of them. Once the stunned expressions had left their faces, howls of laughter followed.

"Okay, I've got this." Karen sent the other parent back into the hall to get everyone organised for starting the session. As expected from a true friend, Karen stopped laughing long enough to get me decent enough to carry on. After all, she was a highly trained individual used to fitting pre-school children of whatever nature and mood swing into undergarments as soon as you could blink.

"I'll go and let the others know we're just coming."

"Thanks. Could you put the music on? I really will be right there, and the bairns can dance around until I get in."

Returning to the hall a few minutes later, I got the distinct impression that most had been made aware of my predicament. A good few heads seemed to be buried in their children's hair, and I could have sworn I heard a stifled laugh somewhere.

Not wanting to appear paranoid, I continued my way up the hall and took hold of one of the puppets. Then something really gross happened – my mallet finger refused to go inside the puppet. Never mind how hard I tried, it just dangled like some scarecrow's appendage waggling about on its own.

"Oh look, Mummy, that finger don't like that puppet; it won't go in," said one helpful child.

Other children were looking more worried, eyes wide, observing my mini tussle.

"I'm sorry," I said. "I've had a little accident in the toilet, and it doesn't look like I'll be able to manage the puppets today. Do you think you can help me work them?" Distraction is an effective technique, and I was living in hope that all anyone would remember was that everyone had a great time working the puppets.

"Oh, yes," said one small voice. "And don't worry about your little accident. My mummy says that they happen to everyone. You'll be dry soon."

I knew then, as parents' laughter filled the hall, that there was no way the community was going to let me forget my tussle with the cludgie and my mallet finger.

Chapter 9

Auntie Lottie's first spring as a full-time resident also heralded in an exceptionally mild break in the weather. We all started to emerge from our hibernation. Big coats and woolly hats were being replaced optimistically with light jackets and jumpers. Villagers also started looking around for some sort of entertainment, preferably close to their own front doorstep. Or somebody else's, if possible.

'Please, come to the grand opening of my garden shed.' The invitation arrived just at the right moment.

Everyone had been following Paul of the Sheds progress since his old hut had finally disintegrated in the first storm of winter. Paul of the Sheds was an important member of our community, being part of the volunteer fire brigade, the mountain rescue and a member of the lifeboat crew. Our very own multi-disciplined rescuer. As and when the weather and his call-outs had allowed, he had reinstated, improved and added to what had become a pile of stones with a missing roof.

Anyone who could, whenever possible, had helped to resurrect it from the ruins. The males of the village, in particular, were eager to assist and see inside this new super-efficient 'man shed'. It was the most up-to-date, ultimate garden outhouse, complete with Paul's ferrets.

Now it was finished, at last, and secretly envied by many of the men in the community who would have loved their very own 'man shed'. Storage had been built in for homemade winemaking and beermaking. A sociable area with plenty of room for having the craic with friends and generally hanging out was also included. Lots of small tools and equipment had been arranged neatly around the walls. All the bigger trappings that were needed for Paul of the Sheds many jobs were still stored under lock and key in his boating shed near the harbour.

It was accepted by all, and good manners dictated, that party food would not be the shop-bought or slaved-over homebaked variety. No, this food would be the real thing, keeping in step with the spirit of the shed. It consisted of burgers and steaks of all kinds, including bunny burgers, venison, beef and salmon, all organically farmed or caught locally. All vegetables were homegrown, but they were a side item, especially at that time of year. The rest was honest to goodness, no-nonsense food. Meat and game – hunted, raised or road-killed. It was a 'vegetarians beware' event. Fruit could be found, but it came mostly in the form of wine or beer.

Entertainment was provided by all who attended, which only seemed fair, especially as the revellers were getting fed and watered. The starting time of 8 p.m. was written on everyone's invitations except, of course, for Peter the Pipes'. His invitation had the start time of 7.15 p.m., in the forlorn hope that, perhaps, he would make it sometime that night. The idea was for him to start the evening off with a piped procession down to the refurbished shed. Unfortunately, true to form, he didn't appear till much later, by which time, many were perhaps a little bit too merry to form anything that resembled a stately procession.

It must be ranked as one of the shortest parades ever. Revellers only had to dance a few steps to reach that monument among sheds. As the dancers in the front reached the shed door, those still waiting in line jigged around behind them. In the end, it turned into a bagpipe conga, mixing a kind of traditional

Scottish dance with the swirl of the pipes and alcohol. Most of us were dancing, continually contorting ourselves round and round the garden past the building's door.

"Ach, look at him, man. He's away with himself." Peter the Pipes was totally lost in his music. The melody grew in its complexity and wildness. Auntie Lottie headed up the front of the procession, dancing in abandonment, much restored to her former health.

Wood smoke flavoured the air as large flames whipped around burning logs. The bright blaze from the fire caused weird shadows to form. Heads, bodies, arms and legs all danced, mixed together in silhouette against the shed. An image, created by our national bard, Robert Burns' epic poem, *Tam o' Shanter*, flashed into my head. Did that mean our Auntie Lottie could be his Cutty-sark? That was a sobering thought. Thankfully, both her age and her form of dress counted her out. Then again, wild music and dancing witches were not that far removed from what was right there in front of me.

The more refined entertainment had gone on beforehand, at a time when people could recall what was happening and give it the attention it so rightly deserved.

Bards came in many guises, often found in the least likely places. At one time, they travelled the roads and entertained communities on their way. The great poets of their time, esteemed for their talents, they were also the keepers of our folklore.

We still had a bard, Mary's Angus. The couple arrived and flowed through the company, toward the centre of the gathering, an expectant hush followed in their wake. Angus was able to construct a poem about anything, cleverly intertwining his knowledge of our history, our todays and predicting what may come to pass. He played with our emotions, leaving us either melancholy or sore with laughter. His 'Ode to the Shed' was a masterpiece in raucous, rhythm and rhyme. He blended-in Auntie Lottie's cottage renovations and the new housing development, both so important, especially to me.

Ode to a Shed

Behold the shed of astounding beauty
Built especially to hide man's bounty.
It started broken and in tatters
Now like a phoenix it has risen from the ashes
Her foundations, true, sturdy and strong
All, hope she will be inhabited before too long
Of course, you realise I talk of the new building
Not the ladies sitting here reverently listening
Her frame was ruined, broken and battered
Weathered, ageing, fallen and in tatters
In case you are wondering again of what I am talking
It's the cottage, not this woman standing here near her dotage.

Auntie Lottie tried to look outraged then burst out laughing; honoured to be immortalised in one of Angus' poems. His words had mingled with the hissing and crackling of the obligatory fire, which was well ignited by the end of his performance.

"Ellen, don't you think the fire is a bit too near that tree?"

"Stop worrying, Stroma. If it falls, it fuels the fire."

"But don't you think that rope swing should have been taken down?"

"Don't fuss so much, Stroma. We are all big boys and girls, just enjoy yourself."

Great-Aunt Lottie jumped back and flicked an ember from her singed cardigan. A faint whiff of burning wool tinged the wood smoke. The level of alcohol consumption was just getting to the point where the partygoers were starting to eye up the rope swing. Most had consumed the homemade wine which is generally the tastiest and most lethal concentrate anyone will ever partake of.

The heavens sensed this and decided to intervene. The wind and rain came from nowhere and grew into a freezing frenzy. My hair was dripping wet and icy on one side, while my other side was toasting in the heat blasting out from the fire. Tatties, roasting in the blaze could be heard exploding, showering the heat-hoggers with baking hot mash.

Inevitably, it came to that time of night when the more adventurous decided that being soaked to the skin by the rain was not enough, only skinny-dipping would do. If they were to get wet anyway, they might as well get wet at the beach, even though it was not a particularly warm night. With the wilder revellers among the party departed, the rest of us could enjoy a quieter time.

The rain had ceased, so it was the perfect excuse for the local storyteller to regale us with tales of honour, legends of old and, of course, accounts of amusing and unbelievable deeds. Angus stood up again. He had been collecting tales and stories about the community since he was a boy. Each year, they seemed to grow in the telling, becoming more woven and complicated with every delivery. Many, however, were older than that and offered warnings to those who listened.

The Tale of Finnian MacPhail

You remember the tale of Finnian MacPhail?
A man of great wealth, shoulders the size of mountains
Legs so long he stood as tall as a tree
A warrior he, a prince, a man of land
On a night like this full of celebration, noble friends and visitors, seated around his table

When all of a sudden there comes a knock at his door
A woman stands, black of dress and round of shoulders
White hair tangled like a bird's nest
She pants and spits almost out of breath
"A crumb from you table," she is heard to gasp
"Away old hag, to bed, be gone, find somewhere else to
rest your head.
My guests are hungry you will have to wait, get gone
now, it is getting late."
"A curse on your house, you greedy man, no fuel for your
belly, no sons for your loins, death will become you before
you are old.
No memories of your heroism will ever be told"
The old sick hag pointed a tremoring finger at the warrior
Now Finnian MacPhail was so filled with rage, he told his
squire to kill her right there
The squire was young and kind and noble
He hid the old hag and fed her from his very own table
Finnian MacPhail rode out the next day, helping his
visitors on their way
He turned for home as day turned to night, and a terrible
scream engulfed his horse into fright
Finnian MacPhail fell to his death as the horse raced
home, his clan now bereft
And what of the squire so young and so noble?
He grew to be great was loved, rich and honourable
So take heed my friends, keep this tale in mind, to
whoever comes seeking help, listen and always be kind
Don't be like the warrior, Finnian MacPhail
Be generous and helpful and in life you will never fail.

By the time he was finished, the bathers had returned loudly
triumphant, shivering violently. Time for hot toddies, coffee

laced with something special, blankets and big towels. Music flowed, and guitars strummed accompaniments to sweet and low songs. All designed to mellow out the revellers and wind down the cèilidh, in the same way a mother used hot chocolate and a lullaby to woo her children to bed and sleep. Just as the levels had quieted down and people had either begun to drift off to sleep or head home, the sun commenced its slow, crimson glide back up into the world. Birds started to compete with the singers, until eventually, their morning recital became too powerful and musical to ignore.

We all sat mesmerised by their choral repertoire. The fire had burnt down to glowing embers and the shed, who's honour the party had been held in, sat restfully outlined by the brightening rays of the rising sun. It had been thoroughly and memorably celebrated and would go on to create and inspire numerous stories to add to its colourful beginning.

Chapter 10

"When's Jack back then?" I filled up Karen's cup with more hot water and passed it over.

"Tomorrow night, hopefully, depending on weather, flights and so on." She helped herself to more cake and placed her cup on top of her thirty-nine-week bump which had grown enormous in the last few weeks.

"Well, see you wait until then; no going into labour tonight. The bridge is closed for repairs, so it would be the long way round. I don't fancy having to get you there, so go home and put your feet up." I hoped she and her bump were listening to my plea.

"Phew, after the way you disgraced yourself the last time, I'm really hoping I don't have to rely on you." Karen laughed.

Since Fergus, their first child had been born almost three years ago, I had been living with the teasing from close friends about my failure as a birthing partner. Things had just been starting to settle down, then Karen had announced her latest pregnancy. That had opened the way for yet more ribbing directed at me. Still, I felt 'disgraced' was rather a strong word. True, it hadn't been one of my best moments, but I felt there had been mitigating circumstances. Anyway, if blame was to be placed at anyone's feet, it should be at Jack's. He was the one who couldn't get home in time for the birth. That had left me with no choice but to step in.

*

I could hear the panic in her voice when Karen phoned me, three years ago, in labour.

"Could you come and keep me company? I'm scared. I've been taken in; they think I'm in labour, and Jack is still on the rig. We don't even know if he will get off anytime soon. Fog's awful out there."

How could I have said no? Poor Karen was a little before her due date, and Jack was working offshore which was a pretty normal state of affairs in the Highlands. Most other people had commitments that couldn't be dropped at the last moment. Besides, what else would I do when my best friend asked for help?

I stupidly thought maybe a few hours or, at worst, until teatime, then I could go home to rest. But like the best laid plans of mice and men and all that, babies, it would seem, have a timetable all of their own. If they can cause any sort of disruption before they arrive, they will.

Karen's firstborn was not going to wait for anyone, no injection was going to stop it coming, no late appearance from dad, persuasion from the soon-to-be mother or any other sort of intervention was stopping that child from making its entrance when and how it liked.

By the time dad arrived at the hospital, I had been there for what felt like days but it had only been about twelve hours. I had had nothing to eat or drink – the cafe was closed. It was in the wee small hours which would mean nothing if you were on a night out but meant everything when you had been closeted in a hospital ward for endless hours.

"Don't go," Karen had pleaded. "You've been with me through most of it now. Please wait until baby is here."

The midwifes ran the unit as if it was still the early twentieth century. On no account would they be outnumbered in the room, and only if they were feeling generous, which they begrudgingly were, could the father of the child be there too. So mum, sisters or anyone resembling support were not allowed in.

That was why I was sitting, at 3 a.m., in a tiny, cold area that joined two corridors together. Someone had put in two chairs which were neither comfy enough nor big enough. The humming refrigerator only had Coke which I knew would give me a sore head. That horrible electric machine switched off and on every few minutes while continually flashing white lights at me. I just knew a migraine was waiting for me around the corner.

Hours dripped by with no news. My electric enemy continued to shake, flash, hum and make itself unbearable. I hated it. If I could have, I would have had it crushed. I'm sure that thing could have been used as a form of torture with great success. I would have told it anything, if it would only have shut up and stopped flashing white lights at me. It sat there, laughing at me. It knew I would buy that fizzy drink eventually, that I didn't want to leave to find water elsewhere with Karen so close to delivery.

A nurse had come to tell me that Karen was just about to deliver, but that had been over two hours ago. I had been watching midwifes and doctors rushing backwards and forwards along the corridor for a while. Had something gone wrong? I couldn't leave. I was on tenterhooks. I hoped they were all okay. It was nearly 5 a.m.

"It's a baby," Jack shouted in glee. "It's here."

"Is Karen okay? What did you have? Is baby okay?"

"Yes, yes everyone is fine. It's a baby."

"Yes, I know that bit – boy or girl?"

"Oh, hold on, be back in a tick."

By the time Jack returned, Karen was being wheeled back to her ward while her beautiful baby boy was sped off to the Special Care Baby Unit.

I followed behind the new parents and realised that the white flashing lights I had been coping with all night were still following me around. I began to feel a bit sick. Karen was put into the ward while I tried to form the words to congratulate them. I started to feel decidedly awful.

"I'm going to be sick," I murmured.

"Grab her," a nurse shouted and stuck a bowl under my face. "Look, that side ward is empty, put her in there for a wee lie down. Someone will come and check on you in a few minutes."

I remember lying on the bed feeling a total sap. I wasn't the one who had just given birth, but I was the one throwing up, and I couldn't even lift my head.

"Get up, get up. You need to get out of here. Get some fresh air, you'll be fine." My pep talk to myself wasn't working. Eventually, I struggled up and headed for the door, said a quick embarrassed goodbye to Karen and started to stagger out of the maternity suite. Jack was also leaving by then and was shadowing me out. I stumbled out of the self-locking maternity doors just as I felt another wave of nausea wash over me and crumpled into a wall. Jack was stuck behind the self-locking doors frantically pressing the release button to no effect.

A doctor came rushing over toward me. "This woman is ill; somebody get her a wheelchair."

"Ach no, she's fine; she's with me. Couldn't stand seeing a birth; she's just got a wee bit of a headache." A wee bit! I could tell from that statement Jack had never suffered from a migraine.

"Well, if you're sure. You need to take better care of her. Get her home."

Jack, being a new dad, had no intention of driving all the way home though. He wanted to be close to his new son and Karen.

I was deposited at his mother's house and put to bed with a bowl strategically placed while they all went to work. It was late afternoon before I was able to get up and sneak away home with my tail between my legs. When all attention should have been on the new family, I had managed to divert some onto myself.

*

Nobody let me forget what had happened. It was a constant source of amusement among both Karen's and Jack's families. I cringed every time it was mentioned. Maybe if I didn't get so embarrassed, they would have let it lie.

I was amazed when Karen had asked me to be ready as a backup if she went into labour before Jack got back again. Unlike Karen, who had yet to pack her bags, I was more prepared. My bag was ready. Fruit was replaced every few days, while the bottles of water and other snacks remained at the ready inside. My migraine tablets took pride of place just to be on the safe side. I had considered taking ear plugs and dark glasses in case of another night spent with that ugly monster in the so-called waiting corner, but I had decided that may be taking things a bit too far.

"You need to come as soon as you can. Jack's mum has the wee man for a sleep over anyway, but I need you to come now." Karen panted down the phone.

"But the bridge is closed. You can't be serious? Are you winding me up after this afternoon?" I crossed my fingers and waited.

"GET HERE NOW." That was more than Karen's normal teacher voice thundering down the phone at me.

Karen was one of those people who never seemed to lose her temper; calm oozed from her like honey from a comb. It would have driven me mad, if she wasn't my friend. I'd never heard her raise her voice before like that, not even the last time she was in labour. This was nothing though compared to the Mrs Hyde she was going to turn into during the night.

"Where the hell have you been?" She stalked past me, slamming the car door. "Come on then; I thought you would have been here ages ago."

"In fairness, it's only been fifteen minutes."

"Fifteen minutes! Have you any idea what fifteen minutes feels like when you have a Heffalump jumping up and down on your bladder?"

Well, actually, I didn't. I really didn't want to know what it felt like.

"Can you not get this piece of junk to move faster? I am HAVING A BABY HERE."

I couldn't believe what was happening to my cool and calm friend. She was turning into a monster before my eyes – panting and yelling, shouting and swearing. My sense of well-being and confidence was rapidly seeping away as this mad woman continued to berate me.

"Fucking bridge! Who the fuck closes a bridge on a night like this? I hate living here. Jesus, the long way round. Oh my God could you drive any slower?"

"I'm doing my best." Which was better than she would have managed given her condition.

"It's all your fault, you know, all yours."

I looked at Karen. "Really? There is no way you can blame your pregnancy on me."

"OH my God! Are you really arguing with a pregnant lady? Aaah, Jesus, just get a move on!"

"She's in labour; she's in pain; she is not herself." I mumbled this mantra under my breath. I was doing her a favour, for goodness sake. If anyone should have been getting lambasted it should have been Jack. He hadn't made it home on time for Karen's labour, again.

Our detour took us through a small town that had two sets of traffic lights, an unusual enough occurrence in the Highlands. I was praying they would be at green.

"Just go through the bloody things. Who's going to be out on a night like this, anyway? Drive through." As it turned out, the who were the police. I'd already spotted them. By then, though, I had already decided who I was most scared of, but thankfully, the lights had turned to green.

"Stupid, stupid, bloody lights," said my companion, panting.

"Not far now; just hold on." Too late I realised that was a major mistake. I spent the next twenty minutes being shouted at, panted at and blamed for everything to nothing but mostly for introducing Karen to that treacherous, scheming monster of a husband who couldn't even be home in time for the birth of his child.

I noticed the nearer we got to the hospital the less this baby seemed to belong to her. It was all to do with Jack, and she was the poor innocent who was having to do all the work. I was secretly glad that Jack was getting his share of castigation too.

The midwifes took one look at Karen and said, "Oh my, you are way further on than we expected. You sounded so calm on the phone."

"You think! Could you … ooh, ooh, ooh … just stop talking and get this thing out?"

"Ah, like that is it? Could you let go of the door handle and we can pop you into something more comfortable? Let go now, come on, just release your fingers." The midwife was prising Karen's death grip from the door when another nurse came past.

"My, we thought you would be ages yet. You look nicely on your way."

"Nicely! There is ... ooh, ooh, ooh ... nothing and ... ooh, ooh, ooh ... I mean nothing nice about THIS!"

The not so secret smile that passed between the professionals was thankfully lost on Karen.

In between contractions, they had Karen changed and sitting up in the delivery bed with monitors bleeping at her side. A midwife was patting her shoulder and trying to encourage her along. "Pant, that's it, you're doing so well. Just pant, well done."

I must admit the calm voice was even getting on my nerves, but at least I didn't pull the midwife forward and say, "I *am* bloody panting, and if you say just once more in ... ooh, ooh, ooh ... in that patronising voice how good I'm doing ... ooh, ooh, ooh ... then I will not be held responsible for what I ... ooh, ooh, ooh—"

"We can't seem to find a vein here," interrupted another midwife.

"Well, I know I've blood running ... ooh, ooh ... in my veins or I would be DEAD. Just bloody ... ooh, ooh, ooh ... find one."

Karen didn't really need to snarl like that. I was slowly sinking into the floor in humiliation. I didn't know who this person was, but I didn't like her. My mantra of 'she's in labour, she's in pain, she is not herself,' had long since departed. I didn't need to be shouted at either, especially when I was there supporting her. I could feel little shoots of annoyance growing toward her as she continued to scold me in waves that were synchronised with her contractions. I was sure she sensed how I felt. Her eyes raged into mine. If looks could kill, I would have been dead. She crushed my hand in a superhuman grip. If I could have pulled my hand away, I would have, and she would have been on her own, and good bloody luck to her too.

"WHAT!" she yelled at me.

I involuntarily jumped just as the senior midwife arrived. "Okay, no time for anything else; let's get baby out. She's well on her way. Yes, look, I can see the hair."

Yuck, was my initial reaction, followed quickly by, *Good, I can be out of here soon.* I could leave her to the company of her own bad temper.

"Push, now, Karen, push. There's a good girl."

"I … am … pushing," a guttural voice boomed out of the creature that used to be Karen as she grunted, screamed and panted her way to motherhood again.

Lindsay arrived in a torment of noise where everything seemed to happen at once. The ferocious Karen vanished in a puff of air. My sidekick had returned – calm, cool and exuberant. My bitterness dispelled in a cloud of happiness as I watched my amazing friend and her truly beautiful baby cosseted together in love.

"Oh, look, she's so bonnie, perfect. Thank you so much everyone. You know I could hear myself and was cringing inside, but I just couldn't stop. It was like something had taken over me. I'm so sorry for being so horrible."

"Not to worry. It's just Mother Nature." The midwife grinned.

Myself, I was just hoping they stuck at two. I didn't know if our friendship could take another labour like that one. I glanced down again at Karen and Lindsay and realised, whatever it took, I would be there.

Chapter 11

Asalmon. What on earth was I going to do with half a side of salmon just won in a raffle? As a visitor, it would look bad if I just handed it back and asked them to redraw the number. I had done the walk of triumph to collect my unknown prize as jealous eyes glared into my back. There was no way I could return it and save face, especially as I was trying to work with the local community, so I received it with good grace, managing to look totally enthralled, and regained my seat beside my colleague at the back of the hall.

"Well done, wish I had won that. What a great prize."

If it had been under any other circumstances, I would have loved to have won a tasty piece of salmon. But this particular side, from its nose to its tail, would have to stay in a warm bedroom overnight, travel over water, not under it, then spend hours on a bus before it got anywhere near a refrigerator. Not a mean feat or impossible for a salmon really, as they undertake much worse journeys in their lifetime, but this was my lifetime, and I hadn't planned on spending an evening with a pink, fleshy fillet. It did, however, remain my confidante for the night as we secretly measured the acts, reciting and singing, against the ones I had heard back home.

It was not a fun-loving, fundraising type of cèilidh with showpieces delivered by local children from the resident primary school. No, it was a seriously charged event, and if there were children present, then they would give prize-winning performances on pain of extra sessions after school. Adults, juniors, duets, quartets, male and female choirs – every act was gratefully received by their home audience as their voices blended together in a melodic dance of songs and words. We also enjoyed and took delight in their delivery as they were not our competition; we didn't have anything like these locally. Soloists were a different thing; we had just as many of those at home.

My silent and, by now, slightly smelly friend was in total agreement – I could tell as he continued his unblinking stare across the table. This was the greatest and most important cèilidh of the year. The unspoken but silently understood official rehearsal for those who would take part in the Royal National Mod, the world companionships of the Gaelic-speaking world.

As the night went on, our fishy friend grew in stature, becoming our very own silent drinking buddy. Relied upon to keep a secret, those staring eyes never blinked once at what myself or my work colleague did or told him. By the end of the night, he wasn't the only one with staring eyes. The fact that I was constantly consulting a fish proved to me it was time to find my bed.

"Bedtime and don't forget our little friend there."

"There's a 'tail' or two to be told about tonight. Tail, ha, do you get it? Well, you did, didn't you? Get the tail, the head, the side." My colleague was in peals of laughter, pointing at our fishy friend.

"On a scale of one to ten, that's not even past two."

"Very funny, I'm off before any other comedians get started."

So, off we went, my winnings firmly clamped under my arm. Not the best move as odour could have been seeping from the packaging. Fortunately, it was a cold, windy night which helped waft away any smell. His natural cologne streaked away in the wind, not allowing him to overpower my rather expensive perfume. My prize had become one of my most valued possessions, at least for that evening. The rather large amount of whisky which had been consumed probably contributed to that feeling.

It was when I got to my hotel room that I realised just how big my fishy friend was. In an attempt to cool him down and give him as close to a natural environment as I could, I decided a little bath in the sink was needed. I could only get his body half submerged; his tail and head were left spilling over. Still, if even a part of him was kept cool, hopefully, he would stay preserved until the morning, when I would start my homeward journey.

To help control everything below smelly temperature point, I forced a window open. The freezing blast hit me in the eyes, and I quickly departed the bathroom, closing the door and laying a towel at the bottom to stop any aroma and icy drafts keeping me awake.

By morning, everything smelt fresh enough. The possibility that I might have got conditioned to any faint whiff didn't cross my mind. The light wind blowing around the bathroom hadn't appeared overly fishy. I wrapped my towel around my lovely side of salmon, which had reverted back to being a mere raffle prize, and placed it inside my overnight bag. Angus and Mary, back in Blàs, would appreciate a piece of the fish when I got back, I was sure.

It was one of those bright blue, clear, crisp, clean April mornings that the Highlands do so well. The sun was shining in the cloudless sky while the water reflected everything in its slow, rhythmic swell. Large northern gannets were putting on a display, sweeping their wings back and diving into the swell. That day's passage was going to be another bonnie crossing of seascape and wildlife. I felt the anticipation as the ferry's engines throbbed beneath my feet.

As we cleared the harbour, the wind perked up, and I watched the spray break across the bow and glisten in the sun. Seabirds, like low-flying aviators, skimmed the crests of the waves, searching for food.

The further we sailed away from the isle, the rougher the sea became. The ferry was now going against the swell and the once gentle movement of the decks was now more like a rock-and-roll motion. Some of my fellow passengers were morphing before my eyes from palest shades of grey to ominous shades of green.

"If only that smell of fish wasn't so strong, I'd be alright," complained one passenger who, right afterward, ran a hasty, if somewhat staggering, race to the toilets.

"Can you not do something about that smell?" asked another green-tinged invalid who lay prostrate along some seats.

"We're trying," said the steward as he passed me, "but we can't find the source." He had started to retrace his steps toward me and stopped close enough that I heard him take in deep breaths. He scented the air, like some spaniel trying to root out a rabbit, or a side of salmon. Sweat broke out on my back, not caused by seasickness but fear, awaiting my certain humiliation when unmasked as the provider of the prevailing smell. Thankfully, just before our friendly 'spaniel' honed in on my bag, he was called away to help clear up after someone who had just lost the race to the nearest toilet.

"For those of you not hanging over the side," came the intercom voice, "if you care to look over to starboard, you will see a school of dolphins. For those of you hanging over the side, please take care and hold on firmly to the rails as we are experiencing a wee bit of a swell at the moment." That was my cue and chance to escape without loss of face. Grabbing my coat and bag, I scuttled outside.

The wind hit me with its fresh, cold, cleansing gust as I staggered toward the side and gripped on. Dolphins leapt, splashed and whizzed under and around the ship, their apparent joy intoxicating. Humiliation, smells and the piercingly stinging cold evaporated in delight while I watched the animals interact with the ferry and each other, a truly amazing sight.

Seeing these animals in their natural environment doing what they do best, racing around, choosing to share their world with us, for even a short time, was magical.

I spent the rest of the voyage outside, huddled against the wind, not caring thanks to the spectacular display of our native sealife. Seals bathed on rugged rocks. In the shallows, herons, stood stock-still in their favourite hunting pose. Ducks of various sizes and colours dipped up and down on the waves as we neared the mainland.

After we disembarked from the ferry, I made my way along to the bus that would take us east.

I sat down and heard a fellow passenger saying, "I can still smell something."

"Can't smell a thing," came the voice from inside a bundle of clothes sitting just behind me. I wasn't that surprised – the smell of alcohol and garlic evaporating from him was even stronger than the pong from my backpack.

At the turn-off to the village, I could see Auntie Lottie's car. This was one of the big benefits of her return to the village. She had taken to looking out for me. Not in an intrusive manner, but in helpful little ways that made my life easier. I don't know if she felt compelled to do this after me allowing her to share my home, but whatever the reason, it saved me a long walk home.

"Oh goodness, what is that awful smell?"

"I won a side of salmon in a raffle."

"Didn't they like you then?"

"I think the seal on the package may be leaking."

"Well, open your window. We'll probably attract all the cats in the area. In fact, we'll drop in at Mary's and Angus'. I'm sure their cat will love it. That thing is not fit for human consumption smelling like that."

I knew she was right.

Chapter 12

It was time to leave. I couldn't be late, although turning up ahead of time would also have its consequences. Getting the balance right was crucial. Hospitality was always difficult to turn down being regarded as quite rude by some. The last time I had arrived too early to pick up the vice-chairperson, paradoxically, we had barely made it to the event on time.

*

"Oh, come on in, Stroma, a quick cup of coffee; we've got ages left before we have to be there." Not, as it turned out, by the time she had taken two phone calls, had a quick twenty-minute talk with her husband and said *oidhche mhath* to her children.

Worse was to come when I took her home afterward. In a spirit of celebration, I succumbed to the offer of a wee dram. Unfortunately, after much searching, she could only find an old bottle of parsley wine that was, in her estimation, at least ten years old. I have vague memories of hugging a particularly large oak tree that resides halfway through the local woods with absolutely no recollection of how we got there or why midnight had seemed the best time to go tramping off through said dark woods. A firm rule I now stand by states: no homemade wine that is older than a primary-five child, no matter if it is marketed as a fun way of taking your five-a-day, will pass my lips.

"It's only gooseberries, raspberries and elderberries after all," really should send out the warning signals instead of the companionable thoughts of, *Yes, great idea, healthy berries, pour me another.*

*

That evening, no homemade brew had been offered yet, and the vice-chairperson of the Development Trust had finished her crofting duties. At that time of year, it was mainly a quick check on the sheep and their lambs and then the cattle. So, we were ready to leave on time.

"The others are meeting us in the car park. We're expecting the usual crowd of competitors. Jack and Paul of the Sheds have been great at persuading new entrants to sign up. Well, they can't really get away from them when they are all cutting the peat together. Local radio have us well established as part of their yearly features, so we've had quite a lot of free publicity from them too. We're hopeful of a good crowd."

Fundraising in a small rural community is difficult. Because it is just that, a small community. If money is being looked for, it is always the same few pockets that it comes out of. Therefore, more and more ingenious and sometimes outrageous ways of finding cash have to be thought up.

We were going to Blàs' big annual Development Trust fundraiser that didn't impinge too much on local pockets. We needed to continually raise money thanks to the housing development eating up our funds at an alarming rate. It was our 'Pie, Pint and Peat' competition. Basically, teams of three entered. One member from each would eat a pie, the second would drink a pint, then both joined the third member who would have started building a peat stack. It was all timed and each team had up to five minutes.

The prize went to the biggest stack that would stay up, more or less, on its own. A degree of surreptitious holding up was allowed. Over the years, a second prize had been developed and was awarded to the most creative stack. It had grown to be as coveted as the prize for the tallest stack.

Neighbouring communities had been entering since the beginning. It was our fourth year, and the number of teams competing continued to grow. Revenue raised helped to fund local projects such as the new housing development. Everyone knew just how important the work of the Development Trust had become. Rumours had been going around before the event that another local family was moving away. They had been staying with their parents on what they had hoped would be a short-term basis, and now, their patience had run out. Desperate to have their own home, they had taken the decision to move to Inverness where accommodation was easier to find.

Their move would affect the school roll. The fundraising event suddenly took on a new level of importance for me. A drop in pupil numbers would mean a drop in the number of teachers employed at the school. I stamped firmly down on my worries. The 'Pie, Pint and Peat' competition was there to be enjoyed.

As we neared the car park, we could see there was indeed a huge turnout. Early on a balmy May evening, the sky was blue, dotted with little puffs of white cloud. On a trailer sat a table complete with pints of beer at the ready and a plate of pork pies. An area was set out nearby where the peat building would take place. This allowed three teams to compete at the same time. Angus was to be the commentator. Those strangers who had turned up could be forgiven for thinking he was either very drunk or completely bonkers.

"*Fàilte*, welcome everyone to our annual pie, pint and peat-stacking competition. The object for the day is to raise as much money as we can for our community group. So, dig deep in your pockets please. For the competing teams, you have a pie, a beer and a pile of peat to stack. Speed and creativity will both be considered in the judging. Are the first three teams ready? Good, let's get started then."

Almost as soon as the whistle went for the teams to start, the first objections could be heard.

"Someone doctored my pie", "He only had foam in his glass", "This beer is warm". Bits and pieces of peat broke from the turfs as they were manhandled into position; dried moss and other bog plants littered the area.

More than half the teams had competed, our neighbouring town and constant rivals, Inbhirasgaidh, looked to be in the lead. They had downed both the pie and the pint in record time. Their stack also looked the highest so far. Although, a gentle nudge in the right place could bring it all down. We needed some local pride restored. Paul of the Sheds' team were up, and the local cheering reached fever pitch. Personally, I have never seen anyone take so long to eat a pie. Didn't he know it was a competition?

Paul of the Sheds had obviously been brought up well and had been told not to gobble his food. He certainly made a meal of it as he took out a small plate from his jacket pocket, and a bottle of sauce and a piece of kitchen roll containing a knife and fork from another pocket. He placed the pie on the plate and slowly cut it into bite-size pieces. The longer this homage to the silent movies went on, the more laugher it generated.

Jack, Karen's husband, had the second phase. He sipped his pint, finger in the air, dabbing gently at his mouth with a tissue. All the while, on his other side, competitor after competitor, leapt onto the trailer, rammed the pie in their mouths, gulped down the pint and raced to stack the peats in what they all hoped was record-breaking time.

DJ had come down from the glen to be their third team member. He had already started laying the peat. So far, it resembled nothing like a tall stack. Ignoring all the heckling and laughter, the three men worked together. They were obviously going all out for the creative prize.

Eventually, just within the allocated time, there stood a small crofter's cottage, complete with a miniature peat stall and Highland cow. There was no doubt who would win the creative prize this year.

The good feeling this produced was taken forward into the raffle. Angus excelled in his poetic description of the prizes in an attempt to squeeze as much money as possible from those watching.

"Pure liquid gold encased within a finely chiselled cut-glass bottle. It will put hairs on your chest, muscles on your arms and is known for its medicinal properties. Not one but four bottles of this pure, sought-after Scottish drink, bottled during one of the best vintages known. It could be yours with the right ticket—"

"Ach away, man. These bottles of Irn Bru were bought fae the shop across the road." Howls of laughter ensued, but so did the clinking of coins. The amount of money raised that night was one of our largest.

Before the evening was done, the vice-chairperson was asking me, "Can you make the next Development Trust meeting? It's on Monday. I know Ellen can't make it again, but I am happy to take this forward. We heard about a great fundraiser held years ago in Bonar Bridge. I've been in touch with the old *cròileagan* committee and asked them for a few tips and some advice. I want to get it started before we lose the momentum."

"Well, you've done really well tonight. Do you think the community can afford to stick their hands in their pockets so quickly again?"

"A lot of the money raised has been from people coming to take part and watch, so we haven't been too badly hit ourselves. Besides, everyone has had such a good time. People are asking when our next event is. Any follow-up peat event has to wait till next year for the peats to dry."

*

Nothing, I felt, could surpass our 'Pie, Pint and Peat' competition, but it appeared that I was wrong. What was put on the table at the meeting the following week was a 'Crofter's Fashion Show'.

There was a lack of males at the meeting due to an organised fishing trip. This meant the women had a free hand in planning and strategic thinking. Auntie Lottie had come along; she had decided, now that she was living here permanently, she wanted to be more involved in community life. She was first to start the ball rolling.

"Since the men are not here, I think we should volunteer some of them in their absence. We may have to be a little conniving if we want to persuade them to take part. Any ideas?"

This was not to be a fashion show of the green wellies and Harris tweed variety.

"Well, I'm pretty sure I can get Jack to do 'sporty crofter'. I'll tell him DJ has volunteered and is keen to do the swimming trunks with welly boots. He would look a right wimp then if he didn't step up to do the sporty crofter. I mean, he'll only have to roll up the legs of his boiler suit, wear his normal wellies and carry a racket." Karen had started the volunteering of the missing men.

"How are you going to get DJ to do the swimming trunks and welly boots?" All eyes swivelled to Helga.

"Just try and stop him showing off his body. He won't be needing asked twice. Anyway, I'll tell DJ that Paul of the Sheds wanted to do it, but I saved the slot for him as he has a nicer body – that should work."

By the end of the meeting, the women of the community had volunteered enough male models. By appealing to their vanity, sense of humour, honour or by using straight-up blackmail, the men would appear in a variety of outfits ranging from boiler suits to shorts to tailored suits, all combined with various different accessories. They'd be showing a little or a lot of bare skin, depending on how outrageous the form of persuasion. Auntie Lottie was enthusiastic in her praise for everyone present and had volunteered herself to act as *fear an taighe*, or female compère, for the event.

*

Much to the 'models' delight, the hall was full on the night. Some, however, were having last-minute nerves. Auntie Lottie was calming the less confident men of the community. She was adorned in a sparkly, dark, evening dress with pink wellies festooned in glitter and tassels. That set the stage for the night.

Crofter models in various fashions, all complete with the required footwear of wellie boots, surrounded her, awaiting their cue.

Jack, under the guise of Sporty Crofter, strutted his stuff while Lady Crofter swished his way past in a pink boiler suit complete with boa and the prerequisite wellie boots. Gentleman Crofter was ambling along behind.

Auntie Lottie had suggested fitting six-inch heels on one pair of boots, but nobody had managed, so far, to walk in them. Even the women crofters taking part had given up trying. Unsurprising really as they were, like their male counterparts, more used to wellies than heels.

The fundraising had gone better than expected. Jack was jubilant, and maybe, perhaps, slightly relieved when it was all over.

"It wouldn't have mattered if nothing had been raised – what a night."

*

Now that the two big fundraising events had passed, Auntie Lottie and I finally had our last meal together in my house. The next day, she was to move into her cottage for good. A small part of me was sorry to see her go. I had enjoyed having some company at night and someone with whom to share how my day had gone. We both needed our own space though. We hadn't got to the stage of annoying each other, and I was glad she was leaving before we did.

"Thanks, Auntie Lottie that was a great dinner. I'll tidy up."

"Not at all. You go and have an early night. What with all your meetings and things, I don't think you've been home before 11 p.m. all week."

She was right, of course. Originally, I had only had one evening meeting pencilled in, but as time had gone on, events had led to four that week alone.

"I'm sorry we haven't had much time together, especially with this being our last week under the same roof."

"Not a problem. I've enjoyed having a roomie but must confess I'm really looking forward to getting into my own cottage. I still can't believe it's finally ready."

I went upstairs, flopped into bed and fell straight to sleep despite the big meal. My dreams, however, were disturbed by constant ringing.

"Stroma, Stroma, there is someone at your door. Stroma, wake up!"

I thought I was dreaming. It slowly started to filter through to my brain that no, that was Auntie Lottie shouting in the real world.

"What?" I struggled up. It was 2.30 a.m. It had to be some sort of emergency. Approaching the door, I noticed the letter box opening.

A voice yelled, "Yoo-hoo, it's us," to confirm that there was definitely someone at my door. It didn't sound like an emergency as this was closely followed by, "If you don't' come down, we're coming up." I felt the panic oozing from Auntie Lottie. "Don't worry, they can't really come up – the door is locked."

I opened the door to see two women dressed as cavewomen, giggling and swaying on the doorstep. I had already recognised their northern lilt before I opened the door which is just as well given their form of dress. The chairperson and fundraiser from my northern community GLADS group smiled drunkenly at me.

"We had our fundraiser and met some boys having a stag do in Thurso." I had forgotten they had organised a fundraiser for that night. Their event had required everyone involved in the group to dress up. Buckets had then been handed out and off they went as a team around all the local pubs, restaurants, social clubs and anywhere else people could be found who would drop some money in their buckets. I suspected some of the restaurants would have been happy to donate just to encourage them on their way.

"That's nice." What else could I say as I dragged the pair in and propped them against the counter in the kitchen. I stuck the kettle on.

"They are from around here, you know, the boys. We told them you were our development officer; they know you too, so they offered us a lift on their bus, so we could visit you and let you know how we got on."

"Yep, they were really nice. They had to drop someone off in your village, so it was no problem."

"So … we took it, the lift that is."

"Yep, I can see that."

"So … we're here."

"Yes, you are." Ever the responsible one, I added, "Does anyone know you're here?" They both had young families and partners, so somebody would be wondering where they were by now. Especially given their fundraiser had consisted of a gigantic pub crawl with buckets.

"Do they?" the first cavewoman turned to her sidekick. "Did you phone home before we left?"

"Don't be daft; they would have talked us out of it. We said we would phone when we got here."

"Ooh yes, that's right, so we did. Can we use your phone then?"

"Right, so you want to phone home at 3 a.m. Do you think anyone will be up?"

"Well, they will be after we've phoned." More hilarity from them both as they slurped their coffee and pushed their bushy hairstyles back out of their eyes.

"How about you just send them a text tonight to let them know you're here, then you can phone them tomorrow?"

"Great! Yep, that would be great."

"Can we stay the night then?"

It was tempting to ask where they had been planning to spend the night anyway as home was over 150 miles straight north. The idea of two tipsy women, dressed like rejects from *The Flintstones* with hair sprayed straight out and make-up an army officer in camouflage gear would be proud of, trying to hitch north was not good. I found myself wondering how many lifts, if any, they would have got. On the other hand, they had done pretty well getting a lift all the way down here in the first place. Auntie Lottie, having assumed rightly that no harm was going to come to either of us, had taken herself back to her warm, snug bed.

"Yep, no problem. I'll have to put you on the couch next door as all the bedrooms are taken upstairs. I've got a relative staying. Thanks for the visit by the way."

"No problem. Couldn't turn down the offer of a free lift, could we?"

"Just a thought, did anyone else come down with you from the group?"

The chance that someone else might be wandering around lost had just fleeted thought my brain.

"No, all the others went home ages ago – dirty stop-outs!"

After much stage whispering and promises of undying love and respect, my two cavewomen were left snoring like the troopers they were.

*

In the morning, Auntie Lottie came through to the kitchen to tell me we had some randoms sleeping in the living room. It was strange hearing her use that term, not so much in response to having strange visitors staying but from someone who was past the age of forty. I hadn't had randoms stay at my house for ages. These are generally people who are known by one person in the household. Or maybe even a friend of a friend who you don't actually know at all. The point is they are unplanned-for visitors who need shelter for the night.

When Iona still lived here, being a few years younger, she was always bringing home someone not well known to me. Beds would be made up for them, normally in the living room. A variety of reasons would be given for their stay including: no one had turned up to take them home after a school dance, there were no taxis at that time of night, they had no money left, their friends left without them to go to a party, somewhere, they were too drunk to be left on the high street, it was snowing too hard for them to get back home to some other rural village. These people were collectively known as randoms, i.e. unexpected guests who can't get home due to difficult or dangerous circumstances ... as perceived by Iona, at least.

Other teenagers brought home little furry animals or birds. The nearest Iona ever came to that was a prickly hedgehog. Iona still collects people and often brings them home on her visits, never to be seen again once they return to the big city. The night before, I had invited in my own randoms, people unknown to Auntie Lottie or Iona but known to me, and my sister wasn't even here to witness it. I had no doubt though that Auntie Lottie would inform both Iona and the rest of village.

Chapter 13

Birdsong is louder than I had realised when there is no traffic, no children, in fact, no one else around. The sun was also up early that morning – it was that time of year when it didn't really go down. Early morning, no one else was around and the promise of a beautiful day lay ahead.

"Morning." I nearly jumped out of my skin. Why would someone else be up so early in the day? It was 5 a.m.

"Morning," I returned. It was a jogger who didn't miss a step. Did they never sleep? He puffed and sweated his way past, complete with headband, sleeveless top, short shorts and running shoes. He was nobody local. The locals wouldn't have been around so early, unless it was for something to do with hunting, shooting, fishing or the ever-present sheep. It was probably one of the many tourists camping, caravanning and touring around the area. I noticed the birds had even quieted down as he made his jumpy progress along the road. They must be used to the crazy humans they share this planet with doing activities that can only appear futile to them.

I looked further along the street to where a movement had caught my eye. Was that Old Tam strolling along? No, surely not at that time in the morning? It was too, and he was heading in my direction. Old Shep, his ancient, lumpy collie lurched along at his side.

"Grand morning fae a walk, but tak my word fae it, it will be raining later, aye."

"Aye, it is that, Tam. Bit early like," I said, continuing on my way.

"Ach, away with you. We're just away hame to hae a bit o breakfast before we're off to the sheeps, aren't we then, Shep? He still likes to look at them. Although his hert isn't in the chasing o them any mair."

Up until then, I had always thought the first anyone saw of Old Tam in a day was at about 10 a.m. when he and his faithful companion hobbled and grumbled their way around the village on their daily visit to the local shop. There they would buy milk and have a wee sneak of the headlines in the paper before placing it back on the shelf. The exception to this was the one day a week when the local paper arrived at the store. Required reading for all the community, especially if you hadn't had the time or inclination to meet up, by accident or design, with Maureen during the week. She could cram anyone full of all the comings and goings in the community, offering a more colourful but definitely less accurate account of all relevant developments.

It was nearing the time when it could be considered early by normal waking hours. I watched as Paul MacQuin or Paul of the Sheds, as he was known locally, sneaked around the back of the three cottages, still dressed in the clothes he had been wearing the night before – smart shirt, jacket and trousers. I knew he hadn't come out of any shed. At his age too! He was fifty-four for goodness sake and still slept around if he could get it. One of the cottages was rented out for summer. No doubt, he had found his mark at the local pub and charmed himself into a short but sweet holiday romance.

Auntie Lottie now lived in one of the three cottages that looked so picturesque. She had been left her home by the last of her blood relatives who had died way before I was even aware.

At one time, nobody wanted or was willing to buy these houses. In fact, you couldn't even give them away, they were so dilapidated. Over time though, one by one, much of the housing stock in the area had been sold to absentee owners. Many of these houses were brought up to date then rented out to holidaymakers anxious to get away from the hustle and bustle of everyday life. Hardly any one of these landlords was ever seen in the village.

My eyes flicked toward the new development that was at last resembling new houses. They wouldn't be available in time to stop the latest family from leaving, but hopefully, it would help keep others here.

Auntie Lottie was lucky; only one of the cottages she lived beside was a holiday let. The middle cottage was owned by a young local couple who squeezed themselves and their three children into what was, for them, a confined space. The huge garden, no doubt, made up for the size of their accommodation.

I was getting tired but would soon be home.

"Oh, aye, and where have you been this fine morning?" It was Maureen. *Does nobody sleep in this damn place?* I thought. It was just after 6 a.m.

"I'm just on my way home."

"Well, I think we can all see that." Maureen opened her arms wide to encompass everyone around which, right then, was just us. "But that's not what I asked. I don't usually see you up and about so early."

"Is this your normal time for being around?" I asked, desperate to distract her before she started to interrogate me further. Weirdly, it made me sound just like her. "Why exactly are you up so early?" I groaned inwardly.

"Me? This isn't early for me, dear. The early bird and all that. Did you see who it was that was sneaking out of the cottages there? I'm sure it was that rascal Paul MacQuin, but I didn't get a proper look. I don't want to be spreading rumours that aren't true now, do I? You didn't see whose cottage he came out of, did you? Wasn't Lottie's now, was it? She's a fine-looking woman for her age. Lots of the men admire her, you know."

"Ach, away and don't be daft. Of course it wasn't Auntie Lottie; she's not interested in any of that now. If someone was sneaking away from the cottages, it would have been from the summer renter, and before you ask, I don't know who's staying in it this week."

"Ach, I know who's renting that cottage; I'm not that ignorant of the facts. But I notice you still haven't answered my original question. I mean, you wouldn't want me to get the wrong impression and start a whole load of gossip that wasn't reasonably accurate, would you? I'm meeting Mary later at the hall. It's the club's coffee morning, you know, and I'm sure Ellen will be there too. They are always interested in hearing how you're getting on."

It wasn't what you would call a direct threat, more of a challenge. I could have lied and said I was just making the most of that beautiful summer day, but I knew Maureen wouldn't be bought off so easily. My clothes were rather wrinkled, my hair was tangled and my face, although splashed with cold water, still bore last night's make-up. My body oozed the unmistakable smell of alcohol.

Old Tam would have known that too. I was not one of them, the early risers, I was one of the other kind that morning. The Paul MacQuin kind. The ones who had stayed up all night, when really, they should have gone home hours ago. The ones who only meant to go out for a drink after work but had stayed for more. The ones who never made it back home, until the next day. The ones who would not make the most of that brilliant summer day, as they had made the most of the summer eve the night before and would spend that day sleeping.

"There was a lock-in at the pub."

"Ah," said Maureen, clearly deflated. Well, it wasn't a total lie, more of a misdirection. If she asked around, there were a fair number of people who would confirm that I was there, at the lock-in – where no one else could come in as it was after closing time, when the bar was technically closed, but still open enough to be called a private party. Thankfully, most would not have taken note of when I left or that I left with anyone else.

In Blàs where most seemed to know everything about everybody, keeping my personal life private, especially from Maureen, was almost impossible. She was a master researcher of potential gossip. It was essential, therefore, to tell her at least a little bit of the truth to keep her speculation to a minimum. I hugged my arms tightly about my body, enclosing my little secret safely within.

Chapter 14

I was freezing again. It was the height of summer and blowing a north-easterly. The rain was threatening, and the sun seemed to have forgotten that it was supposed to shine, hot, clear and strong. It didn't help that I was stuck in a field at the end of the village.

Highland gatherings, Highland Games and galas, they were all squeezed into the so-called blazing summer months. Unfortunately, it felt like more of these events were held during unseasonably cold spells than during the dreamt of hot, scorching weather.

I was stuck at a stall to promote GLADS rather than the Development Trust for a change. Most locals knew about the work of GLADS. It was the tourists and visitors who I seemed to spend my time talking to. This made their visit more informative and enjoyable, but it didn't bring in more volunteers to help promote the Gaelic language and culture, locally or, indeed, across the Highlands. However, it was interesting hearing where they all had come from and how their holidays were going. They just laughed about the weather and told me they didn't come to Scotland for that anyway. Mostly, they could find warm, hot weather at home.

GLADS HQ insisted on my presence at these types of events, so who was I to argue? On the rare occasions that the sun shone and locals braved the sizzling elements, it could be an enjoyable experience which I got paid for anyway. Not that day though. It was a normal cold and windy summer day. As such, there were not many people about. More would come later with the parade but waiting was making the day drag.

The various crafts tents stood in a windswept row, down toward the beach. Being familiar with craft people, I wondered how many of them had only just finished their wares either the day before or that morning, the sand blowing around that day attaching itself to the still wet glue and tacky paint adding another element to their offerings.

I saw Jill had finally made it. She was struggling to put up her display units. I'd had to call on her the week before about providing a stall for a Development Trust fundraiser.

*

Her house was conveniently situated right in the middle of the village. Colourful baubles, knits and bric-a-brac adorned the windows, walls and door, making the cottage feel colourful, eclectic and arty. However, looking past all the bits and pieces, the paint was cracking around the windows and front door. In fact, if all the colourful camouflage was stripped out, the little house would have appeared rather run-down.

"No time for doing that sort of stuff, you know. I have to get this lot finished for a craft fair and someone is coming for this tomorrow too." She took commissions, but I didn't think she had enough work to do that would fill up a normal person's working day. Like most of her ilk, she left everything to the last possible moment.

"I've been trying out this new technique," or "I've got loads of time for that I'll do it later." Only, later came, and she still wouldn't have started it, so she would spend the next two days and nights working continually without a break, until remarkably, her embellished shawls, wall hangings and tapestries would be finished just in time. She would have lost half a stone in weight as she hadn't had time to eat, and mugs would line her sink.

I had knocked on her door and waited then knocked and waited again, knowing that she would probably need to clean her hands before she could come to the door.

Her cottage, as usual, was in a *bùrach* that far into the craft fair season. Coloured buttons lined the work surfaces, beads and glittery jewels were mixed together on a table in a kaleidoscope of colour. Glue of all sorts was lined up in tubs and saucers that lay under and over old newspapers. Paint, colour mixes for enamel and clay, littered the whole room.

There was nowhere to sit that didn't have something on it, either in a stage of being made or drying out. Her clothes dryer was covered in an assortment of items at various stages of drying, none of these items appeared to be clothing, or more correctly, clothing of the size and sort she would wear.

There was one space, however, right in the middle of her sitting room, directly opposite her front window, that was totally clear of any clutter. A desk with a lamp and a chair stood in among the clutter like a desert island, safe from the storm of craftsmanship and chaos that reigned around. Her workstation proudly bore evidence that space and organisation were hiding within all that confusion.

*

Another cold gust of wind, scattered with rain droplets, brought my focus back to the Highland gathering. The pipe band had finally arrived along with the parade from the middle of the village.

It had taken them longer than usual. Mainly, I suspected, because Old Tam had been given the honour and title of Chieftain for that year's games. This meant that he headed up the whole parade which, strangely or perhaps not so strangely, knowing Old Tam, included Shep lumbering along beside him.

Maureen had been the one to put forward Old Tam's claim to be the Chieftain for that year's event. It was a ceremonial title and most people would have wrongly assumed that Old Tam would have been awarded it long before then. He may have been dour and a bit grumpy, but he was generally viewed with affection and respect throughout the area.

Apart from leading the parade, he would officially open the games and oversee the sports, dancing and Highland events, such as tossing the caber.

Old Tam, I suspected, would rather have been watching from the sidelines or at least from the beer tent. Maureen had heard, as usual, from some friend of a distant relative's friend, someone who was supposed to know these things, that Old Tam was in danger of being whisked away, like many before him, to live a warm and safe existence in the bosom of his family.

"We have to let him know how important he is to us all before he leaves. What's Blàs without his presence? He's the life and soul ..." Maureen had stopped herself there. Even she had to admit that, even though Old Tam may have been embedded in the psyche of the village, its life and soul, he never was, more like the voice of doom and gloom.

He was seen in the village most days and was always one of the first to offer help and advice. His delivery though was invariably wrapped around a sense of foreboding and pessimism. His clothing reflected his personality in that it was dark, old and a little musty. He was never without his tammy which perched on his head come rain, sun or snow.

So, there he was, limping toward us. One ancient man and his equally ancient dog out in front of our local pipe band. The heavyweights stomped behind, uniformed in their kilts and vest tops, not one of them looked the least bit cold or stood under 1.98 metres. The Highland dancers followed on behind, shivering in their colourful outfits. Cyclists and the mostly local field athletes were next. A large number of spectators and the general public brought up the rear.

"In the name of the wee man, what on earth has he got on? If it wasn't for Shep at his side, I would never have recognised him." Maureen's wheelchair bumped up and down on the uneven surface as she drove up to join us.

"Maybe he has taken up golf," quipped Jill. "I like colour myself, as you know, but wow, he is bright."

Old Tam was sporting a dazzling yellow, orange and purple tartan suit that may well have looked edgy on the fashion catwalks of Milan or Paris. But there, in a field in Blàs, it mainly just stood out.

"I told him he had to look smart, but I wasn't expecting this." Maureen pulled out a pair of sunglasses and put them on.

"Could he not have worn a kilt? And will you just look at that hat?" I was sure my mouth was hanging open. Old Tam had replaced his beloved tammy with a bigger one that matched his suit. His new hat sat at a jaunty angle with the addition of two tall, brown pheasant feathers sprouting straight up. I looked accusingly at Maureen.

"Don't look at me like that. He said his kilt was too *robach* to see the light of day again so I just told him to make an effort and left it up to him what to wear." Maureen peeked out from under her sunglasses. "Anyway, I think he looks just grand, sort of—"

"Colourful," interjected Jill.

"You are sure that is Old Tam?" I asked as I watched the gaudily clad character who stopped to smile and speak to the crowd that was waiting on the official start of proceedings. "He's smiling, I mean, properly smiling."

"Of course, it's him. He's obviously loving his role. I'm beginning to wish we had nominated him years ago, if it can bring such a sea change in him." Maureen looked very happy with herself as her gaze followed the procession's progress across the field. It was time for the opening ceremony and speeches.

"Well, this should bring the tone down a bit. Let's hope he isn't too dour." I was still trying to get over this amazing change in Old Tam when he stood up at the mike.

"*Fàilte* yin ain an all to Blàs Highland Games. Afore we start, I'm going to squash a few wee rumours that have been going hereabouts. I am nae movin or going awa. Here is where I was born and here is where I will be takin my last breath, ach nae for a while yit, am hoping." Old Tam was setting the record straight. He even cracked a few jokes. Visitors to the games must have thought he was quite a happy character what with his sense of dress and his sunny delivery.

Most of the locals were looking a bit shell-shocked but laughed at his jokes. They seemed to embrace this new lively version of Old Tam. Could his new vivid suit really have brought about such a change in him? It was difficult to believe. The crowd roared their approval as his speech ended.

My stomach rumbled. The smell of homebaking and hot drinks wafted around me. Auntie Lottie, Ellen and Mary were working in the tea tent that afternoon. I was dying to know what they thought of Old Tam's transformation. First though, I needed something to keep me warm on the outside. Why, after all these years, I didn't wear a thick winter coat or at least one that had a lining and was waterproof, I didn't know. Then again, it was Scotland and the sun could come out in the next five minutes.

The cold was getting to me as I turned around and signalled to Jill to see if she wanted me to bring her back a cup of tea. That's when I saw it. A beautiful, bright, colourful plaid spread across Jill's stall. It was waving in the wind, beckoning me forward. I rubbed my hand gently across the fabric. It felt warm and soft to the touch. The colours were far brighter than I would normally wear, but I felt it – that shawl had my name on it.

"How much for the shawl then, Jill?" Not that the price made any difference; in my heart, it was already bought and paid for. I wobbled fractionally as the intensity of the colour invaded my senses. Out of the corner of my eye, I noted Old Tam in his eye-watering suit as he hobbled past. He smiled in my direction. I shook my head, still unused to the sunny personality that he was radiating. Had loud colours really affected the change in his demeanour? Could it happen to me?

I paid for the shawl and swirled it around my shoulders. Immediately, I stood straighter and instantly became warmer. I made my way toward the tea tent and reflected that, really, I didn't care what Auntie Lottie, Ellen and Mary thought of Old Tam's transformation into colour. Wrapped in my new dazzling shawl, I found I totally understood how that could happen.

Chapter 15

I was headed north, trailing around Loch Shin. Glad to be away from the demands and extra work the housing project had placed on me. The importance of its success followed me like a shadow. I had no idea that the cost of volunteering to help would be so high. I was suffering from many a sleepless night, worried about budgets and grants, not to mention the threat of more people moving away. I now knew how many of my volunteer GLADS committee members felt.

My trip took in part of the North Coast 500 route, or NC500 as it was usually referred to. Marketed to tourists to entice them north, it had almost overwhelmed our local population with its success. No road, toilet or any other sort of upgrades had been undertaken before the marketing campaign started, leaving tourists and locals alike struggling to deal with its popularity.

I looked forward to winter, when hopefully, things might quieten down. My once tranquil roads were heaving with traffic. Not as bad as a city, right enough, but busy for here. I could no longer speed along deserted roads, because there was always something coming from the other direction. Generally, nothing as big as the Screen Machine, but at least that knew its own width. No, campervans were way worse. Perhaps because most were being driven by tourists who only drove them once a year or maybe had never driven one before. They had no concept of the width of their vehicle or the road.

Four years before, it would have been a car pulling a caravan that would be gently moseying along at thirty-five miles an hour. Not a care in the world, no notion that locals had to get to their work on time so couldn't afford to sit at that speed all day, caravanners totally oblivious to the shortening tempers as drivers fumed and yelled at them from behind.

Passing places were used, not for letting others overtake but to partake of morning coffee or afternoon tea. If only they'd have known that two minutes further along the road they could have pulled into a bonnie village, like Scourie, and watched the tide flow in and out, enjoyed the sea birds circling and diving, instead of eating car fumes and listening to engines roaring past. Taking one small fork off the main road, when you are used to houses at every turn, can be a step too far for some.

The single-track road was left behind as I once more returned to the modern world of two-lane traffic. I was making good time, rolling along the A838. The sky was blue, the sand was white, and the mountains looked inviting. I took a deep breath and looked around, reminding myself how truly magnificent Scotland was.

Rounding the bend to Durness, I discovered that all traffic was stopped. There were cars and motorbikes everywhere. My first thought: *Has there been some sort of accident?* People were milling around, walking backwards and forwards across the road. Cars were pulled up on the roadside. Where had all these people come from and what were they doing?

These fellow travellers had all come to an abrupt stop. Campervans nestled alongside Harley Davidsons, tiny Fiats rested bumper to bumper with large four-wheel drives, and at least two tour buses were squeezed along the main road.

I crept by and thankfully saw no sign of an accident. I began to take it all in, and suddenly, it dawned on me. This sight to behold, among spectacular countryside, on the edge of the wilds and wonderment, was a shop. Not just any shop, I'll grant you. No, here was the only outlet for the starving consumers of this age who had been deprived of the mere sight of one for miles. Better than the average store, it was, behold, the Village Shop. The bonus attraction – the post-box on a stick nestled beside a petrol pump.

In their panicked need to reconnect with their purchasing power, tourists marched with purpose into the shop, only to meander out after their fix, licking ice cream without a care in the world. They stepped out in front of traffic and treated this main throughway like a traffic-free country estate.

A traffic jam had developed where it shouldn't have. It felt peculiar to arrive so suddenly back into consumer country. In winter, outwith the holiday season, two cars parked there would have been deemed busy. Okay, so you could buy essentials like ice cream, chocolate and petrol, but this amount of shoppers seemed absurd.

It was the most north-westerly village on the mainland of Scotland, with a population of about 400 spread about, not the middle of Glasgow. It felt like the entire tourist population navigating the NC500 had seen that little outlet and slammed on their brakes to stop and shop.

I practised my swerving as I dodged the people wandering around. They held up hands to stop me, smiled and carried on walking in holiday mode, unaware of the danger they were in.

That village shop appeared to be more wondrous to them than Smoo Cave that resided just below on the shoreline. Ironically, it had been inhabited by the original hunter gatherers.

*

For me, Smoo Cave had more importance than any geologist could ever place on it. It held memories of life before the loss of my parents. We'd walked along the beach for miles, played in the sand and tasted the salt air on our lips. Seagulls had cried over our heads and nobody else appeared for miles around. We had the whole place to ourselves, nature the only sound as the sea rushed onto the shore. I could have done without the crushed sand between my teeth though.

Smoo itself always seemed to appear out of nowhere, a deep cut in the cliff. As we came up from the beach, the cave would grow and grow while we appeared to shrink in size, until I would stand, holding Iona's hand, looking up at that enormous hole where the sand met the cliff.

Scrambling inside, the cave would echo with our voices. What a great place to have a secret den. We could play there undisturbed forever, sheltered from the tide, wind and rain.

Strangely, I have many more memories of walking and playing on deserted beaches in cold, wet and windy weather. I always thought it strange that we only went to the beach when the weather was awful. Was this to avoid the crowds? Bitter, sodden and stormy was the norm for beach weather in winter, or so I was convinced for many years. In fact, this could also be the description for many a day in summer. Perhaps, we did beachcomb in the summer, when the elements chose to pretend it was dreary winter.

Sutherland, with its spectacular scenery and wildlife, is beyond doubt the empress supreme for beaches on the mainland. We could have our pick, there are so many to choose from, all impressive in their own way.

*

As I left the metropolis of the village where buyers could get their fix, I noticed that, although some souls had opted to go and see Smoo Cave itself, there was not the same bustle or queues either in the car park or waiting to walk down to the beach as was on the road.

I skimmed the north coast like I was a blip on the map. My meeting would take place that night with parents from Tongue and Bettyhill who could arguably have said that they had the best beaches around. I wouldn't have liked to choose between them.

Chapter 16

People were dashing about everywhere, mainly on and around the beach at Blàs. I saw someone on horseback and heard the noise of a quarrelsome quad bike. Voices carried on the soft breeze. Vibrant blue sky competed with the cool aquamarine of the shimmering sea. Waves topped with white, creamy foam crashed onto the shore. Glowing sunshine mocked the early chill. A few hours later, and it would have ceased its taunting, turning into one of those hot, glorious summer moments.

There was, however, a manic atmosphere prevailing upwind from the seashore. Something was definitely happening. Toward the village, people seemed to be walking just a bit too fast for a typical holiday. Three figures were outlined against the sea at the start of the beach. Old Tam, Mary and Auntie Lottie surveyed the scene. I crossed the road toward them and noticed a tourist holding onto two large mongrels.

"I'm so sorry, they don't usually do things like that. They are normally so friendly and obedient."

Goodness knows how many times we had heard this. Wide open spaces, complete with all the sights, sounds and smells of a Highland beach, can override even the best-trained mutts. I was hoping this was simply a non-serious dog incident and not some surfer or wader gone missing from the beach.

"Morning all. I take it nobody's missing."

"Oh no, no, lass, way worse n that." Old Tam's rheumy eyes filled up even more. "It's Shep. Them giants chased him, and I cannae find him ony-whair."

Old Tam had reverted straight back to his normal dark mode of dress and dour personality as soon as the games were over.

I tried to imagine Shep running at all, never mind outstripping the two large hounds who could, in one bound, be halfway along the beach. It turned out that Old Tam had been taking his morning walk back from the village when two large dogs appeared to land at his feet. They ran a couple of circles around Shep, following up with doggie play bows, obviously trying to entice Shep to join them in some fun. Shep, whose eyesight was not at its best, took fright and ran or, I expect, hobbled away at a faster rate of knots than Old Tam could keep up with.

All three had disappeared down the beach as confirmed by the owner of the hounds. She had been in a distressed state herself before she had found her own dogs twenty minutes later. Finding out they had chased poor old Shep made her appear just this side of hysterical. Her dogs, however, although totally exhausted with their tongues lolling out of their mouths, were ecstatically happy to be reunited with their owner. Of Shep, there was no sign.

His hearing was almost as bad as his eyesight, so shouting his name would have been a useless exercise. The local canine walkers, turning up at various times during the morning, had heard of the missing Shep and were now spread along the beach in an effort to find the poor old dog. I looked closely and saw small specks out near the sand bank.

"Tides on the turn, richt enough." Old Tam had seen where I was looking. "Them people better get out o thar fast, or they'll be caught."

I ran down the beach and flagged the quad bike down. "DJ, get out there and tell them to get back now. We don't want any drownings looking for Shep. We'd be able to see him if he was out there."

Thankfully, he asked no questions and sped out and rounded up the stragglers before the tide could rush in and carry them off.

"Has anyone spoken to Paul of the Sheds yet?" I asked Auntie Lottie.

"Nope, we didn't want to get the boat out. We thought we would have found him by now."

One of Paul of the Sheds many jobs was inshore rescue. His other jobs included mountain rescue, lifeboat crew and volunteer fireman. He was also a trained paramedic and inshore fisherman. Hence the need for all his sheds, or so he said. The name had just naturally evolved around him, and he was stuck with it. Phoning Paul always made a thing feel more official. On that occasion though, he couldn't have taken his boat out even if he had wanted to. Unfortunately, he was on one of his other call-outs and wouldn't make it back before the tide came in.

"I'm sure Shep isn't out there. Someone would have seen him."

A car screeched up and slammed on its brakes beside us. It was one of the local dog walkers. "I've just been out to the turn-off. Sorry, Tam, there was no sign of him."

"Aye, thank ye, lass, thank ye." Tam looked back out to the tide eating its way up to the shore. I had no idea what the woman in the car had been thinking. Shep was an old collie, not a young greyhound. Even the big dogs that had chased him wouldn't have made it as far as the turn-off in less than half a day, even going at full speed.

A large timber lorry rumbled past. We all looked at each other, thinking the same thing. Since the workers had started felling some of the woods nearby, these large, fume-gushing lorries had been careering along our roads at vicious speeds. Shep would have no chance against them.

Engrossed in searching the skyline for Shep, I hadn't noticed that Auntie Lottie had disappeared. A high-pitched screech followed by an obvious scrunch of gears grabbed our attention. Auntie Lottie's car, black and brown, which in other cars would have killed any sense of style, arrived yelling out its character for all to see.

"Right, Mary, you stay with Old Tam here. Stroma and I are going to take a look around." She motioned me to get into her passenger seat.

I climbed in beside Auntie Lottie and left Mary to comfort Old Tam as he stared out at the beach.

"I'm thinking the distillery, maybe he's there. His sense of smell would recognise it's the same thing Old Tam often reeks of." Personally, I thought this a bit rude. It was highly unlikely that Shep would be there, but anything was worth a try.

"Don't you think it may be a bit far for him to have travelled?" I asked.

"Not a bit of it. He's been away for a few hours now. If he did hobble along the beach, he could have come out anywhere near here and crossed the road without anyone noticing. He's probably gone to ground and is snoozing in the sun."

Auntie Lottie dropped me off beside the whisky warehouses while she looked for a member of staff. Maybe one of them had seen something. As I rounded the second big shed, I saw something shaggy standing stock-still beside the next building. Bubbles of excitement and joy raced up from my feet to my head. I tried to shout to him, but what left my lips was a deep, relief-filled sigh containing his name. "Shep." He tilted his head, a lost expression on his face.

I gently crouched down and held out my arms. "Shep, Shep, here boy, come on, come for a cuddle." He regarded me for a few moments, then his tail wagged slowly as he hobbled into my waiting arms.

"Have you been trying to breathe in some of the evaporating whisky then?" Shep leaned further into me. "They won't be happy, you know, the angels, if you pinch their share." I ruffled his ears. Auntie Lottie came screaming back around the corner. Another lorry rumbled up and out of the village.

"Aye, old fellow, you been getting your angels' share then?" She bent down to help him into her car. "Those angels must have been looking out for you, right enough, despite you stealing their whisky. Come on, old fella, you can get a sniff of the real thing at home. I'm pretty sure Old Tam will be having a wee nip himself when he sees you."

Chapter 17

Summertime, and it felt colder than the worst winter's day. My hands were turning blue; I could no longer feel my feet. While the sun shone outside, we were once more condemned to freeze inside a beautiful church. Elaborately decorated ceilings and an extravagant interior alone were not enough to take away the shivers from the congregation.

Auntie Lottie, ever the optimist, along with most of the revellers, had dressed according to the outside weather, not the inside church.

We shivered in our spruced-up clothes, high heels and light jackets. Many of us were praying for the fires of hell, so we could get even a little warmth. The longest marriage service in history continued around us. I doubt even a royal wedding would be longer. Every time we thought it was finished, a new couple emerged from the congregation to say a few words on how important their own marriage was and how much in love they were.

A middle-aged couple stepped up to the pulpit; it was the bride's auntie and uncle. Not the best couple they could have picked to tell us about a successful marriage. There was an audible gasp from the congregation. People were beginning to shift uncomfortably on their pews.

Ross Smith had had more affairs than I would think possible, if Maureen was right. His wife, Jean, had refused to accept all the rumours, even though her own son and Debbie Mackay's boy could pass for identical twins. In a place where red hair, blue eyes and freckles were not unusual traits in themselves, you could be forgiven for not believing everything you heard. But Ross Smith had a very distinctive look, even given his red hair. He had a small star-shaped birthmark on his left cheek. All Ross and Jean's children displayed the star somewhere on their face. The number of children outwith their marriage who also had the star birthmark and resembled Ross Smith was uncanny. After his last escapade ended in a DNA test and claims for support, even Jean could no longer bury her head in the sand. Jean stepped forward.

"Some of you will be surprised to see us here. Despite everything, I love my husband. I understand his weaknesses." An audible sob was heard from the congregation. "With the help of Father Antonio, together we have found strength in God." Jean looked down toward the bride and groom. "Marriage is full of challenges, but trust in God and your love for each other, and you will find your own path through. We wish you love and happiness on your path together through life." She stepped back.

"Ach well, she may well trust in love and marriage, but I would nae trust that swine with any women." This was muttered in the pew behind by a granny who had made no secret over the years of just who the father of her red-haired, freckled and star-faced little granddaughter was. It was Ross' turn to speak.

"My wife and I are still married to each other. I love her, and with the help of God and Jean at my side, I can overcome my weaknesses." A smartly dressed woman clutching a hankie to her face rose and fled from the church. Cheeks flaming and clashing with his vibrant hair, Ross struggled on. "I too wish you both love, happiness and a fateful marriage." A snigger ran around the pews. Jean stood frozen to the spot. Anger radiated from her body. The priest moved quickly and whispered to Ross. "What? What's wrong? Oh God, sorry, shit, shit, sorry, faithful, sorry, that's *faithful* marriage."

"Well that certainly heated things up." Auntie Lottie whispered to me as the priest asked us to bow our heads in prayer.

It was a long and laborious address. An attempt to bring us all back to the business at hand of celebrating the couple's marriage. We no longer cared though if they hated each other and less still how important their love of God was. *Just please finish, and let us get some heat,* I pleaded silently. I had watched some of the elderly fall asleep. They shivered awake again before they disgraced themselves by snoring. On reflection, perhaps they were not falling asleep because of the length of the service; maybe it was hypothermia setting in.

Resentment oozed toward the priest as he revelled in his long, heavy garments while we shivered and shook our way through his service. Other signs of desperation were settling over the congregation, the requirements of the bladder shifting priority over the cold.

I had no idea where the toilets were, but I bet they were warmer. There was going to be an almighty scramble for them the moment the service was over. Photographs would have to wait, unless the photographer was prepared to enter the loos.

I heard a sigh from Auntie Lottie as she turned her head away from the freezing but happy couple. She was enviously following the progress of Karen and Fergus as they made their way through the rows of pews, apologising as they went. They were going to the toilet! The priest chose that moment to throw in yet another prayer.

"God help us ..." the priest started.

"Indeed," I heard Auntie Lottie whisper as she scrambled to her feet and scurried in the direction recently taken by our path-finding friends.

"… who helps himself …"

I heard another scramble up and the quick clack, clack of high heels racing along. That, I suspected, would be Ellen.

The priest, realising he was fast losing his audience, sped through the remainder of the prayer. The service finished very shortly afterward. The photographs, on the other hand, were taken much later, after the queues for the loos had gone down, goose pimples had receded, and warmth and relaxation had returned to the day.

*

Two months later, arriving home after a long trip north, Auntie Lottie appeared at the back door.

"I've brought homemade cake. Not mine, of course; Ellen made it."

"Come in then, I'll put the kettle on."

I knew she had news to tell. There was no other reason for a late-night visit.

"You won't have heard then?"

"Well, if what you are about to tell me only happened today, I expect I haven't."

"That's good then. Only, Maureen stopped me …"

Whatever was going to come next, may or may not be true then.

"You remember that wedding we were at? You know, the bride was lovely."

That didn't exactly help, but as it happened, I had only been to one wedding recently and that hadn't been that long ago.

"You know, the one where poor Jean Smith tried to tell us that Ross had mended his ways. Well, just like the season, it's over. Already. Would you believe? With all those people getting up to speak on their behalf too. Maureen says—"

"She's hardly a reliable fountain of knowledge. So, Jean finally gave him the push – good for her."

"No, no, Jean, poor deluded woman that she is, is still with that charmer of a husband of hers. No, not them, the bride and groom. Maureen says, and she should know being that it's her nephew's uncle's brother's cousin or something like that. Well, the bride she's off to Australia with another man. Just left a note, and off she went. Left the house, the furniture and the poor man. What do you think of that?"

"Well, given that it's come from Maureen, not much really." I didn't want to be caught spreading rumours. "Why are you so sure it's true?"

"Well, it runs in the family, it's in their DNA along with that family birthmark. After all, look at her Uncle Ross. Having him and his wife standing up saying how good marriage is, it was like cursing them from the start. I mean, who in their right mind would have asked the Smiths to stand up for them. Oh, Stroma, you'll see. Maureen's more often right than wrong. Anyway, we've another wedding to go to in December, but I'll tell you about that later. I reckon that one will last longer than the turning of the season."

Chapter 18

Peep, peep. The sound of a van horn could be heard all morning throughout the burgh. It wasn't one of the usual days for any of the visiting mobile vans. After being stuck on the computer for most of the morning, it seemed a legitimate excuse to stop what I was doing and take a look. Maybe something new was being offered to the district.

There, right outside the village shop, were Old Tam and Auntie Lottie, deep in conversation with a man in a blue boiler suit and white wellies. A small white van was parked nearby.

"Weel lad, it's a bit like takin coals to Newcastle." The lad looked blank, too young to relate to the once thriving coal industry and where it had been. "We dae that ouresells. Mair likely to sel ye oure ane catches."

"Well, not really. Paul deals with all that, doesn't he?"

I was impressed, I didn't think Auntie Lottie took much notice of who bought and sold the local catch of salmon, prawns and shellfish.

"Aye, yer richt thar, lass. He deals wi that ither mun wi the van on Wednesday, see. Cannae see mony wanting to buy yer fish."

The lad thanked them, jumped into his vehicle and took off. We hadn't had anyone else trying to sell fish in the village for years. Someone new must have taken over the route, not realising that we were not a forgotten village. We were, in fact, quite capable of catching more than enough fish to keep the needs of the villagers happy. Apart from that, the thought of having to face our own fishermen after buying from a rival was justification enough for buying local. Anyway, nobody could possibly beat them on the freshness of their catches, straight from boat to table.

Apart from the Screen Machine, we had visits from a bank, a butcher and the mobile library.

"Weel, that was a bit strange. Cannae imagine why he thought we would want to buy his fish. He comes fae Inbhirasgaidh, ye ken." Old Tam shook his head disbelievingly at the effrontery of the next village. "What's the world coming to? As if we would buy fae them. Maybe we should get oure ane van and go to his patch."

Rivalry between the two communities was legendary. If there was nothing to dispute, the population from both villages would eventually find something to disagree about. In the long winter months, it gave us something to do and kept us from going insane. Or, then again, the disputes, in the light of day, raised a large question mark as to the sanity of the whole area.

*

Fishing Competition. Meeting tonight in the hall. Looking for competitors to fish for a large variety and volume of sea life.

There was a phone number and contact e-mail address on the poster. The normal proviso of 'just ask at the shop' had been added at the bottom.

It was now August, and things had progressed as steadily as a rising tide. Paul of the Sheds had taken his boat into Inbhirasgaidh harbour for the day and sold some of his catch to tourists walking along the pier. Their fish van had made repeated trips to our village and sold, in turn, to newcomers unaware of the danger they were putting themselves in.

The fishing competition had been suggested by the local priest who served both areas. He regularly found himself in the middle of these conflicts and wanted to stop the 'fishy selling', as it was dubbed locally, before it got to the silly stage. I felt he had already lost that battle.

Inbhirasgaidh were well ahead in the scale of things, having already recruited their best fishermen. Rumour was rife that champion anglers had decided to holiday nearby the week of the competition. Dirty games were obviously afoot.

Slow to get off the mark, the rodmen of Blàs were meeting to discuss how best to beat their opposition. Fishing and competition between the two communities didn't sit well with me, so I didn't go to the meeting. Like the priest, I had to work with both sets of villagers. My livelihood depended on my neutrality; there was no way I was taking sides.

Free entertainment throughout the day and the cèilidh at night though would maybe make it all worthwhile. All jealousy and enmity would be washed away in a wave of dancing, laughter and the odd drop of the refreshing liquid.

The day of the competition dawned damp, windy and cold. Paul of the Sheds' boat was out early with eight rods on board. This was in accordance with the rules set down by Father Antonio. Only eight rods per boat. One other boat could dive for scallops or other forms of shellfish. Three was the maximum on the shellfish boat.

Obviously, hearing about the tourists' arrival in Inbhirasgaidh, Father Antonio had taken action to avoid any bending of the rules. No mention of the champion fishermen was heard as the boats set out.

The population of both villages was left to build up fires, set up barbeques and raise a food tent along the shoreline.

Somehow, a beer tent had also made its way into the area; a sound system and teenagers littered the beach.

The catch was to be given to the village's best cooks. They, in turn, would prepare snacks and meals that could be handed out to those in need and the elderly who always seemed to enjoy their fish. An assortment of dishes was then to be sold off in individual portions to both sets of villagers, tourists or anyone else who came along. Money raised would be split between the Development Trust and repairs to the church's stained-glass window.

The cooks of the day had started out friendly and amiable. By late afternoon, the tension of the rivalry had seeped and simmered through to the chefs. Simple fish dishes served with fresh butter and herbs had developed into more and more eccentric meals. Flounder stuffed with spinach and cheese served on a bed of duchess potatoes with an exotic salad was on offer. Salmon fillet on a bed of blueberries, served with a raspberry and herb coulis, had also found its way onto the menu.

Before the proposed simple banquet of seafood could turn into a cordon bleu extravaganza, the priest and judges once more stepped in and brought expectations down to earth.

The boats arrived back. The fishermen of both villages dripped their way onto the quay. Catches were weighed and separated to see how much of the variety was edible. As soon as they possibly could, the chefs grabbed what they wanted and marched off to the tents to begin the cooking. Everyone was hungry by then and eager to see the outcome of the competition.

"Oh wait, wait a minute. Wait for us, we've got some." A troop of unfamiliar anglers led by the local gillie, all in waders, jackets and carrying fishing rods marched up the street.

A judge, complete with notebook and pen walked alongside them. These were the professional fishermen who we had heard about and eventually dismissed as rumour. None of them were from the villages or the local area. Who were they representing then? Both Blàs and Inbhirasgaidh had their quota of competitors.

"They fished according to the rules. Eight rods plus three for shellfish. Got a good haul too."

Mutters went through the crowd.

"There is nothing in the rules that precludes any team from entering this competition as long as they stick by the rules regulating the number of boats and rods," Father Antonio declared. "These men represent neither Inbhirasgaidh nor Blàs. They are independent with no alliance to anyone but themselves."

The ante had suddenly been upped. Local honour and pride were at stake. All of a sudden, it didn't matter which of the villages won, as long as it was one of them. Neither Blàs nor Inbhirasgaidh would be happy to see outsiders win. They were the expert fishermen with local knowledge; no visitors, be they professionals or not, were going to take that from them.

Without thought, locals from both communities shuffled closer to each other, now standing shoulder to shoulder, eager to see who would win. All rivalry forgotten, the need for either Blàs or Inbhirasgaidh to win was overriding any of the usual antagonism between the two communities. It was a quiet and anxious wait.

Eventually, one of the judges stepped forward, clipboard in hand. "Well, it's a close-run thing. It was the shellfish that made the difference, Inbhirasgaidh is declared the winner."

A yell of relief and happiness rang around the harbour. People started to make their way toward the food tents. A fiddle could be heard, and mercifully, the rain had stopped. I watched the priest hang back, have a quick word with the strange fishermen and shake their hands.

"That was a clever thing you did there, Father."

"Everyone needs a little help now and again. You will be glad also that things will be settling down for a bit I believe."

Of that he was right.

Chapter 19

Germany, Canada, Spain and all points of the compass in Scotland were to be represented at GLADS' next language programme. Our European cousins were mainly over here on holiday and had seen the course advertised. They wanted a taste of the language to take home with them. Our Canadian student was over for a year, working and tracing her roots. Her ancestors were one of the many families that had been forced off the land and shipped abroad during the dark days of the Highland Clearances.

GLADS courses were originally set up to help parents learn the language of their forbears. More and more learners, however, appeared not to have a family connection with the language. Hillwalkers, for example, often wanted to know what the Gaelic names of the mountains meant. Other students came from a musical background, their initial interest sparked by joining a choir or learning a Gaelic song. Whatever reason they had for learning our language, we were just happy to give them the opportunity.

GLADS courses could last a weekend, three days, five days or a week. They had to be flexible to fit around people's busy lives. I also had to spread the courses all around the north of Scotland to entice as many participants as possible. Making it easy for those with children who could pass on Gaelic to their offspring was considered one of our most important aims.

I covered an area larger than Belgium, so time was a precious commodity. Going west was always breathtakingly beautiful, but it had to be rationed out. A training course, however, was a legitimate reason to leave Blàs and head that way.

Long before I had started this job, Auntie Lottie had established herself as one of the most sought-after tutors of GLADS' Gaelic language learning courses. She had always made herself available to deliver GLADS technique throughout the Highlands. Her homecomings to Blàs were built around most of the courses' scheduled long weekends or weeks. Now that she lived in Blàs permanently, we had scheduled more courses with her as the lead tutor.

GLADS sometimes had several classes running at the same time to reflect the different fluency level – beginners, intermediate and advanced. Although, there were occasions when we only focused on the one group. Visits to various places in the area where Gaelic and its culture could be seen, heard and then talked about were built in. These trips might consist of a visit to a battlefield, museum, croft or distillery, depending on where the course was being held. Transport could be by boat, minibus or car.

I wasn't sure if it was the concept GLADS had developed or if it was that Auntie Lottie should have come with a large warning sign, but her classes appeared to turn the scholars into wild and crazy students. Although by the end of each course, her students generally had outperformed any of the other classes in terms of Gaelic language acquisition.

They would also surpass most of the other classes in their lack of concern for their livers, as alcohol seemed to feature strongly in one way or another during or after their lessons. That was combined with a, now legendary, belief in the survival of the fittest and fending for yourself. It meant not going back for anyone left behind after a cèilidh or sightseeing trip. It didn't matter if a student was lost somewhere on the road, in the woods, on the ferry or a combination of all three. Evening or daytime, it made no difference. If left behind, you found your own way back. Auntie Lottie seemed to grow their passion to become more fluent to an almost zealous level. Nothing got in their way, not late or lost students; her classes stopped for no one.

We had booked the nearest accommodation to the course, a small cottage which was about a mile from the actual delivery centre. Most of the attendees who didn't live locally had found accommodation in the township another mile along the road from us. This was not unusual given that people would travel a fair distance to attend. Auntie Lottie and I were once again sharing a cottage, due the length of the course.

"We were learning to ask for drinks and our preferences today." I knew what was coming next. "So, we're having an impromptu cèilidh tonight. It will give the students a chance to use some of the language we learnt."

I had noticed, since working with Auntie Lottie, that the day that her class learnt about drink preferences a cèilidh would be held. During class, her disciples had learnt to ask for coffee, tea, milk, biscuits and cake in a variety of ways. So why was it not a coffee evening that was held afterwards?

I once asked her this and got the reply, "No point in doing what we learnt this morning, tonight is about developing their language to ask for something other than coffee and tea."

It sounded reasonable to most ears, but I had seen the carnage mid-course ceilidhs could lead to.

"Okay, I take it that means we are leaving the car here."

"Well, it looks like a nice night, so we could walk back with the students."

We both knew what that meant. Alcohol would be on the menu along with the singing and dancing. At that very moment, the students would be at the village shop buying up all the beer and snacks they could. If they heard of any local musicians, and there were always some around, they too would be invited along.

"You know they may not make it to class tomorrow."

"Oh, they will, and if not, I guarantee they will have had enough fun that they remember all the language they learnt." Not if the amount of drink that was going to flow was taken into consideration – a lot of brain cells were going to take a massive hit.

By the time we had danced our last dance, drunk our last pint and all the staff had left (apart from Auntie Lottie and myself) it was pushing some unearthly time in the morning. We would have a long walk home.

Directly after leaving the hall, there was a small hill which ran down to join the single-track road. Thanks to Auntie Lottie, I found out that there was a very deep ditch running alongside the lane.

Students, Auntie Lottie and myself all trooped merrily out of the hall. Very quickly, we scattered into small groups. It appeared, by some unspoken word, that we should impersonate tacking boats on our windy way home. It was about halfway along this zig-zag route that I found myself wondering about Auntie Lottie. I approached the only other person who was just short of tipsy and asked if he had seen her, only to find out that he too had started to wonder where she was. Mark you, it was probably only because he was hoping for some extra language practice.

The villagers from Blàs, in particular Ellen and Mary, had installed it in me the exact opposite philosophy to the one Auntie Lottie followed. It had been drummed into me that you never leave a person behind on a night out, and if necessary, you took them home.

Keith, Auntie Lottie's student, was quickly sobering up. Not relishing the loss of his tutor, he agreed that we should head back along the road toward the hall. It was at this point that it became really obvious that the zig-zag dance home would have taken all night as we had barely left the hall behind. As we neared the turn-off at the bottom of the hill, we could hear a muffled cry.

"Help! I'm over here. Help!"

"Where, over where?" I yelled back.

"Here, down here."

Down here? In the pitch dark with trees on both sides and no moon, how were we going to find anyone down anywhere?

"I can't see you. Can you try and sit up?"

"No, I can't. I'm down here and already standing up."

By that time, I was crawling, inching my way along the edge of the track, patting down the bracken as I went. That's when I felt something hairy brushing my hand. Letting out an almighty yell, I scuttled backward only to be grappled again.

"It's me, you idiot. I'm down here; that was me."

Well, it wasn't me who was trapped down a six-foot ditch, so just who was the idiot here! I reached forward and grabbed hold of the hair again just to make sure.

"Ouch, you fool. Let go, that hurts." That was enough to convince me that, yes, that was Auntie Lottie trapped in the ditch, unable to move as it was so narrow. She, not being that tall, couldn't get out. Keith, by this time, was so doubled up with laughter that he could not move or offer much assistance. After a great deal of pulling, pushing and puffing, we eventually managed to extract her from her prison.

"How on earth did you manage to get in there?" I asked her

"No idea," she said. "I was just looking up at the bonnie sky, taking in the heavens, and next thing I knew I was at the bottom of that ditch."

"Well, next time, eyes front, never mind the celestial beauty above."

We spent the rest of the journey picking bits and pieces out of her hair. Taking the lead position on the road seemed like a good idea, or we were never going to reach home before we had to leave for class.

Once we reached the cottage, the students decided that it was not worth their collective time going back to their accommodation, just to turn around and come back again. Keith informed the class with his newly acquired vocabulary the next day that he had found the bath he had slept in, comfy enough but rather cold.

He ended up sharing our accommodation for the rest of the course, partly because he had helped pull Auntie Lottie out of the ditch, but also, on seeing how substandard his lodgings actually were, we felt compelled to offer him a room at ours.

As it turned out, he had an amazing sense of humour in his first language, English. By the end of five days, both Auntie Lottie and I had sore ribs and faces from all the laughter. He offered to guide us up a hill on the way back east as a thank you. Keith, as it turned out, was a keen hillwalker, so the 'walk' turned out to be a frog march up a mountain. This had the benefit of sweating every drop of alcohol that we had consumed over the last five days out of all of our systems.

Both Auntie Lottie and I loved views, but unfortunately, we were also scared of heights. When we got to the top and saw the amazing scenery we had to sit down before we fell down. Shimmying part of the way back on our backsides did not go down well with Keith.

"Why didn't you tell me you couldn't do heights?" The sensible part of him had obviously come out once we left the course behind. Or maybe, the seasoned hillwalker in him could see the dangers presented by taking day trippers like us out on the mountains. All this did was add to his conclusion that we were only just this side of sane.

"We didn't want to appear like wimps," Auntie Lottie replied.

Keith could be heard muttering under his breath.

"Where has his sense of humour gone? It must have stayed back with the others we left at the cottage."

Two other students had joined us for the last three days after they had found worms in their bath. This wasn't the entire reason they had eventually given up on their accommodation. There was also the lack of power and heating. They had turned up cold, wet and miserable, wanting to go home. I moved to share the bedroom with Auntie Lottie, and they moved into mine and completed their course. We had left the cottage before them, and Keith kept voicing his concern about this as we trooped downhill.

"You know, we didn't know them before the course, what if they don't tidy up properly or pay the remaining bill?" Our landlord had noticed that we had taken Keith in and then two more. We were pretty sure the other landlords had told him. So, Keith had had to sign a contract taking responsibility for them all.

Once we were back in the car and on our way, Auntie Lottie was feeling rather put out.

"You know, I had thought he had a good sense of humour. But he can be such a grouch. Maybe I should help him see the error of his ways."

"I think you should leave the poor man alone. He was one of your best students and kept us laughing with all his stories."

Auntie Lottie didn't reply, and I thought she had left it there. I should have known better.

*

Two months down the line, I received a phone call from Keith.

"I can't believe you did that. I thought that landlord was losing his mind."

"Keith, I have no idea what you're talking about. What's going on?"

I don't know whether he believed me or not. He did go on to explain that he had received a letter stating that the landlord thought it was, at worst, a case of theft and, at best, bad manners that, after offering his high quality house for such a reasonable rent, Keith and his companions had then had a party in it, not cleared up and had taken the expensive towels.

He was told that the landlord would normally have vetted renters since they had only just built the house and were going for an up-market clientele. They had thought him trustworthy, but obviously, they had been mistaken and were very disappointed in him and his companions. Auntie Lottie and I were excused from this as they knew we had no connection with the troublesome tenants and had left a day earlier.

Keith, despite data protection, had managed to track down our other two house guests who thought he had gone nuts, totally denying having a party and stealing the towels. Keith, feeling desperate and not wanting to lose his good reputation, had left messages on the landlord's phone apologising profusely and asking him to let him know how much it would cost to replace said towels.

The poor landlord must have thought that here was someone who had totally lost the plot or, worse still, someone who was playing a joke on him. So, he had just ignored the messages and gone about his normal life. It must have been lying heavily on Keith's conscience though, as he then wrote to the landlord asking for the costs to be forwarded to him, so he could settle up. By this point in his serious narration, I was completely at a loss.

"I finally got through to the landlord. He said he felt sorry for me, and did I think perhaps that someone had maybe played a wee trick on me. There had been no party and no towels were missing. I dug out the envelope and knew it had to be you. The stamp clearing says Highlands."

A slight niggle pushed at my memory. Auntie Lottie, late one night, coming to the door.

"Have you got Keith's address? I wanted to send him some word exercises, and I have a few further suggestions on courses and books for him. My computer's not up and running yet, so it will have to go in the slow post."

"What can I say, Keith? I'll look into it."

I arrived at Auntie Lottie's door completely out of breath.

"I've just had a phone call from Keith."

"Keith who, dear?"

"You know, Keith. Keith, the one you wrote the letter to about parties and missing expensive towels."

I relayed the story. After she had wiped the tears of laughter from her face, she said, "Who in their right mind would go so far as to try and repay a debt that was not his and actually didn't even exist at all? This is priceless. I hope he's got his sense of humour back. I'll send him some language programmes; that will cheer him up again."

Try as I might, I couldn't stay angry with her.

Chapter 20

I tasted the salt on my lips.

"I'm off for a pot of tea." Auntie Lottie was worryingly becoming my best friend on work trips. We were travelling by ferry. All worries of Blàs and the Development Trust left at the quayside. Sea travel whether by ferry, sail or motorboat was normally one of the few times when nobody could track me down. Not in the case of Auntie Lottie though. One mention of ferries and the Isle of Lewis, and she was around to my house like a hungry seal hunting its prey.

"I'll just hitch a lift with you then. I haven't seen Jess for ages. It will do you good to have some company." Now that she was living permanently in the village, she rarely left it without being in the company of at least one of us. How she had managed to holiday abroad so often on her own was a mystery to me. I hadn't realised just how many 'friends' she had. Not that I minded most of the time as it was still enough of a novelty to have a travelling companion. Once we were out of the car and on the ferry, we could go our own separate ways.

Ferries, being the only form of transport to get off and on some of the islands, are looked at differently by the islanders than us day trippers and holidaymakers. As part of a holiday, it's a novelty to take the ferry. To the islanders, it is often the only way to get off or onto the island. Locals need the ferries to be reliable, to bring in food and materials, to take their goods to markets, to attend hospital appointments or go to and from work. As a lifeline, the ferry becomes a completely different thing. Like them, I have watched and waited for ferries to take me home or off on holiday only to be disappointed.

I had been keeping an eye on the weather for days. Not that that really does much good, as sometimes, when I least expect them to run, they do. Then, without reason, they break down or sail off in a different direction. Marooned at the end of a pier in stormy, wet weather, no view thanks to the weather, no shops, no cafe, in fact, not another soul … It can be a long and lonely wait.

Despite this, if I have to travel, boat is by far my preferred mode of transport. No heights involved, no ridiculously early times in airports or paying for cups of horrendously bitter coffee. Yes, ferries for me are the ultimate mode of travel. Whether they resemble a tart's boudoir or a scruffy cafe, I'm always up for the journey.

Home, for me, is being surrounded by water, whether it is the sea, the loch or falling from the sky above. It is fortunate then that I live in a water-logged nation. The rain sparkles in the sunshine and causes great rainbows to form all over the countryside. Ross-shire is the Rainbow County with its swooping, large skies striped with double and single rainbows stretching across the firths, mountains and moorland. All that water gives us mirror-like images all around. Day or night, the reflections continue.

*

Karen and I often walked the narrow path around the loch in early spring, autumn or winter when the sky is dark, and the big watching moon and stars reflect on the loch's surface. No torch, just her two mad dogs leading the way. We would be immersed in the brilliance of the night sky and our lively conversation, taking little notice of where our feet were actually heading. We tramped up and down the trails and in and out of the trees, their forms silhouetted against the dark sky. Night sounds all around us, undisturbed by our passing. Owls speaking to one another, warning of where their territory began. The canines would take no notice of this, firmly attached to their leads, sniffing and foraging their way in the hope of frightening deer to chase or some small furry animal to pounce on.

*

A sudden lunge from the ferry pulled me back from my reminiscing. Despite the sparkle and shimmer of the water, all I could see around me was grey sky merging into grey seascape. To keep my spirits up, I peered at the bow to see white waves break, disrupting the murky grey of the sea as we passed. Were we even moving at all? All around us was low cloud; it was like being in a colourless, misty snow globe.

Ferries, never mind how decked out in finery, are designed primarily by pessimists. The interiors can be bright and shiny, new and uplifting, no sign that a crossing could result in the loss of dinner. That's until you enter the toilets where the layout has a hose gleefully fastened to a tap, silently warning the passengers not to become too complacent.

To avoid feeling seasick, going outside on deck can work, as long as it is on the leeward side, otherwise being blown to bits by the wind is a real possibility. On the sheltered side, you'll hardly feel any wind.

I licked my lips, tasting the salty sea again, my hair whipping around my face – not in that romantic way you see in films. No, my locks were more like long trails of Velcro, fastened firmly to my face, making it almost impossible to see. While I struggled to free my eyes, a voice sounded in my ear.

"Ach, I know, the salt's always getting in my hair." A bald-headed crewman with a smile as wide as the ocean swaggered confidently past.

Passengers seemed to fall into five categories. The smokers and the seasickers were the two groups normally found outside. Both groups could be found huddled outside in a spot that could provide some shelter from the onslaught of the winds, their faces pale and pinched from the cold. That is where the similarities stopped. The 'seasickers', hats on and hoods up, tried to keep away from the cafe and food smells. They had that look about them that could mistakenly be perceived as recovering from partying hard the night before. Tired, unshaven and hunkered down. Unfortunately, there was usually one wearing a red hat which did nothing for the slightly green-tinged face peering out from underneath.

The locals form the third group. They tend to have gadgets or books to keep them occupied or will be lying down fast asleep, getting some downtime before an equally long journey on the other side.

Then there are the watchers like me who watch the sky, the sea, the people but definitely not anything that resembles technology. Even I, though, had had enough of watching; a cup of tea beckoned. I headed to the cafe to meet up with Auntie Lottie.

Since she hadn't returned to find me, she obviously had not been content with just a cup of tea. The reason for her long absence soon became evident. She was deep in conversation with a couple who were clearly not dressed for travel. They stood out in a way that only those in business suits could on a ferry, especially one in the depth of winter with the rain lashing down outside and the sea bubbling like a pan of tatties. This did not strike me as the best place to be the best dressed.

Like Auntie Lottie, they were in the fifth and final group – the jumbles, those not fitting neatly into any of the previous groups. Sometimes tourists, sometimes not, all differently strange in their own way. All I wanted to do was put my head down and concentrate on my cup of tea. I was cold and wet, and my nose had started to run.

"Are you from these parts?" one asked in a strong American accent.

The temptation to say, "Yes, actually, I am a mermaid and live right here in the middle of the sea," was strong. Luckily my mouth was occupied by a slurp of tea.

I was not going to admit I was from the Highlands as that would lead to an exchange I really didn't want to have. I had been stuck in conversations so often with many others of their ilk – enthusiastic and overly sincere disciples of one form or another. I didn't need to be saved, see the error of my ways, as they saw it, or be preached to. So, truthfully, I answered that I was just there on business. I thought I should use the right facial expression to convey I was indeed a professional, even though I was decked out in a big, warm, thick, soaked waterproof jacket.

"We're here to work too. We're Mormons, here doing God's work." Matching smiles and overly white teeth beamed in my direction. An image of a crocodile briefly flirted across my brain.

"Really?" What else could I have said?

"Yes, we are missionaries on our way to Stornoway."

I'm sure there is a song somewhere with a similar title but it's questionable whether 'missionaries' is part of the lyrics.

"You do know that the Western Isles already have a strong religious ethos running through them?"

"Oh yes, ma'am, we do. We just have to help them understand the real truth behind it all."

I had just managed to stop myself from saying, "God help you," when Auntie Lottie asked, "You don't think someone is maybe playing a joke on you? I mean, these islands are renowned for their devotion. It's only recently that they allowed ferries to sail on a Sunday, for goodness sake."

The two clean-shaven heads looked at each other, smiled benevolently and rose from their chairs.

"Thank you, ma'am, for the company. We have to put in some study time before we dock."

We watched them leave.

"How do you think they'll do?" I asked Auntie Lottie.

"I have no idea. But they have to be the most ill-placed people I've ever met. Taking their religion to Lewis is a bit like taking a poor wee lamb to slaughter I'm thinking."

Chapter 21

"Is hair is becoming as wild as his nature." Mary grabbed hold of the ten-year-old's head and ruffled his curls. "You'll be mistaken for a lassie soon enough if your mum doesn't do something about it."

"Ach away, Mary, it's no that bad yet. I just wish we had a hairdresser here. I can't be bothered going all the way to town just to get the lad a haircut," his mum replied.

"I think we all miss George. It's a shame he left, but he just couldn't take the midges, poor soul." Mary shook her head sadly.

George, a highly acclaimed hairdresser, had moved to the area three years ago, seeking a better work-life balance. He'd been keen to take up fishing and other outdoor pursuits when time allowed. The only problems were: it rained a lot more that he expected, was colder that he expected, the winters and dark nights were definitely not what he expected and, in the summer, when teams of midges played tag and engulfed the population on warm, dull days, he had taken their attacks personally. It had to be said, his reaction to bites had been a bit more dramatic than the norm. Large, round, inflamed spots the size of a twenty pence piece that hung around for days were not a good look.

Everyone had loved George though. The villagers had never been so well turned out. Fringes were straight but not in the novice, horizontal, directly across the forehead style. Hair was trimmed on a regular basis and nobody sported the bowl on the head look. Hairstyles were colourful and of the latest fashions. The inhabitants could primp and pose with their beautifully manicured coiffure styles in the best of places but, more usually, out on the moor, it has to be said. Until George, unable to take the long winters and large bites any longer, sold his house, closed his business and went off to live in Spain where the heat, sun and winters were exactly as he expected.

Ellen had now called a coffee evening at her house. Maureen, Auntie Lottie, Jill, Mary and I had dutifully turned up. It was an easy decision – she was the best baker in the village, and we all knew her homemade cakes would be served. Old Tam had wanted to come too, but Ellen couldn't put up with Old Shep smelling out her kitchen.

"We have to do something about the state of our folk's hair," Mary said, opening the proceedings.

Some were worse than others. The residents who regularly had to leave the community to work were, on the whole, looking much the same as always. Others did not fare so well. Old Tam, for example, would have done better going bald with age. He resembled a demented wizard with white flowing locks swirling around his head. Shep's coat was in better condition.

"I can't see how we can force anyone to come here," I muttered.

"Have you tried the college? Maybe they have an outreach hairdressing programme. Someone could maybe come along to the hall. We could set up appointments." Jill suggested.

"Nope. I rang them; no one was interested in coming out here. Costs too much in petrol, so they say." Ellen, as always, was way ahead of the rest of us.

"How about the community bus? We could arrange a day and take anyone who wants a haircut into town." This was Mary's suggestion.

"We tried that before, remember? Too many wanted different days. Just won't work. What we need is to attract someone to the district. We could use the web to advertise. There's still George's old shop. It would only need cleaning out. We could run it as a community enterprise through our Development Trust. That's if we can find someone to run it properly." Ellen had obviously given this a lot more thought than the rest of us.

Auntie Lottie, who had been quiet for some time, piped up. "I could do that, you know. I have done some snipping and cutting in my time."

We all looked at Auntie Lottie. Her hair, as usual, was immaculate – styled and set to within an inch of its life.

"Mind, I couldn't do too much fancy stuff, but I could definitely trim hair."

There followed much discussion about funding and buying any equipment needed to start this venture. Ellen felt sure this was something the Development Trust could cover without too much trouble or money. All it would take was a quick meeting to release the start-up costs. Although the housing project was eating up most of our funds, everyone felt the benefit of having a hairdresser again outweighed any other considerations.

We were concerned, though, at how quickly the costs of the housing project were rising. Would our gamble pay off? Would locals be willing to rent and part-buy the houses when they were completed? Or was there another reason why families and the elderly were leaving that we hadn't thought of? It had seemed so straightforward when we started – provide the houses and our population would grow.

146

*

Auntie Lottie set up a system of regular appointments at the hall. Sticking to quick trims, a share of the local gossip, serviced with a cup of tea and cake – it seemed to be working a treat. The wild man image that the locals had been sporting was finally being brought under scissors and spray.

"I just can't wait until I get into the shop. I've ordered colours of all descriptions, perming stuff and lots of other bits and pieces I can't wait to get my hands on." Auntie Lottie had only been working out of the hall for a couple of weeks, already long enough in her estimation to have developed her creative skills in hairdressing. She was ready for the next level.

We hadn't been listening properly. If we had been, we would have taken what she said as a statement of intent. But caught up in our optimism at having our own hairdressing business back in the community, we failed to hear what she was really saying.

The excitement could be felt in the village in the run-up to the shop opening. Appointments had been booked, and Auntie Lottie was raring to go. She had even bought herself her own uniform.

Auntie Lottie had been in power for a week, and the temptation to use new products and colours that she had no training in had become too much. Now, around the village, instead of the long and unkempt look, the locals were emerging with exotic and wonderful hair colours and styles, all germinating from Auntie Lottie's ability to talk most people around to what she wanted.

New hairstyles never seen before in these parts – or, thankfully, anywhere else – could be seen at the sheep pens. Bright oranges and purples that couldn't even begin to blend in with their originating colours found in the heathers and on the moors. Fringes where now cut into sharp angles. Even Old Tam was hiding a new hairstyle under his cap.

Another emergency meeting was called at Ellen's without Auntie Lottie but with a few other locals including Old Tam and Shep this time. As more and more hats and caps were removed, more and more outrageous hairstyles were revealed.

"I only went in for a trim and look what she's done." Curls filled the space around Struan's head.

"You have to talk to her, Ellen; it was your idea."

"I've tried. She just won't listen. I'm sorry, but we seem to have created a monster."

Mary put up her hand. "Don't you be telling her I said this, but you know Robert, Angus' second cousin once removed? Well, his niece, you know the one that ran away with the postie from Inbhirasgaidh, ooh must be six or seven years back." Blank faces stared back at her. "Well, her friend's son's daughter, Heather, she's just started up a mobile hairdressing business. I know she goes into Inbhirasgaidh once a week, maybe she could come here. We could let her have the use of the shop for that day. Might be enough to entice her."

"Sorry, did you say son's daughter or friend's daughter?" asked Paul of the Sheds.

"I don't think that's the point, Paul, do you? Could you ask her, Mary, and let us know? I can't see Lottie complaining if we can get a real hairdresser back." Ellen sounded relieved.

Auntie Lottie, as it turned out, was more than willing to step down. She had enjoyed running her little empire but was starting to find it a bit too demanding on her time. She graciously received her flowers and thanks from the community and hung up her scissors for good. Much to the relief of the inhabitants at large.

Chapter 22

"We remember your parents so well, of course." That's all it took; the thrust of their words stabbing my soul. I knew as well as they did that I couldn't say no. Mary and Angus remembered my parents as children, often filling in the blanks with stories about their lives that Iona and I hungered after.

Being starved of our parents' presence for so long, we devoured tales of their youth and their lives before us. That was why, thirty-six hours later, I found myself with eighty-six-year-old Angus and his elderly wife, Mary (with her bad knees), stumbling around a graveyard in the depth of night. Our only companions were a torch, an umbrella, a mini garden spade, a walking stick and an indistinguishable urn. The umbrella was being firmly gripped by the aforementioned elderly woman, while her other hand held on to the walking stick like grim death.

Rain poured down relentlessly, making our passage even more hazardous. Water pooled, making the ground as slippery as if the first ice of winter had arrived. My female companion was determined not to trip over 'some poor soul's last resting place'. I, on the other hand, was determined she wouldn't fall and become one of those poor souls. She … they were, of course, the reason why I was there in the first place. My own fault really. Apart from the need to hear tales of my mum and dad, it had been drilled into me by my parents as a child, to automatically answer yes, if some old biddy asked me to give them a hand. Saying no to anyone who asks for help is a difficult feat for someone like me. That pair had done a great deal to help in my rehabilitation though. It had been a difficult journey, but I knew, after this, I would be able to press down hard on any rising guilt that came from saying that almost impossible no in answer to any plea for help.

'We were wondering if you could do us a wee favour?' Such an innocent start to a conversation that could have led to me and two determined pensioners becoming jailbirds.

A cousin had died, apparently a long-ago playmate who had vanished into the big wide world in his early teens, never to return, until now, having bequeathed his ashes to the only living relative who he knew and liked. After this request, I could well understand why the others hadn't liked him much; they had probably suspected what might be coming.

He, like many others of his generation, wanted his remains firmly interred in the *seann dùthaich* or old country. And here's the rub: he wanted this done without any of the other family members, who he didn't like, knowing that he had returned, even if that was only in an urn. Added to which, of course, he had supplied no funds whatsoever to cover the costs of said internment.

These two pillars of the community had taken it upon themselves to fulfil the cousin's last desire to be buried beside his kin in the old churchyard. Not a difficult demand you would think, but as the graveyard was no longer used for new burials and requests to add his ashes to the site had already been denied, we were left with little choice. That was the first time I was even aware that you could stop burying people in graveyards, but I suppose it makes sense. There was only one option left open to Angus and Mary. Gone was any thought of a small ceremony with an even quicker internment.

If necessary, just open a hole and throw me in was written on the letter they received. I'm still not sure if he had actually meant it, but Angus and Mary had taken it as read. Still, they were left with a dilemma. They knew that permission had not been granted but felt honour-bound to do the decent thing. Despite lacking any outward sign of emotions, they genuinely wanted to return him to the family fold, in a manner of speaking.

They had no intention whatsoever of trying to seek anyone's permission to do something in their own cemetery, not again anyway. On top of which, our dynamic duo reckoned any paperwork could take a longer time to process through the correct channels than they had time left on this plane of existence. A valid point in my estimation, especially if midnight walks, under darkened skies, atop slippery mud, on a very cold, wet and blustery late autumnal night was a normal pastime for them.

Rumour had it that, if his side of the tribe hadn't fallen out with the other side of the clan decades ago, this problem would never have arisen. But the officials who could have said yes were the direct descendants of the 'other side of the family'. In Angus and Mary's eyes, they were just righting a wrong that had only surfaced due to a long-running clan dispute.

It had also meant that no one else in the community, most of whom, apart from Iona and I, were connected in one way or another, could be asked for help. It even ruled out both Ellen and Maureen. Auntie Lottie was a non-starter as she couldn't do anything quietly. So, really, in the end, who else could they have asked?

"He left it too late to die, you see. I can't ask Angus to drive; he can't move his leg properly now." Harsh but true.

"We can use our car. It's not as obvious as yours."

That depends very much on what you consider obvious. My car was large, true, but as far as getaway motors go, it was fairly dependable when asked to start. It did not sound like an overheated lawnmower, nor did it backfire on the odd occasion. Angus and Mary's automobile was now so old it had gone through the whole cycle of losing money as soon as it was bought, to bottoming out a few years later, to now being worth a small fortune as it had journeyed from new, to used, to classic. One owner, 20,000 miles, good condition (if you're not bothered that there might have been a few sheep in the back on occasion) vintage car. The fact that it could now be classed as vintage tended to turn heads, so as an undercover or getaway vehicle, it was completely useless.

"His mam always wanted him back. But he never came, silly sod, until it was too late." I was picking up on a rather unsympathetic attitude toward Angus' deceased playmate. "Ach, why he asked me, I'll never know. Maybe I'm the only one left who's fit enough to bury him."

"I can't see that being the reason. It's not as if you have to lift a spade and dig him in." I laughed, stupidly as it turns out, as that is exactly what these two old biddies had in mind.

An ancient church that had long-ago ceased any sort of religious sermons hovered over the grounds, the roof completely lost to time. An owl hooted. I ducked, goodness knows why. Thankfully, neither of my companions seemed to notice. A lot of rustling was going on in the bushes and trees nearby. I normally loved the big skies at night through autumn and winter, the multi-coloured aurora borealis waving lazily across glittering stars. The harder you looked the more of the Milky Way, galaxies, constellations and drifting satellites, you saw. That night, however, even if I could have seen through the colossal cloud formations, there was no way I was looking up from our illicit act. All attention was being placed firmly on keeping myself and my companions upright.

"I think they are around here somewhere," stage-whispered a voice from the background of my focus. I, at that point, had been distracted from my efforts by a car's headlights searching along the road. Thankfully, it had carried on, but adrenaline was rushing the blood through my ears, and it took a while before I realised that someone had spoken.

"Are you sure, dear? There are an awful lot of stones here with the same names on them." She was right, of course. The tradition of calling your son after yourself and your father and your father's father before that, right back in a continuous, unbroken line through time, did not help.

Most had been Gaelic speakers, and since they had insisted on conferring their names on their sons in the traditional way, why oh why had they not insisted too on having their headstones engraved in Gaelic? It would have been easy to see whose son, cousin, or brother rested there, if they had been carved using the Gaelic language, because in that, your relationships were part of your name. Then again, the headstones would have had to have been a lot larger. Right then though, that would have suited me fine.

"This *is* the right graveyard, dear, isn't it?"

Now, this I hadn't even considered; I had just assumed they both knew what they were about. Really, when all is said and done, who would get the wrong graveyard? It was at that point I started thinking of Iona. I suppose, if you can go to the wrong funeral, the logical next step would be that you could easily end up in the wrong graveyard.

"Of course it is, you daft bat. How many cemeteries do you think we have here? Look, there's Alan."

I found myself praying he was referring to a headstone and not a person. Angus shone the torch at some more very old headstones, all dripping with the cold water that continued to stream from the sky. Some of the writing had been weathered so badly that I could barely see the names. But Angus seemed to know what, or rather who, he was looking for.

"No, that's not the right one," he mumbled to himself. "Right name, wrong side of the family." Yes, that would be the 'other side of the family' who would be having a fit right now, if they knew what we were about to do, the other side who had fallen out with our urn-encased companion.

Rumour had it, the fallout was part of the reason he had left and lived his life many hundreds of miles away, across an ocean in a strange and foreign land. Although compared to what we were doing, I wondered how much stranger another county could possibly be.

"Won't that do, dear? It's still family, after all. It's getting awfully wet and cold." That was rather an understatement; it was very cold and had been soaking wet since we started out. Mary was shaking now, not due to any age impediment but the cold. I was becoming more and more convinced that, if we didn't get this job done and soon, I might not be able to get her out of there, ever! As she turned around, she slipped on the drenched ground, and I grabbed her arm. "I'm okay, dear, you look after Angus. He'll need you; he's not as young as he thinks."

"Shh, is that her?" Oh God, there was someone else there. They never said someone else would be coming. I thought the whole idea was that no one else could know. The torch was again shone onto a gravestone.

"She'd be so happy to know that her son returned to her, you see. Such an awful time they had, being apart. This way they will be together forever. We promised her too, you see. That would have meant two promises we would have broken, if you hadn't helped us." Mary was beginning to recount our conversation at the house. The cold and wet were obviously getting to her. They had been so distressed when they had asked for my help and had already informed me that, if necessary, they would do it themselves. I didn't want to feel responsible for the community finding two bodies collapsed in the local graveyard if I could help it. So, there I was, holding up a frail woman, who no longer had the shovel to help keep her upright as her husband had finally found the grave they were looking for.

"Are you sure it's her; it's been a long time."

"Of course I am. It's not like she would have been moved now, is it."

"Yes, but there are a lot of them about."

"This is it. I'm almost sure."

Almost? Oh for the love of God, please don't bury this poor soul in with the wrong side of the family. Although from the way my companion was shivering so violently, I was starting not to care whose grave it was as long as the urn got buried before she too joined it.

"Look, read what it says. It clearly states mother of ... Aye, this will do. The dates fit. Aye, this is definitely his mam."

"Ooh, alright then. Would you like to take a turn at digging, dear?"

No, no, absolutely not. What if we dug too deep and found someone? Clamping down on my increasing fear, I shook my head. Then I noticed how long this was going to take with Angus shovelling. His balance wasn't so great either. I grabbed the spade and started scooping out the soil, putting all the worst horror films out of my head. Here I was excavating a mixture of water and dirt from a grave that I knew contained someone's remains, on a dark, wet and windy night. I wouldn't have believed anyone could be so silly if this had been a plot in a film.

"I think that's almost deep enough, or we might be meeting up with something we'd rather not, don't you think? Here, let me finish off."

Thank you, thank you whoever made the universe work in its quirky way. No hand had grabbed my feet, nothing had tried to pull me under, and so far, no one had appeared to eat, bite, rip or maim us in any way.

"Come under the brolly, dear," said Mary. Really, staying dry was the least of my worries. What if someone came along? What if we were caught? I was not altogether sure if we were breaking the law, but the fact we were in a graveyard, trying to bury an urn in the middle of an awful night did not fill me with any confidence that we weren't. If this was to go to court, we'd hardly look innocent, would we? Anyway, if I was to go to court, at least being caught in a fast getaway car would give me more street cred than getting caught doing something illegal with a couple of geriatrics whose getaway car barely reached forty miles per hour.

The reason they wanted me there was as the getaway driver, at least that was how I regarded my role. Neither one of them was able to drive anymore due to an assortment of ailments ranging from bad knees to failing eyesight. Well, that wasn't strictly true; Angus could have managed to drive – it was stopping that would have been his major problem.

He had had a tin leg for as long as I knew him and kept many children enthralled and slightly in awe by clunking things off his leg with ghoulish glee. Driving around with him, on the other hand, required nerves of steel as he would have to manually lift his leg off the accelerator to place it on the brake. He had no concept of speed, or rather, he did but just loved it too much to worry about how to stop. Then age had stepped in and forced him to hang up his car keys. His gammy leg moved too slow even for his nerves. So, that was where I came in – getaway driver extraordinaire, more than capable of keeping their car on the road at the top speed of forty point five miles per hour.

Angus had finally stopped dredging out muddy water and soil. We knew we would have to dig a lot deeper to find the original occupant, but we were not taking any more chances.

"Would you like to take some time to say a few words?" I asked.

"No, I think we used enough words concocting this whole plan for him. I'll just take a minute to have a wee think though." Angus handed me back the spade.

"You do that, dear; we'll start making our way back to the car."

The journey back to the car was even more of a nightmare than the expedition out. Angus had the only torch, and there was no light from the moon to guide us as we stumbled and slithered our way along where we thought the path might be. Mary was using her walking stick like a large spear, sticking it into the wet mud and pulling herself forward. My exterior was calm and confident, while I looked after Mary's welfare. My heart, however, had raced into my ears and was beating so loudly I swore I could hear music keeping time with it. Meanwhile, the hollow left in my chest had filled up with butterflies dancing and fluttering to their own rhythm. I felt sick.

"Are you managing there okay?" I asked for the hundredth time.

"Yes, dear, fine. Is that our car, do you think?"

It better be, I thought. Who else would be out on a night like this, or rather, who else would be out on a night like this and not be up to no good?

"Have you got the car keys, Mary?"

"No, Angus has them. Is that something coming out of the hedge?"

A large, dark shape was emerging from the bushes just behind the car. My heart increased its pounding which increased the tempo and volume of the music swirling around my head. The butterflies, no longer content with fluttering in my chest, were going wild as they joined the music swelling around us. The thing from the bushes lumbered forward, at least six feet tall, reeking of something awful and dripping with heaven knew what. I struggled for breath while the music and my heart hammered and clashed together. The shape came nearer.

"Hey."

We screamed and would have run but physical impairment combined with the sight, the smell and the sound of the music were overpowering. A raging storm engulfed us as my common sense deserted me, gone in search of a safe haven.

"Mary." Oh good God, it knew her name. Nothing was making sense. I barely heard the music now as adrenaline thundered through my body.

"Stop being so daft. Who do you think stands before you?" Now it was being philosophical, asking riddles – help, I had never been good at them. Although, if my memory served me well, this was not the usual way a scene like this unfolded. Normally, there would have been a messy murder, not an asking for the name of an ethereal, or not, being.

"I fell in this muddy ditch, and I couldn't get out. Will you no give me a hand?" The creature held out a slimy, smelly paw.

"Ach, away with you, dear; there's no need to be frightened. See, it's just Angus in a wee bit of bother."

Suddenly, my musical ear keyed into the melody, and I started to recognise Wagner's 'Ride of the Valkyries'. It appeared to be coming from the large, looming, smelly figure which had stopped in front of us.

"I thought I would take a short cut and get back to the car before you. But I slipped into a ditch, soaking I am, and the smell … Can't you smell it?"

"Only a little, dear." Must have been one of the understatements of the century.

"I can't hear myself think. Wait a minute." Angus turned around and heaved a large box from his back which he fiddled with for a while. Abruptly, we became aware of the sound of the wind howling through the trees and the crackle and snaps among the dead leaves and branches. I thought I had been going mad, hearing music in my head, but it turned out it was Angus with his old-fashioned music box.

"I thought he'd like this music played as I put him in. We used to screech around the croft scaring all the cousins while playing this piece. Seems it can still have that effect on some of youse even now." He actually chuckled. That was the point when I realised that I could seriously contemplate the murder of another human being. All that time I had been worrying about Mary not making it out alive and in one piece, and here was her husband completely unrepentant after nearly scaring us both to death. The assassination of her husband was a real consideration for the fleeting seconds it took before the cold and wet seeping through my clothes registered its stormy protest.

We all clambered into the car as quickly as old stiff limbs would allow. Never had such an old banger been loved quite as much as when it sheltered us from the outside elements that night. A warm steam started to rise from our sodden clothes and reinvented itself as condensation which streamed and misted down the windscreen and blocked any view of the road in front.

Auntie Lottie would have loved the impression of old-time atmospherics it created. We, however, had to suffer all the modern special effects, including the awful smell emanating from Angus and the musical score supplied by his battery-operated music box now resting comfortably at his muddy feet.

In the end, we had to open the windows just enough to stop the condensation totally taking over the windscreen. A little patch cleared for me to see out. Any poor soul who saw the car would only have been able to see my unblinking eyes staring back at them. I repeatedly rubbed at the windscreen with the freshly laundered cotton hankie that Mary gave me, in an attempt to see out. We raced along, homeward bound at our blurring forty point five miles per hour, trailing muck and music in our wake.

Chapter 23

Early morning in October, the shells of the new houses loomed ahead, empty and uninviting. They looked like deserted ruins. It was hard to believe they could be the stimuli that would help regenerate our village.

Within the woods, the atmosphere was so different. Frost had outlined the branches, and a kaleidoscope of gold, red, orange and brown leaves littered the path. A slight mist hung just below the level of the trees. It was easy to see from where writers took their inspiration for fantasy books, legends and fairy tales.

I hoped I had timed it right – too early and nothing would be ready, too late and someone else would have reaped the harvest. I had thought I was the only one who knew of this horde, but last year, it had been obvious that some other gatherer had beaten me to it.

I slipped on the wet tree roots, the worst culprits for tripping unsuspecting walkers. Thankfully, the drizzle of rain had stopped. On top of the ice, it made for treacherous walking. It kept other people away though. There was a tiny part of me that was a bit put out – after all these years of quietly picking my harvest, someone had found my secret patch.

I wouldn't have minded, but the previous year, they had taken the lot. It had always been accepted practice that you just took as much as you needed and left the rest so others could harvest them too. Of course, I had always been sure that no one else had noticed *my* patch in its overgrown stretch of woodland. But still, I always left some for others even if that was just the wildlife that frequented the magical place.

I was slightly earlier than usual. Even with that in mind, it all depended on the weather. The harvest could be ready a week earlier or later dependant on what sort of weather was around during the flowering and growing season. I smiled to myself, remembering the other forest harvest, not much talked about.

*

It took place just as sad winter was turning into hopeful spring. Nature knows and understands the early signs that longer, warmer days are coming. Trees, in particular, feel the change. It is then that strange beings begin to enter the woods.

If you happen to be up early enough you can catch your first sighting of them making their way into the middle of the forest. They will be wrapped up against the wind and rain, in dark green jackets and large rubber wellies.

They hobble together through the undergrowth until they come to a prearranged place where they suddenly part, searching for their own share of the quarry. If you are quiet, you will hear them calling to each other in their soft Highland lilt.

Each carries a battered metal bucket that contains tubing and piping. On closer inspection, a drill and mallet can be spotted along with wooden plugs, a spike and a sort of hook. These elusive mortals are the Sap Seekers. They have only, at best, three weeks to harvest their crop, or more correctly, the Forestry Commission's or absentee landlord's crop. Angus and Mary were Sap Seekers; they would not have considered getting anyone's approval to harvest anything from the land.

The correct way to handle these beings, should you unexpectedly come across them, is to ignore whatever they are doing, say a polite hello and carry on walking as if nothing unusual or untoward were taking place. You see, technically, they shouldn't really be there, at least not without permission.

"Nice tree you have there," would be frowned upon, as would, "I take it it's syrup you'll be making and not that dreaded wine, ha-ha."

Nope, a, "Morning, Angus, nice day for a walk. Mary, nice to see you about too," and carry on, is the correct cultural way to deal with this situation.

As a child, I came across Angus and Mary in the woods. Being curious, as is the nature of children, and not knowing the accepted way of greeting on a day like that, I walked over and studied what they were doing with interest.

"We're just gathering sap, child. Angus likes to make syrup to put on his toast. Here, I'll show you what to do." And there followed my indoctrination into birch sap gathering.

I learnt it is important, if after hammering in a spike nothing comes out of the trunk, to seal the hole very carefully with a wooden nail then wax. After three trees have been tried and all are dry, then the gathering stops, and the gatherers will wait a week. In childhood, I would be on tenterhooks all week for fear they would go back without me. If sap does come out, you rig up the bucket with the hoses, pipes and hook to the tree. The bucket comes complete with a hole near the top for the sap to flow through. It is always exciting returning the next day to find sap in the bucket ready to take home and put in the fridge.

"Here, have a taste." Mary offered me my first ever sip of silver birch sap.

It was the freshest thing I had ever tasted. As a child, I felt like I was tasting the woods. In reality, it tastes like slightly sweetened fresh water. Nothing like the sugary syrup that eventually makes its way to the table.

The syrup making or winemaking has to take place quickly thereafter or the sap will go off. Over the years, I was taught the way of collecting birch sap in a sustainable way. Both Angus and Mary always stressed the importance of sealing off the tree properly after harvest to prevent it from continuing to leak and eventually dying. Nothing was ever mentioned about the legal ramifications or the need to seek permission to drill holes.

It became an annual event for us. Following in the footsteps of generations before us. It was years later before I found out that Angus and Mary had only started making birch syrup especially for my benefit. Before that, all their harvest had gone straight into their homemade wine.

*

I heard voices directly ahead, bringing my focus back to my autumnal harvest. It sounded like someone had beaten me to my patch after all.

"Don't you dare leave me here."

"I've got to get help. I'm not so steady on my feet these days, and I can't get you unstuck on me own."

I turned the corner in the path and saw Mary struggling her way back along toward me.

"Come back, you old besom. I could get eaten by crows … or die of cold. I'll never forgive you if I die with my hair like this." It was Auntie Lottie, not sounding happy.

"Hello, Mary. Is it not a bit difficult underfoot for you in these parts?" I asked. Auntie Lottie could wait, of that I was sure.

"Ach, I manage fine. It's that daft old goat, Lottie. She's got herself all caught up in them bramble bushes, and I can't get her out."

I walked down to my patch and there was Auntie Lottie resembling a rather depressed scarecrow. Her hair was wound tightly around the sharp barbs. Her skirt – God forbid she would wear trousers – was twisted and caught fast.

It took the combined efforts of both Mary and me to eventually untangle her from her thorny prison. Our fingers were sore with the constant pricks from the spiky points. Auntie Lottie kept up her one-sided flow of conversation as if she was sitting at a table sharing a pot of tea with us instead of ungainly dangling from the bramble bushes.

"I see you found my berry patch then. I used to come down here as a girl. It's moved slightly, but still, I think you get the best brambles here. I'm happy to think it was you all these years who was harvesting them. I was never here at the right time until my short stay last year. I'm sorry I got a bit greedy; it was my first visit in a while. I've left you some this year." After we had finally freed her, we gathered our share of the sweet taste of autumn together, our fingers staining purple like when we were children.

"I had to come with Lottie this year. Angus is not feeling so great, so our patch is hardly touched, if you are wanting more to take home."

"Ach, we have well enough here."

"Well, come away back to mine the pair of you. Angus will enjoy the company. We'll have a nice cup of tea and some of those bannocks I made for him this morning."

On the way back, we swapped recipes for bramble wine, bramble and apple pie and bramble fool.

Chapter 24

My face felt like it was being ripped open by the sand as it rushed toward me in waves of stinging crystals. The wind howled its annoyance at all who had braved the elements. Whitecaps crashed and clamoured onto the beach, while the community stood solemnly just out of reach of the grasping swirls.

I had no idea who was there. Only quick glimpses of eyes could be made out under the layers and layers of jumpers, coats, hats and scarves wrapped around necks, heads and faces. At least we were dressed for the cold.

Why and on whose insistence were we standing in the middle of an autumn storm cloud on that desolate beach? Who else but Angus would have insisted on being thrown into the sea from this beach? This was to be his last stand, so to speak.

One of his young cousins had finally stopped speaking, not that anyone had heard anything over the howling gale. He held up the urn, and as one, the assembly took a step back. Much as we had loved and appreciated Angus as a member of our community, we didn't want to inhale him.

The grey mist raced from the urn up into the darkened sky and off into the turbulent water. A sandpiper screeched past as rays of sunlight escaped through the clouds to search out the sea. A sudden wild gust blew Angus toward us again, Mary took an involuntary step forward, while the rest of us started running up the beach determined not to be caught in his far-flung reach. And then he was gone, and Mary's body and soul sagged toward the ground.

"Come on, hen, he wouldn't want you to stay here," yelled Findlay and gripped her arm firmly. We struggled through the gale, half carrying, half supporting Mary on our way toward the village hall. Maureen hurtled toward us, wrestling to keep her wheelchair upright.

"I'm so sorry, Mary, but I couldn't get my chair down the beach." Mary just stared back through vacant eyes. "I can come to the hall though."

Through a distant darkness, a faint gleam struggled to ignite Mary's soul as she caught a flapping movement at the back of Maureen's wheelchair. Her voice, hoarse against the strength of the wind but cold and dead at her loss, battered into Maureen.

"I know you always had your eye on my Angus but could you not, for the love of God, go flaunting it about on such a day."

"Oh Mary, you know we were all friends; how can you say that?"

"Well, if you didn't have to go flaunting your underwear in such a public place maybe I wouldn't. There it is for all to see."

Maureen was stunned. She quickly looked down to ensure she was properly clad, but nothing was showing as far as she could tell. Silence was an unusual state for her to find herself in, a far cry from her normal role of local newscaster.

"Take no notice of her," Findlay said. "She's just upset."

"You be quiet, Findlay. This is between her and me. Just look at her knickers, there for all to see."

Another strong blast of wind whipped around Maureen's wheelchair. A red lacy bra flew past and soared like a pair of giant cupcakes into the sky. For a few seconds, we were all mesmerised by the sight as it bobbed and winged its way up, up and away.

"That's me best bra!" cried Maureen.

"And if you're not fast enough, your knickers will be joining it," Mary said. "They are flapping about at the back of your wheelchair like an advertisement. There's no hiding them."

"No, no, oh, Findlay, grab them quick before I lose my knickers entirely."

Findlay, not a man to normally refuse an offer of any sort, suddenly succumbed to a dreadful bout of shyness and scurried away to the hall. Mary dashed forward and grabbed the pants from the back of the wheelchair.

"Thank you, Mary, what would I have done without them?"

"What indeed. Why did you hang them on your wheelchair? Today of all days, Maureen, you should be showing only respect for my Angus."

"Ach, I just forgot. I hung them there to dry and forgot in my rush to get ready."

"It's been a horrible day. One I hoped never to see. But you, Maureen, with your knickers in the air and your bra floating about in the sky, well, I can just see the smile on my Angus' face right now."

"I'm just so relieved to see you didn't think I was after Angus."

"I felt a rush of anger when I saw your undies fighting in the wind. It's the first thing other than despair that I've felt since Angus went. I didn't want to feel anything. But I'm glad I have. Of course I knew you were never after Angus. We've been friends for too long for any of that stuff."

"Ach, I should have been more careful with my things. My best undies too. I just hope Findlay doesn't find me good bra anywhere. It might just give him a heart attack."

"I think one of them is enough for now. Come on, Maureen, let's get this hall business over with. You'll come back with me to the house afterward, won't you?"

"Course, Mary. I've got a lovely bottle of homebrew with me just waiting for a bit of peace and quiet to be drunk. Onwards and upwards."

We all looked up at the sky as the clouds screamed their way overhead. A tiny dot could be seen snaking its way upward toward the deep, dark heavens.

Chapter 25

"It was like the Wild West. Bullets whizzing everywhere. They sent armed police from Inverness, but there was nobody to shoot at. Apparently, the shed is completely burned down, nothing left but a blackened, sooty mess. Thank goodness, Jimmy Mac had moved his sheep out of the field next door, or they'd all be dead. Shot by a dead man's bullets; how weird is that? Heard his missus needs to be bailed out o the jail."

I knew all this, of course. Only, mine was a slightly more accurate version. They, on the other hand, had obviously spoken to and had Maureen's version. The real version may not have been quite so dramatic, but I was not about to douse the fire. It wasn't the Black Widow I was dealing with or some notorious mafia mama. No, the perpetrator here was a wee, old lady who though it could be said she had a temper, it didn't run to shooting up the neighbourhood. The phone call I had received had gone like this.

"I've been arrested." My first thoughts were that someone had found out about her original plan regarding Angus' ashes. But we hadn't done that in the end. So that was just ridiculous, it was more likely the illegal burying of his cousin's ashes before that.

"Is this to do with Angus?"

"Well, yes and no." By now I was convinced it was the ashes scandal, or at least, it would soon be a scandal when everyone found out what we had done

"Is it to do with his death?"

"Well, more because of his death. Will you come and bail me out? This is my one phone call that I am allowed."

I heard the phone being removed from her hand, and a voice which sounded authoritative, exasperated and fed up, all at the same time came on.

"Mrs Craig is not under arrest, neither is she needing to be 'bailed out' or only allowed one phone call. We merely need someone to come and pick her up as our car is fully engaged at another incident, and we really, really, need to get Mrs Craig off the premises, now."

I didn't quite skid to a halt outside, but I got there as fast as I possibly could before Mary could cause any more harm by admitting to one of the crimes that she actually *had* committed. The cause of this 'bail out' *had* been a combination Angus and ashes but not in the way I had anticipated.

*

Angus, before he retired, had run a shop, well more like an Aladdin's cave of treasure. There was everything from tall, black waders to toilet roll, tomato sauce to handcrafted fishing flies. Everything and anything that locals or passing tourists could want or afford. The knowledge and enticing tales supplied with each acquisition, free of charge, were priceless. All the local children loved going into there, Iona and myself included. We were convinced that there was real treasure hidden inside.

Angus cultivated the belief that, like many a male of his generation, he hunted and fished. To further cement this belief, he sold the kind of nick-nacks that any decent hunter or fisherman would want. When Angus came to retire, he had taken

171

a lot of the stock with him. This had consisted mainly, although not exclusively, of all sorts of packets of cartridges, an occasional gas cylinder, spare petrol cans and other objects that he could not envisage living without. After all, he would now have the time to indulge in his favourite pastimes.

Most had been stored in the shed where they remained, long forgotten about. As the years went by, this bundle was added to as tools acquired for projects never completed were piled on top. Wood, glue, nails, bits of cupboards and furniture, camping equipment and various other paraphernalia that could have fetched a fortune with the right label if displayed in the Tate Modern – all had rested together, gathering dust over the years.

Mary had had no knowledge of what lay beneath the pile that she referred to affectionately as 'his junk'.

After Angus' death, she had responsibly disposed of the rifles to dealers and given his small stash of cartridges to one of his friends who she knew hunted. Everything Mary considered dangerous had been tidied away or sold in a safe manner. But she had known nothing of the packets of cartridges that lay on the bottom of Angus' junk pile.

*

Once retrieved and firmly ensconced in my car, I asked her what was going on and how she had landed up at the police station.

"It's the shed. Angus' shed; it burned down."

"Oh, Mary, I am sorry. What happened?"

"Well, I heard a crack then a whizz … I thought it might be thunder and lightning. But when I went outside, I could see the shed was on fire, so I called the fire brigade. The police arrived first seeing as the boys were all away, busy helping out DJ with that wall that collapsed, so it took them a while to man the fire engine. And before you know it, Constable Jim is hiding behind the bonnet of his car telling me to go back inside, telling me bullets are cracking and banging all over the place

"Nothing could have been coming out of the shed though. I mean, who did he think was shooting at him? There were plenty of other noises, I can tell you. But no actual cartridges could have been flying about. I mean, they don't, do they? Not unless they have been inside a rifle, and I've sold all of the firearms. They wouldn't listen to me though. Told me they had to be careful and to stay inside where it was safe. It was all a bit too much for me, even then; I could still hear it from inside the house. The boys on the engine weren't taking any chances either – they were hiding behind their big red truck. Nobody could do anything. They just kept everyone away, shut our road to the croft in case of visitors and sat it out until the last crack and pop had gone off. Lost his shed and everything he loved. They wouldn't go near it until it lay in a pile of ashes on the ground."

"Oh, Mary, I'm so sorry. They're not blaming you for the fire, are they? You're not going to be charged with anything, surely?"

"Well, that nice constable said as I hadn't known anything about the ammunition, everyone has agreed that it can be recorded as a garage fire, so I won't be charged or held responsible for having so many cartridges. But if Angus had been alive, he would have been charged and maybe even jailed. You're only allowed to keep so much ammunition at home, and Angus obviously had way more that he was supposed to. Imagine that! My poor Angus, I couldn't have let that happen."

"Ach, I don't think it would have come to that. It's lucky that no one was hurt. Was it the cartridges that started the fire?"

"Oh no … well, I don't think so. They never said. But do you know what Constable Jim said? He reckoned that Angus had stashed more ammunition in there than they had in the British Army."

I couldn't help but snigger. After a moment of two, I said, "You know, Mary, I know Angus had all those guns and fishing rods, but I don't ever remember him going to the shoots or even fishing come to that."

"Well, dear, of course you wouldn't. Just between you and me, Angus didn't like blood sports of any kind. We had to make a living, so he had to sell all that kind of stuff in the shop and know all about it. But he never went shooting. His friends understood, you see; they played along with him being one of the hunting and shooting crowd. But they knew he couldn't hurt a fly. He didn't want to appear like a hippy or one of them New Age sorts. So, you see, you are quite right, dear, my Angus was a pacifist."

Chapter 26

Iona's trips home were always peppered with delays. These delays could be caused by work commitments or transport problems. Anything, in fact, could be used to explain why she never arrived as planned. I had long given up expecting her at the agreed time.

"They didn't arrive. Have they been in touch with you?" It was one of my neighbours who had gone shopping in Inverness. He had kindly offered to collect Iona and her friend, but it seemed Iona and company hadn't got off the train from Edinburgh.

"No, no contact. I did try and phone her earlier but no reply. Look, thanks for trying, just come away home, and I will wait to hear from her." In the age of mobile phones, it is almost impossible to be out of reach, but Iona had perfected the art to degree level.

"Ach, I've a few things to do in Inverness yet. I'll go back for the next train at midday and see if they're on that."

I thanked him again and put the phone down.

Local transport is limited when you get off the beaten track or, in this case, the rail track. Connecting buses are few and far between, so when someone is due for a visit, friends, family and neighbours often offer to pick visitors up on their way back from Inverness. If they're going to be there for the day anyway, it's never a problem. I shouldn't have been at all surprised really. Once more, Iona was a no-show.

*

We had been persuaded as children that the 8 p.m. curfew bell that still rang every night in Blàs was to make sure that children returned home on time. It was actually left over from the curfew imposed on the village after the battle of Culloden in 1746. But we didn't know that. All we knew was, if we were late home, the consequences would be dire. I had had no intention of finding out what those dire consequences were; I was not really a rule-breaker. Iona, on the other hand, was never scared of anything. She wanted to know what the dire consequences were. There was no way she was going to live her life, even then, to the sound of a bell.

*

I finally got a phone call from Iona and her friend at 10.30 that night.

"Can you come and pick us up? You'll never guess what happened. I'll tell you when you get here."

What had happened was, of course, a few drinks that had got out of control and ended up lasting throughout the night. That had been followed by a decision that the best place to be visiting right then was Paris and not the Highlands of Scotland. This, even though she was supposed to be coming north to raise money for some charities. The fact that neither Iona nor Patrick, her Irish friend, had had any photographic identification that would have allowed them to travel to Europe didn't seem to have figured in their plans.

In the end, it hadn't mattered, as halfway to the railway station an alternative decision had been reached. They had remembered they were taking part in a sponsored walk up north so had better stay in Scotland after all.

Minutes after jumping on the first available train, they were fast asleep. Unfortunately for them, the train only did a loop around a few towns before heading back to Edinburgh. The dynamic duo had awoken to find themselves back where they had started. Not to be outdone, they had jumped onto another train, where once more, no doubt tired from their previous journey, they had promptly fallen asleep again.

A conductor finally put them off at Stirling. Lucky for them, as this was where they could get a connection to Inverness. Their travel time by train should have been somewhere between three and a half and four hours, depending on stops. Iona and her companion had managed to build this up to twelve and a half hours. Almost a record, I believe.

*

Travelling around the Highlands has improved a lot, although I suppose that depends on what your notions are of improvements. Summertime, with its increase in tourists, means it now takes longer to reach Caithness and the north then than it does in the bad weather. Tourists are not really the biggest problem though.

Nope, most of them just brake hard in front of you and pull off, so they can see the view better. Knowing that this will probably happen means that everything is usually fine. They spend money and get to enjoy our amazing country for a short time, while we get to live here and enjoy it all the time.

The biggest problem is 'sponsor' time when charity fundraisers travel from Land's End in southwest England to John O Groats in northeast Scotland, causing huge hold-ups. I don't know why this distance of 874 miles has become the 'chosen' route for charity fundraising over the decades, but it has.

Legions of foot soldiers march toward the north under one banner or another, trying to raise money for their chosen cause. This phenomenon generally runs between when the weather is expected to get better until just before the weather closes in again. Or so they think. Snow in June is not unheard of and neither is a heatwave in February, although blizzards in April are more the norm.

The road they take snakes its way around every bend and rock in the region, taking you on a breathtaking tour out of Sutherland. There are only about two safe places to pass on the whole stretch up through the area until you are well into Caithness.

Of course, it is never at the safe overtaking areas where you find yourself coming up behind the barely moving fundraising vehicles. The participants don't only walk, cycle or run the length of the British Isles, oh no, they come on horse-drawn carts or a battery-operated toilet complete with driver, or a bicycle that lies almost flat on the road or a person placed on a bed that a fellow fundraiser pushed along – all in the name of charity. The crazier the transport the more publicity they are likely to get which then, hopefully, leads to more supporters and ultimately more money for their cause. This could go on for months, from late spring through autumn.

*

Two days after Iona and Patrick had finally arrived in Blàs, I found myself waiting for them again. Inspired by all the fundraisers over the years heading south and north, Iona had come up with her own version. She intended to use a different route and cross Scotland from west to east. Two charities would benefit.

I looked along the track. She was over two hours late. It had all sounded well-planned, but knowing how unpredictable she could be, I was a bit concerned. This was to be her way of commemorating Angus.

*

One of Iona's most endearing qualities was her openness with people. She was willing to believe the most outrageous stories. Angus, most of all, loved this in her and would spin her tales that captivated and encircled them both.

"See that tree over there," he said as he walked us to school one day. "That's a eucalyptus tree, and the people who used to stay in that house kept koalas in the garden. Don't you remember seeing them when you were younger?" He left it at that, but the seed had been planted. The house was literally falling down at that point, and the garden was overgrown. Angus and Iona spent a whole summer searching around for evidence of this cuddly-looking Australian marsupial.

Angus had long since forgotten his tale by the time Iona went to high school. She, however, hadn't and arrived home on her first day, all indignant

"I was speaking to Steve on the bus. He said his grandparents never had koalas in their garden, and he should know, because they were *his* grandparents. I told him he was talking rubbish and that everyone knows the koalas lived there."

The koalas were never mentioned again, and her interest in them got condemned along with the ruined house. I thought she would have learnt from that incident to be a bit more cautious about believing what people told her, but it just wasn't the case. She continued to love Angus' tales, the more preposterous they were, the more she enjoyed them.

*

Iona was desperate to have something positive come from his loss and so had decided to raise money for both Chest, Heart and Stroke Scotland and the Blàs Development Trust.

"Look, if you take us to Ullapool on a Friday, we can stay with some friends. They have offered to drop us off at Inverleal early the following Saturday morning. We'll see what the weather's like. If we want a short day, we'll stay the night at the Glenbeg bothy. If not, we'll push on a bit further, pop up our tent and then walk in from there to Ardgay on the Sunday. All you have to do is pick us up when we get there."

She had voiced this idea shortly after Angus had died. So, there I was on the allotted Sunday, anxiously awaiting her and Patrick. I rechecked my watch; she was over two and a half hours late, and still there was no sign of them.

"She'll be fine." Auntie Lottie was there with me as I looked down the glen. I felt Mary and Ellen at my back. They had come to celebrate Iona's achievement and cheer her home. She and her companion had raised £10,000 between them, a remarkable effort.

There was no sign of life heading toward us. Where were they? I could have lost her to the mountains or bogs or … well, anything could have happened in the wilds of Scotland. A fine drizzle was obscuring my view. It might have been snowing higher up. Angus wouldn't have wanted her to put herself at risk.

"My Angus would have been so proud of her." Mary had sensed my thoughts. "She's so strong and determined, Stroma. She's trained for this. Angus would be cheering her on if he could. He was always her biggest fan, whatever she was doing, and it's such a lovely thing she is doing in his memory."

Nothing yet. Iona should have arrived over three hours ago. It was starting to get dark. Ellen had been running her car to keep herself, Mary and Auntie Lottie warm. I couldn't sit still. I paced around. Where was she?

When do you call out the rescue services? I tried to ignore the constant patter of my heart. Then I saw them coming out of the gloom. Two figures, slowly making their way toward us. My companions were out of the car, hot chocolate being poured out of flasks. They were cheering loudly and clapping the duo home. Iona and her friend sped up when they heard us. I wanted to cry. I was so proud of my little sister who couldn't find her way home on time but had just completed the shortest crossing from the west coast of Scotland to the east on foot – through the wilds, over moorland and glen, all togged out in the proper outdoor clothing, rucksack on her back and a broad smile on her face.

"You finally made it." I threw my arms around her neck.

"Ach well, I didn't want to break a habit of a lifetime. Had to keep you waiting." She hugged me back.

Mary was right – Angus would have been so proud of her.

Chapter 27

Red and yellow and pink and green, purple and orange and blue, with stars and planets and asteroids too. An autumnal night, a big sky, there's nothing quite like the sky on a dark and clear Highland evening. No background light to dilute the spectacle. Not damp and murky but clear and fresh. Frosty and so cold it takes the breath away, leaving a feeling of being invigorated and glad to be alive.

I was on my way back from a meeting with a parents' committee. One, for once, that I could walk to and from without the need to travel miles along uncharted single-track roads. The meeting had been productive which helped with the all-round feeling of well-being. I wasn't often on my own patch. Needs around the wider region and beyond regularly overrode more local issues. A bit like the cobbler's children whose shoes are always the last to get mended, everyone else's problems around the Highlands had to be nailed before those of my local area.

The theory was, because I lived in Blàs, I could deal with any issues that might arise when at home. If only that were true. To be totally honest, working in my own locality had always felt a bit more awkward than anywhere else. Perhaps it was because I had gone to school with a lot of the parents, they felt they knew all there was to know about me. What gave me the right to advise them on how to introduce Gaelic to their families?

Even though I had been my sister's guardian, in their eyes, that did not qualify me as any sort of real parent. They would never have voiced this opinion, as the idea of losing your parents, when they had young children themselves, was way too disturbing to contemplate.

The meeting that night, however, seemed to have run smoothly. The agenda had been stuck to without much "did you hear about?" or "were you speaking to Maureen?" or "Maureen said". The parents there were mostly slightly younger than me. Perhaps that made them more likely to accept what I was saying. If my counterparts were all finished with having children that would make my life so much easier at meetings.

The aurora borealis continued to twinkle and sparkle, lighting up the sky to illuminate my pathway home. This phenomenon happens way more regularly than people imagine. To the extent that I always expected to see it on a clear night. That's not to say I didn't appreciate it. I did, but if I didn't see it one night, I knew I would catch it another time.

It's never exactly the same though. Sometimes, it's like searchlights illuminating the sky in strobes. Other times, it dances daintily across the surface of the heavens. That night, it just exploded with colour that radiated down from the universe onto the land that highlanders called home, bathing it in a spectacular performance.

I was so busy looking up and out at the universe that I failed to notice the potholes that littered the road. Before I knew what had happened, I was on my knees not caring how amazing the Northern Lights were or if they would ever appear again.

"Ouch, ouch, ouch." All my notes and completed forms were spread all over the track. Thankfully, because the puddles were frozen, most weren't soaking and useless. These forms were important. They would allow the committee to hand over a percentage of their fundraising to the Development Trust in order to give a much-needed cash injection to the trust until the rents started coming in from the new housing development.

As the voluntary treasurer of the Development Trust, I knew we were at a critical stage regarding expenditure and income. Grants had helped, but we were coming dangerously close to losing all we had achieved so far. Balancing the cash was giving me many a sleepless night. Scared to look in the mirror, I was sure I looked closer to Mary's age than my own from all the worry. Thankfully, most of our community groups understood the importance of what the trust was trying to do and were keen to help out. We had to make this work before we lost any more families from the area.

"You okay? Can I help?" I looked up. There was a witch looking down at me. Had I bumped my head? Was I dreaming?

"Can you get up?" A skeleton hovered in the background. What was going on?

"I've picked up all the papers I can see, so you should be okay with these. Lucky no rain tonight, just this frost." This was delivered by a spectre or rather a ghost-like figure who smelt surprisingly of a mixture of burnt turnip and aftershave.

Just go with the flow my fuzzy brain told me. My hands were numb with the cold now and the rest of my body was not far behind them.

"Can you lend me your hand for a minute, so I can get up?"

One green-gloved hand, one bony hand and one white-sheeted hand immediately appeared as if from nowhere. They were, however, still attached to their respective arms.

"Lucky we were passing. We're just off to the pub. They said, if we wore fancy dress, we would get a free drink, so no competition. Got our robes off the children after they'd finished guising, and here we are. A motley crew of heroes to your rescue."

"I reckon you'll do. Thanks for that. You the only ones going then?"

"Ach no, there's a whole crowd of us meeting up there. Too old for going around the houses now and much prefer a wee nip to a couple of sweeties. You be okay walking home like this? Or we could take you home first if you like."

These were turning out to be the nicest motley crew I had ever met.

"No, that's okay, thanks. I should be able to make it from here. No bones hurt." I threw this in the direction of the skeleton.

"Aye, aye, very funny. If you're feeling up to it, you can join us for a drink in the pub later."

"Okay, I'll think about it. See you around."

Off they went, my three rescuers – the witch, the skeleton and the ghost. I was feeling a bit like Alice down the rabbit hole until it dawned on me: of course, it was Halloween!

It also explained why the parents had been so happy to escape their homes that night. Those left at home would have had to deal with the dressing their children in costumes to go guising, other guisers visiting, the dooking for apples and sticky treacle-covered pancakes dangling from strings.

Halloween became a regular night for committee meetings after that. It turned out to be one of our best attended meetings each year.

Chapter 28

It was not officially a Bonfire Night celebration. This community wouldn't have stooped to that. They didn't particularly care what had happened in London all those years ago or, if truth be told, what was happening there even today.

Commemorations for the turning of the seasons, equinox, solstice and harvest had been going on way longer than the modern Bonfire Night. No guy would ever be placed on top of the fire here and the date was sacrosanct. It didn't matter what day of the week it fell on it never changed. Moving it to the closest weekend to accommodate the working week or anything else for that matter, would have been frowned upon.

Claims had been made that bonfires and celebrations had been going on at that very spot for millennia. Not to be outdone by any other festival or community, our wee village had been partying on the sixth of November since time began. Or at least that is what the ancients and the locals born and bred would have us all believe.

"Ach, it's just a leftover from *Oidhche Shamhna*. Halloween was the start of it all. The partying, I mean. Tonight's fire was intended to end the week of merriment. Kind of like a full stop at the end of a sentence, so people could get back to sobriety and work." Angus had been a great one for collecting stories and myths from the area. I just hoped someone had written them all down. The only thing was, no one was ever sure which ones had some modicum of truth and which had come totally from his imagination. Even Mary wasn't sure.

It was the first year without Angus, and so, at the one time of year when it was rumoured the dead could visit, it seemed only fitting that Angus' life should be honoured.

"Ach, he would have loved this." Mary was sipping a steaming hot toddy. I wasn't so sure – latterly, he was never that happy in wet weather.

"The cold, you can always stick an extra layer on. But this rain, it's awful, can't do nothing about staying dry. It just creeps in everywhere," he'd grumble as he collected his weekly paper from the shop.

"Good turnout," someone yelled as they walked past under a large umbrella. It was too, despite the horrendous rain, rivers of which ran past the bystanders as it thundered down in a constant stream. All out to honour one of the worthies of the village.

*

To qualify for this coveted title, normally, individuals would have to be born and bred, if not in the village itself, then at least local enough to have attended the local school at some point. Many stories had to be attached to the recipient's name. These accounts had to be about incidents that had taken place down through the years, the more outrageous and unbelievable the better.

However, like life itself, there are always exceptions to this rule. Qualification could be gained through your everyday activities and characteristics, if they tended toward the quirky side of life. Some sort of irregularity had to exist, or as in the case of the old couple who lived at the other end of the village, it could be the regularity of their existence that brought them this prestigious honour.

Both ex-service people, they materialised into their cottage on a day and year no one recalls. Where they came from still remains a mystery to this day. Maureen's patience finally ran out, and she once asked them as directly as politeness would allow where they came from. After forty-five minutes of a predominantly one-sided conversation, she still didn't have any idea other than they had once been stationed somewhere in England.

They obviously had never attended the local school, therefore were never expected to enter into the more colourful tales of the community. At no time seen apart, they never varied their routine. Rain or shine, winter or summer, you could set your clocks by them. The only variations arose when an unplanned-for community event was taking place. Then they would leave their highly restricted timetable and attend, which was rather quirky in itself. This, however, was not the main reason for their inclusion into the esteemed group of worthies. Oh no, their admittance was for something way more fundamental than that.

"Ach, I see its pants day then," would be the cry as locals passed by their garden, the washing line dragging the eye in. Pants day, we all knew, fell on a Wednesday. Helpful to those who perhaps were apt to lose track of which day we were on.

It was difficult to miss as gigantic knickers and humongous Y-fronts billowed in the wind like flags proclaiming 'all here is clean'. The community became fascinated by these voluminous undergarments, as the couple they were supposed to fit were tiny. Not so much notice would have been taken if the underwear in question had more resembled colourful bunting.

Lingerie was not a word that could be attached to the items. No, these were industrial-grade, working undergarments that would have been left standing if the world had blown apart.

Not a drop of colour was seen – that would be way too frivolous. White, pure, clean, bleached, startling fabric that could be seen for miles. The garments were like runway lights dragging our eyes in to lock onto them when really all we wanted was to avoid staring if at all possible.

Unintentionally, this quiet and rather dull couple had, over time, become part of the colourful variety of individuals upon whom the community bestowed the title: worthies of the village.

They were unaware of achieving this sought-after acclaim. Many others who coveted the title would weave tales about themselves which would become legends. These stories often started off, as many do, as relatively truthful anecdotes. Later, they would mature like wine into something much more enjoyable and entertaining. Less truthful it could be said, but what's truth in the world of the storyteller?

The most respected worthies, however, were those like the old couple who had not gone seeking the title. Through deeds and lifestyle, the title had been bestowed upon them by the unspoken consensus of the community. Angus was one of those. A worthie of great respect and renown, cherished and revered by both young and old, whose stories and escapades would continue to grow and thrive throughout the generations to come.

The rain had stopped, thankfully, and moving away from the ever-increasing heat of the bonfire was becoming inevitable. One side of me was in danger of steaming while the other, facing away from the blaze, remained wet and cold. Now that I was no longer being soaked to the skin, I had to move on.

The sky suddenly lit up with bright, colourful lights. Engines could be heard revving and horns blaring. Crofters with every conceivable sort of tractors, trailers, all-terrain vehicles and trucks had switched on their lights and revved up their engines. Quad bikes stood side by side with motorbikes. Maureen, not to be outdone, was sitting resplendent in her motorised wheelchair adorned with multi-coloured fairy lights. Auntie Lottie, also compelled to commemorate her friend's late husband and worthie of the village, had brought along her decorated lawnmower with lights and crafts donated by Jill. Even the youngest in the community had torches blinking in the dark attached to their bikes and buggies. Paul of the Sheds had managed to load his vessel onto a trailer and had lamps festooned around his boat.

Illuminated by the boat, stood the old couple – compelled out of their strict routine by this important event. Like two mini lighthouses, they stood erect at attention, head torches proclaiming their presence, determined to pay homage to such a beloved character in this place they had chosen to call home.

Angus had lit up the lives of our community with his tales, songs and poems. He had warmed the hearts of our fellow villagers with his good humour, fun and sheer love of life. On a night when spirits could be free among us, when a fire could warm our bodies if not our souls, when colourful lights exploded above us, what better way to remember and recall a man who radiated both light and noise wherever he went?

The sound and glittering spectacular went on for a full five minutes, until one by one, the lights tweeted out and the engines hushed. Two small head torches remained, unmoving, their steady beams a haven in the dark, until they too went out. Silence loomed in the inky sky, and for a split second, the earth lay quiet. Then a huge roar erupted from the fire as it blazed and thundered toward the sky in a gigantic inferno of orange and red.

"Well, my Angus would have loved that. Much better than any fireworks. I need something hot and sweet now." Mary turned toward the hot chocolate stall, the flames of the fire reflecting in her unshed tears.

That was the last community-led remembrance for Angus. Mary was determined all sadness associated with him should be finished before the start of all the next month's festivities.

Chapter 29

"Oh, come on, Mary, you have to come. I need the company. When was the last time you went to the city?" Although Auntie Lottie had settled into the community and had no intention of living elsewhere again, she still craved the big city at times, especially if that meant clothes shopping.

"I've no decent underwear left, and I need a new bag. You could do with a new winter coat before the weather gets any worse. Remember the state that one got into last winter? It couldn't keep a drizzle out, let alone a downpour. Two nights, I promise. Two at the most. I'll drive down, tasty dinner and sleep. One day at the shops. Then nice wee breakfast the following morning, and we'll be back in time for tea." I could see Mary weakening. She had barely left the village since Angus had died and then only when someone else took her.

Mary had never learnt to drive ... well, she could drive a tractor, of course – what woman from a crofting community couldn't? However, she had never sat an official driving test or bothered to learn the rules of the road. That had been Angus' job.

"How about one night then, Mary? We'll leave early in the morning, do some shopping before we book into the B & B, finish our shopping before a nice meal and head back the next morning. Come on, what do you say? One night only?"

Mary capitulated rather reluctantly.

As the time for the trip drew nearer, it emerged that Auntie Lottie had booked two nights, and Ellen would be accompanying them both.

"Just to make sure nobody leads them astray you understand." Ellen was trying to hide behind a veil of responsibility, when in fact, everybody knew she loved a visit to the shops. Anyway, Mary was senior by thirty years to both Ellen and Auntie Lottie, so it was hard to envisage her letting anyone lead her astray. It would more than likely be the other way around.

*

Friday morning, they were all set. I put the computer on sleep mode and went to wave them off along with half the village. Auntie Lottie's car, like herself, was rather unique.

That classic car was the love of her life. She had spent a small fortune on it over the years, including having the engine taken out of the boot and replacing it with a more modern V8 which now resided under the bonnet. This gave her luggage-room in the compact boot.

It was what my parents had referred to as a 'punch car'. If you saw one, you punched your friend's arm, hence the name. A Volkswagen Beetle, full of fun with as much character as anyone could wish for.

Auntie Lottie's car was a classic black with brown bumpers and large, high-set headlights. She had customised these by adding dark eyelashes around them. Full of angles and high in style, her car was also somewhat temperamental but had always taken her from A to B in relative safety. The screech as they took off confirmed she hadn't yet tightened the fan belt.

*

The village felt quieter over the next two days. The noise that had been generated by the building work had become such a part of everyday life that is was noticeable in its absence. Work was continuing inside the new houses so could no longer be heard. Old Tam, glad to be back after a stay with his son and daughter-in-law in Glasgow, was especially happy with the peace and quiet.

"Ach, it wasn't to be, peur auld Shep, he didnae like the city at all." Old Shep just wagged his tail. It was difficult to imagine the old dog not liking or even noticing where he was. As long as he was with Old Tam, he was happy and content.

*

It hadn't been that long ago that Old Tam had reluctantly left the community. His cottage, it had to be said, was rather run-down. It leaked in a few places, and the only reason he didn't freeze to death during winter was thanks to the big range in the kitchen that blasted out enough heat to easily warm a much larger house. Nobody could remember a time when Old Tam hadn't inhabited the old cottage. According to his son, no upgrading had taken place that he could remember. Finally, Old Tam's family had called a halt to it all.

On his son's last trip north, he had come prepared. What the community had feared since summer was coming to pass. Another of our senior residents was to be whisked away. A corporeal melancholy had engulfed the community. Old Tam's dour spirit appeared to infect everyone and seeped into the everyday fabric of life before his departure. The atmosphere was bleak.

"This old place is not fit for a dog, let alone an elderly man. You are coming with us, lock, stock and old dog. We've got a room all ready for you."

So off Old Tam and Shep were carted. It had been happening more and more often in the village, our old folk vanishing overnight. The sons and daughters who years before had left the area for college, work and pastures new, never quite able to cut ties completely, would return for holidays over the years, until they deemed their parents too frail to stay by themselves. The elderly relatives were then spirited away with them, lost to the village residents forever.

When Old Tam and his equally old dog got to their new place, both were waited on hand and foot. They had their own wee corner of the house to make their home, got fed hot, well-balanced meals and had grandchildren come to visit.

But Old Tam was not a city man nor was he the sort to be waited upon or left without anything to do all day. Both his son and daughter-in-law were out working from morning until night. Their children had already flown the nest, so Old Tam was left to his own company.

He was well missed in the village too. Everyone was so used to seeing him at certain times of the day going about his business that they hardly ever needed to check the time; he was as reliable as the speaking clock, given a minute or two to compensate for any conversation stops during his rounds.

Two months after he left, someone snapped up his old house, and a large renovation swung into action. The outhouses were incorporated into the original building which created a rather nice courtyard that was bound to be a lovely suntrap.

Then, mere months after he left, Old Tam, without any preamble, was spotted ambling along the road as if he had never been away. He was also seen leaving the not entirely finished cottage, only by a different door.

His relatives, having seen how miserable he was with his city life, had called a family meeting without his knowledge.

One of his granddaughters, a district midwife in Argyll, had recently accepted a job in the Highlands. She was quite happy to take the opportunity to buy his cottage and get it renovated for her own use. Her dad, Old Tam's son, had agreed to help with the cost as long as a granny annexe or, in this case, a granddad annexe was included in the work. This was all agreed and put to Old Tam who almost jumped on the next bus home.

Morag – his granddaughter, Old Tam and Shep all arrived unannounced back in the village and settled into their routine as if this had been the arrangement for years. It would still be quite a while before the cottage was finished, but it was windtight and watertight, and that was all the excuse Old Tam needed.

His return reversed the feelings that had heralded his departure. Hope surged and spread through the community. Who would have thought that Old Tam, the very picture of gloom and doom, would be the catalyst for sparking the feeling of optimism that now prevailed? It did help that his return also coincided with the final phase of the housing development. Perhaps our community could be saved after all. Even I had started to genuinely believe we might be winning.

*

Unfortunately, the arrival of Auntie Lottie, Mary and Ellen back from their trip to the city did not go quite so unannounced. It would have been hard to miss their arrival. Into the midst of the village drove a large four-by-four police car which pulled up right outside Auntie Lottie's cottage. Ellen and Mary were ensconced in the back with Auntie Lottie squeezed in-between. When the policeman opened the rear door to the trio, Auntie Lottie could be heard saying, "Ach, are you sure you won't come in for a wee cup of tea?"

The reply couldn't be heard. The policeman then helped the others from the back and put their suitcases on the ground before heading back through the village. Curtains twitched around the community. What had the three of them been up to that they needed to be brought home by police escort? Where was Auntie Lottie's car? Two shamefaced women hurried away toward their homes before I got a chance to speak to them, so I made my way into Auntie Lottie's house.

"I've just put the kettle on. The other two just wanted to get home. I don't think they were very happy at getting a run home from the police. I can't understand why. Such a nice young man. Wouldn't even come inside for a cup of tea, you know."

"Where's your car Auntie Lottie? You didn't have an accident, did you?"

"What? Goodness, no. But it was all my fault really." This did not surprise me in the least. "I had bought some drinks and food which I put in the boot to eat on the way up. After such a large breakfast, we didn't really want anything at the start of the journey, so we decided we would stop quite near to home. Once we got on the quiet roads again, the car was being a bit more temperamental than usual, so we pulled in to have a cuppa. I thought I would try and fix the problem with the engine, but the others were having none of it, so I put everything back in the boot.

"After about a mile or so, a big police car with blue, flashing lights pulled in front of us and signalled for me to pull over. My heart was in my mouth. I knew I couldn't outrun them. Mary and Ellen were shouting at me from the back to stop. I was getting quite flustered, I can tell you. I was pretty sure I wasn't speeding." So was I. Auntie Lottie was more likely to be pulled over for driving too slowly than too fast. As for outrunning the police car, that was a complete non-starter.

"I pulled in just as my car screeched for the last time. It didn't sound very healthy. Anyway, tea?" Auntie Lottie handed me a mug, and we sat at the table.

"'Are these yours, madam?' In that authoritarian voice policemen put on, holding up a large, fawn pair of knickers? I was that embarrassed, I can tell you. Here you go, dear, use that to mop up the tea."

"What? The policeman pulled you over to check if you had lost you knickers?"

"Not just any old knickers, you understand. These were new ones from that expensive underwear shop. Still had the labels on. Glad the size wasn't visible. I didn't recognise them at first, see, as they were new. Took me a moment to realise they were the ones I had bought. When I told him, yes. He said, 'I take it these are all yours as well.' All my new underwear. Bras and pants, all with the labels on. I hadn't realised I had bought so much. Mary and Ellen were that embarrassed, you'd have thought the undies belonged to them.

"It turns out that the catch on my boot had broken when I put the snack stuff back. When I drove off, all my new underwear had started streaming out of the back of the car. That nice policeman had spotted this all happening and picked up the lot before he stopped me." Auntie Lottie calmly took a sip of tea.

My mind was struggling to process what she had said. For some reason it had decided to centre on how the policeman would have reported this incident to headquarters: 'Motorists should be aware of free flying debris on the main road east, consisting, although not exclusively, of loose flying knickers and expensive lacy bras.' I decided to focus on more mundane things.

"Okay, but why did you end up getting a lift back?"

"Well, I maybe could have sorted out a way of keeping the boot closed, but the car refused to start. All that screeching I thought was the fan belt, turns out it may have been the starter motor. So, I'll need to get Paul to fetch the car down and fix it. That nice policeman took pity on us. Well, he could see the age of Mary. I don't suppose his superiors would have been too happy with him if he had abandoned us to the elements, especially at this time of year. So, he offered to drive us here, seeing as he had business in the village anyway. How else would we have got home otherwise? You know there is no signal up there. The others didn't like the idea of arriving in a police car. Me, I was tired after so much driving, and after all, he was such a nice boy."

Auntie Lottie's car was eventually fixed, and she was right, it had been the starter motor. It took Ellen and Mary a lot longer to get over their embarrassment of arriving back in a police car. Eventually, they could laugh about it, mainly, I suspect, because it wasn't their underwear that had been picked up by the local constabulary.

Chapter 30

"I'm so glad you let me come. I haven't seen Agnes since she moved away." Auntie Lottie had hitched a lift north with me to visit a friend. Agnes was yet another Blàs resident who had left to be nearer younger family members. It felt like for every month it took to build the housing development, we were losing yet more of the community to other places. It was concerning, but there was not much more we could have done. We had to hold our nerve and wait until the housing development was signed off before we could offer accommodation to anyone, officially.

I comforted myself with the knowledge that the sale of one of the houses through the shared owner's scheme was well under way, unofficially.

One of the young joiners who had been working on our project had asked if he could be considered for the shared ownership scheme. We couldn't ask him to wait until the application process opened as it felt so right. His purchase was being used as a way to check our systems before we opened the process for everyone the next month. He would be in before Christmas.

Agnes had increased the population in the far north by one. She had moved to Caithness instead of south to the city of Inverness which, in my eyes, was an added bonus. One more person in Inverness made no difference, but a person choosing to move north when so many were moving south, well, that was a reason to celebrate. Caithness and Sutherland's concerns about depopulation reflected out own.

The Caithness road stretched out before us. As we hugged the rugged coastline, it felt like we were driving up the familiar TV weather map. Flat, high, on top of the world, no trees or towns to obscure the uninterrupted miles north. Tiny fishing boats sailed on the big sea to our right, and the outline of oil and gas rigs could be seen in the distance.

The northern visits were always interesting, entertaining, frustrating and interspersed with hysterical laughter. I was never quite sure if that was because you had to be half mad to put up with the weather and general remoteness of the area, or if it was just that the people there grew to be as wild, generous and unpredictable as their surroundings.

Or perhaps it was because you had to drive the Berriedale Braes before you entered the area. Such a charming name that conjured up thoughts of all types of wild flowers, delicate herbs and sweet wild berries. Then you reached the Braes, and with them the realisation that the name and place did not sit so snugly together. Moorland Ravine would have been a better description; at least that would have hinted at what lay ahead. Taking a massive detour up around the north-west of Scotland with its single-track roads and amazing scenery was not an option when I was on a time limit. So, the main A9 north it was, including the Braes which lie in wait just before you enter Caithness.

What they consist of is an incredibly steep hill with double bends on the way down, the North Sea on your right and a drop I try not to think about on your left, with a not very reassuring emergency layby for use in case you can't stop in time or your brakes fail. That never really comforted me. It just concerned me that they felt the need for measures like that in the first place.

Those 'soothing' measures are followed by a tight corner on a sharp incline. Cars have to scramble up it toward a hairpin bend. For safety sake, before you reach this bend, it is essential to ensure that no lorry is coming down toward you, thus it requires a quick glance up and to the right. Then you have to change down gear to crawl around the aforementioned hairpin bend, as any lorry heading south will need the whole road to get around the corner and won't be able to stop. All this on the steepest part of any brae you are ever likely to encounter, anywhere. It is a lot worse on the way back. I could not avoid the Berriedale Braes on a trip north-east.

Auntie Lottie was prepared to face this with me, just to meet up with an old friend. I, on the other hand, had to meet up with officialdom, mainly bureaucrats from the council, to get the parents what they wanted: the next stage in their families' Gaelic language education. The Holy Grail of the Gaelic world and just as elusive is the setting up of a stand-alone Gaelic Medium Primary School. This would allow their children to receive their primary school education through the medium of Gaelic. The end result would be an increase in the number of Gaelic speakers and bilingual children fluent in Gaelic and English.

These meetings were impressively boring and normally staged by both the council officials and GLADS. It was comparable to a dance where one moved forward while the other took a bigger step backward. Sometimes it was ladies' choice – outwit them quickly and complete the dance before they realise that you've got them on the floor. However, there are some things and people even we cannot control.

Most business books would say, be motivated, uplifting, smile, engage with people and be upbeat when trying to sell an idea to the general public. So why was I there on a cold and, yet again, snowy winter's night listening to a dour, demoralising but sincere expert in multilingualism trying to persuade parents to put their children into Gaelic Medium Education? That much-loved, Scottish, comical TV character, the Reverend I.M. Jolly, was more up lifting, and this was someone who was supposed to be on our side!

Thankfully, I had done a tonne of work with my parents, who laughed and commented, "Well, I'd be more likely to put my bairns to English Medium after hearing that. Just as well we go our own way up here."

"Why, what did he say?" asked another. "I sort of switched off halfway through."

This meeting was a simple case of turning up for the parents, so the education authority could tick all their boxes. "Yes, there are actual families here who want it." Tick. "Yes, they have the required number of children." Tick. "Yes, they are stroppy enough to fight for it and have that annoying GLADS backing them." Okay that is maybe not an official tick in a box, more a mental assessment, and finally, "Yes, damn it, we will have to provide it then." Tick.

I had to be there in case an unplanned-for tango was laid on for the parents. They could get left as wallflowers without hope of a Gaelic Medium Primary opening any time soon without our presence there.

"Well, we're off to the pub; want to come?" The meeting was over, the parents jubilant. They wanted to celebrate; they were finally to get their stand-alone Gaelic School.

I declined as the snow, by now, was making its presence felt, and I had an almost two-hour trip back home with a fellow passenger … when I could track her down. As it turned out, this task was surprisingly easy. Auntie Lottie was waiting beside my car.

"Agnes saw the start of the snow and couldn't wait to get back to her nice warm flat. She ditched me at the pub and headed home. That woman is way old before her time." Auntie Lottie shook the melting snow off her coat and curled into the front seat. As we set off home, the pavements were still wet, the snow unable to get a grip on them yet.

Once outside the town, the temperature dropped enough for the snow to get a better footing. We turned right onto the main road south, and the snow started in earnest. Very quickly the A9 became almost too difficult to navigate. The top of the moor, the Causeymire as it is known, is very open and winds whip across it with a ferocity and strength that can take drivers by surprise. What was taking me by surprise was the lack of road surface and the presence of all the snow across the road and not on the moors. I was in the position of being too far along the track to turn back as we crawled forward like a three-toed sloth.

"If we get, sorry, when we get to the coastal road, I'll stop and see if we can find somewhere to stay," I told Auntie Lottie.

"Not to worry, I've been driven in worse." I didn't hear the rest of what she said, but it probably involved a romance and some foreign, exotic destination. My attention was firmly on the road and the conditions. I didn't want to bash the car again with Auntie Lottie at my side. Each mistake would be gone over with a fine tooth comb the next time Ellen, Mary, she and I were in the same room. It was imperative that I got us home safely, even if just for my own sanity in the years to come.

Just as we started heading out toward the coast, the weather lifted, the moon broke through and the snow disappeared. The countryside glowed from the illuminations, the moon in all her glory taking on the mantle of giant, bright spotlight. The dark, cold North Sea mirrored the sky, and everything around became defined and sharply outlined in its glow. The main road was clear, no white blanket blocked our passage, hardly any cars, only slightly icy, just two lorries sweeping past. Awaiting our turn to join this pathway south, we could start to dream of our nice, warm beds that were beckoning us homeward.

Unfortunately, that was one sweet dream not to be realised, at least not that night. As we neared the Braes, I tried not to tense up. It's actually not as bad at night, because I can't make out the sheer drop down to the sea on the left-hand side. In daylight, I feel like I am going to go right over. I have to slow down and take the corner carefully, while trying not to look at the drop.

I was closing on the two transporters which were also obscuring my view, an added bonus as far as I was concerned. We all slowed down, then slowed down even further, then stopped and stayed stopped. That was unusual.

Cars can momentarily stop there while larger vehicles try to get around the hairpin bend, but by my calculations we, or at least the lorries, hadn't quite made it to the hairpin bend. Well, more accurately, our south-bound lorries hadn't quite made it to the hairpin bend. It turned out, a juggernaut coming north had but had not quite managed to manoeuvre around the corner properly and was slowly sliding off the road.

My heart was thudding for the poor driver. We could hear the engine of the north-bound transporter being revved and revved again, coughing and spluttering like an old man who smoked sixty cigarettes a day.

The gargantuan battle went on for what seemed like hours, until, after a final gasp, the engine seized. All went silent, and I was grateful that I couldn't hear a female screaming, because that would have been me. The monster going north, fortunately, was stuck fast which meant neither it nor its driver would be plummeting to their destruction on the rocks below.

Not so fortunately for us as it turned out. It was grounded just at the point on the hairpin bend where other lorries couldn't get past and neither could our proportionately smaller car. It was 10.45 p.m., and all was not well. Though, I suppose that depended on how you looked at it. The truck heading north was still hanging on in there and had not totally toppled off the road, so the driver was unhurt which was a blessing. I can't say how his head or heart were feeling after seeing that drop and having felt his vehicle slither toward it.

The driver in front came to tell me that the road was completely blocked in both directions, but the police had been informed and were on their way.

Unfortunately, the police coming from Sutherland couldn't get up to view the incident because of said lorry, but they were going to call the police in Caithness to get a recovery vehicle out to move it. This would obviously take some time.

How to whittle away time on the A9 Berriedale Braes past midnight at the end of November with a pile of cars stretching back behind you and the expansive, black sea in front?

Well, surprisingly, we were easily entertained thanks to our adventurous male population, though to begin with, it was my passenger who provided the distraction.

It was a big northern sky with thousands of stars and planets helping the moon illuminate the heavens, cool, icy and beautiful. In the only layby to our right, a twisted bare tree was silhouetted against the crystal shining night sky. My passenger, however, didn't seem to be appreciating this glorious splendour as she shuffled and shifted around in her seat.

"Are you cold? I can switch the engine on for a while to heat us up a bit." I said.

"Nope, nope, it's not that."

"Well, what is it? We should try and get some sleep."

"I'm bursting."

"What! Didn't you go before we left?"

"Of course, but we've been on the road now for a couple of hours." This, of course, was correct, and we would have been back home by now under normal conditions. "I really, really need to go." Given that we were trapped on a vertical, icy road with no level ground this was going to prove challenging. One small tree clinging desperately to the sheer side of a precarious layby was not going to provide privacy.

We decided, for decency's sake, that the only way to allow for some relief was to switch off any interior lights, open the front and back passenger-side doors and try to slip unobtrusively out to achieve relief. This was easier said than done as the beautiful, illuminating moon was acting like a searchlight and, soon, would be irradiating more than any female may have expected. But desperate measures were needed and quickly, so we switched off the interior lights, opened the two doors quietly and Auntie Lottie gently leaned out, slipping flat on the ground as soon as her feet landed on the surface.

"Hurry up," I whispered, hoping the other drivers were not so bored that any form of activity would provide welcome entertainment.

"I can't."

"What do you mean, can't? Just do it; you're letting in a draft."

"I can't. I'm coming back in."

"What's wrong with you? Are you finished?" In truth, I didn't really want the answer to that question, but sometimes, the mouth works before the brain gets into gear.

She clambered back, gripping firmly to the door handles as she could barely keep her footing on the steep, icy road.

"I couldn't." She laughed. "It's so, so cold out there that I don't need to go anymore. I think I've frozen up from the waist down."

That's more than could be said for the all the male drivers in the cars behind us. All night, we watched as men came down to see what was happening in front, which was nothing really. Then we watched as each male took out their mobile phone, held it aloft and tried to find a signal. To my knowledge, none of them did, but they continued to do this all night. It did not seem to matter if the previous person hadn't got a signal. They would, of course, be the one to succeed where everyone else had failed, because they were the one with a much better phone than anyone else!

Their business would conclude by doing just that – their business in the layby right across from us. We did try not to watch that bit, but we weren't that successful. There weren't really many places you could go when there was a drop on either side, and maybe, we were a little bit jealous of how easy it was for them in the first place.

It did help to pass the night away and keep us entertained, especially the mobile phone bit. Well, until a man knocked on our window to tell us that the tow truck driver had refused to get out of his bed the first time the police had phoned his house. The police were now on their way, personally, to his home to persuade him to get up and come and open this main road, so we could get away. We had been stuck for hours by then.

It was just after this point in the night that the males all stopped coming down the hill. The driver who had knocked on our window originally had looked a bit taken aback when he realised that we were women. Not surprisingly, considering he had just done the hold the mobile phone in the air act followed by the compulsory toilet stop. Word soon spread that two women were right across from the twisted tree layby that had so frequently been used as a public convenience by all males north of our car. I swear you could have almost heard a collective gasp in the still air. Regrettably, that put a stop to our entertainment for the rest of the night.

Finally, at 6 a.m., we were on our way. The police had eventually turned up at the pickup truck driver's door and suggested firmly to him that he get up, get dressed and come and do his job. It took probably about ten minutes to open the road. From that day onward, Auntie Lottie opted for the train north whenever she could.

Chapter 31

It was the beginning of December, and I couldn't see a thing but snow. Great blobs of it raced toward the windscreen. The wipers barely coped. *Air ais air adhart*, backwards and forwards just like my thoughts that jumped between the new housing scheme and all I needed to prepare for the festive season. I should have been concentrating on the conditions as I headed into darkness obliterated by white, freezing clumps.

I noticed no one had offered to accompany me. Auntie Lottie had opted to have a cosy night in with a drink and some good friendship. I, on the other hand, was trying to navigate yet another single-track road, although winter conditions made every road seem like it was single-track.

The reason for this desperate journey that risked life and limb was a quarterly visit. These visits to GLADS groups were to check on how their funding, language development and numbers were holding up. Nothing was allowed to interfere with these visits, not even the Highland weather.

Was that dark form a tree? Nope … nope … oh great, a stag! It was a big stag too, massive in fact, standing along with its herd, staring motionless at me through the snow. Perhaps they were frozen solid. I hoped they would stay that way, ice-covered and immobile, at least until I passed.

Going anywhere near the brakes in those conditions could result in spending a very cold night in a car-shaped igloo.

The seasons, or more correctly, the weather determines how to react when confronted with these majestic beasts. If it had been springtime, the whole mob would have plunged across the road in one mad rush just as I passed. Surging, running and leaping in what would appear to be a collective suicide attempt. Legs, hooves and haunches plummeting across the byway with little to spare between them and the car.

There were no other headlights to be seen in any direction that night. A quick glance in the rear-view mirror confirmed there was only snow. The joy of a car-free road wasn't really hitting the mark. I would have given my life savings to have seen some friendly lights heading straight for me. Perhaps I should have listened to all the warnings saying 'Don't drive unless you have to'.

At the time, I had felt I really had to. That particular quarterly meeting coincided with a crisis meeting. Without my input, our GLADS group was in danger of closing. My 'parents' needed me. Of course, there was always that part of my brain that whispered, *You've never had to turn back before, you've always managed to get there in the end, and you know what you're doing.*

That traitorous part of me was secretly excited about matching my wits against nature, but even it was starting to admit that perhaps, maybe, this time nature had the upper hand. Was that a glow in the distance? Halfway up the darkness, I saw a few small beacons of light beckoning. As I grew closer, the number of lights increased. My breathing returned to normal.

I optimistically moved up a gear. I was now speeding along at perhaps thirty miles per hour, though it felt like sixty. Car beams were heading in my direction. Great, nearly there. But the car lights disappeared. Where had they gone? It was at that point my numbed brain kicked in and remembered how the road bent, twisted and dropped down. The lights were still there inviting me forward, but I knew that it would take me at least another twenty minutes of driving before I was anywhere near the village.

Sanctuary was in sight, and so I pressed on. I really had no choice in the situation anyway. I couldn't have stopped there in the middle of nowhere, dark, cold and silent – there was no radio to keep me company as there was no signal. I had forgotten to put music on before I left, and I dared not remove my hands from the steering wheel. Even Auntie Lottie's constant chit-chat would have been a welcome relief. Darkness surrounded me as snow fell constantly from the sky.

All of a sudden, the blizzard eased. The village was nearer, and out of nowhere, I saw car lights again. Only, they were coming straight at me. *Breathe,* I thought. *Take your foot off the accelerator, swerve gracefully into the side.* Mirror, signal, manoeuvre just wouldn't have worked. My car gently hit a bank of snow then glided right back into the centre of the road again. I roundly cursed the idiot in the other car for being out on a night like that, while hoping any bump to the car would just blend into the general bodywork.

*

The hotel was normally shut at that time of year for renovations. Ellen, on hearing that I needed somewhere to stay, had called in a favour. The result was that the hotel I ended up staying in had a unique selling point – it allowed me and others to book in for bed and breakfast when it was officially closed. A friend of a friend sometimes comes in very handy.

As I climbed up the hotel's creaking stairs, I followed a sort of paper trail made up of small pieces of stripped wallpaper. The walls themselves were all half-covered in old pieces of flaking paper. The corridors were difficult to pass through due to the pots of paint, brushes and rolls of new paper that lined the whole area. All of which, I and any other fellow travellers were truly grateful for – at least it was open while technically being still closed.

Another bonus was I got the whole before and after effect. A few months into the new year, after the snows had plied their hardest, I went back to sort out a few leftover hiccups with the committee. The effect then was a warm, cosy, newly-finished, newly-refurbished establishment … well, until the following winter anyway.

I mulled over a travel brochure left in my room that marketed the area as 'an opportunity to roam through unique, beautiful and remote destinations'. It cleverly ignored all mention of winter which often meant that any hotels that are 'warm, friendly, comfortable and hospitable with a wide and varied menu' were freezing, unmanned, and you could count yourself very lucky (or not, depending on the food!) if they were serving any food at all.

I tried to text a thank you to Ellen as I was truly grateful to have any sort of accommodation. It could have been the only available room for miles, and I didn't fancy another trip through glen and mountain that night. Travelling back east at a starting time of 10 p.m. on a winter night was sometimes even beyond my intrepid skills.

I looked out the dark windows at the horizontal snow that hid the boats in the harbour from view and felt thankful it was only December and that I was inside. Winter often became a lot worse at the beginning of the new year.

I wondered who in their right mind would come along to a meeting on a night like that. But I knew they would, by four-by-four, tractor, trailer or snowshoes, they would come. Some complete with a child (which wasn't strictly supposed to happen). It was always good to see new members even if they were only a few days or weeks old. The meeting, like many others before, would be full of personalities, enthusiasm, tension, hilarity and goodwill, at least to me. It was officialdom who held the ultimate power though and caused the endless red tape that was generally the root of most of the group's problems. Goodwill was hardly ever directed at them.

*

After a couple of hours, it was over, with a new list of must-do's for me and a promise of seeing them all at the group the following morning. The chairperson, who was the linchpin of the group, voiced her concern that she might not make the session the next day. Her husband, who had dropped her off and was picking her up in the tractor, was also the person who gritted the roads. This would leave her without any transport. Goodness knows what possessed me, but I offered to pick her up and take her to the group.

Parent committee members gave up their precious time for free to run the family language groups, while I was being paid a small but precious salary. Therefore, I often felt honour-bound to be extra helpful.

The meeting over, I trudged triumphantly back to my digs, which was a fairly accurate description as it turned out. My car was blocked in on all sides by heaps of newly ploughed snow (courtesy of the chairperson's husband who had made a lovely clear, black, mushy road on his way past with the tractor). On the upside, the falling snow looked like it was turning to rain.

I was looking forward to a warm, soft, comfy bed complete with a stress-free sleep. Disappointment tinged with cold soon took over these thoughts when I started to change into my pyjamas. The room was at the top of the building, and when I say top of the building, really it was more like an almost refurbished attic directly under the wind and snow, and it was freezing. I thought some feeble heat was creeping from the radiator, but it was hard to tell. A force ten gale, however, was screaming through the five-centimetre gap under the door. It howled toward my bed.

On top of that, I realised my phone still did not have a signal, it was losing charge, and I hadn't brought my charger.

Damn, I thought, *my alarm may not go off in the morning. I can't afford to be late and missing breakfast is not an option.*

I knew the consequences of missing breakfast at that time of year. I had learnt my lesson on previous winter visits. Nothing would be open along the road on the journey home. No food shops, no cafe, nothing, until I got back to the east. I wasn't going to be leaving the group until almost lunchtime – I needed to eat breakfast.

Normally, panicking about not waking up in time would have been enough to keep me awake all night. When the bitter cold was added in, I knew there was no chance of getting any sleep.

In an attempt to combat the freezing temperature, I got out of bed and put my socks back on. When that didn't work, I got out of bed again and put on my jumper. No matter how cold I got, I refused point-blank to put my trousers back on again, so the next item to accompany me to bed was my warm jacket which I lay on the top of all the bedclothes. I reasoned in my numb state that I would feel a bit overdressed under the covers with a jacket on. Turning over would also have been a bit of a problem.

I must have dozed off eventually, because I was woken by the sound of what appeared to be my next-door neighbour having a shower. The humming of the pump and the gurgling of the pipes had dripped into my sub-conscious. I dragged myself out of my warm cocoon and bravely stripped off again. I rushed into the shower, which surprisingly was lukewarm. In fact, it was miles warmer than the room. It was, however, extremely noisy. At least any other fellow travellers lucky enough to have secured a bed in the technically closed hotel would know I was clean.

Still, throwing my clothes on felt wonderfully warm, and I was cosy at last. I stuck the kettle on and checked my phone again, 5.15 a.m.! On the plus side, the snow had mostly gone. Scotland's weather is as mad and crazy as our population.

My bed still beckoned, but there was no point in climbing back into that cold sanctuary. The thought of having to put on more clothes to go back to bed did not really appeal to me. My hair was also soaking wet after the shower, and I stupidly hadn't bothered to bring a hairdryer. I had forgotten, when I was packing, that I was going to a December technically closed hotel and not a March definitely open one. In March, after the refurbishment, a hairdryer, fluffy towel and warmer weather would all have been waiting for me.

By the time I was due to pick up the chairperson, I had been up for hours and was full from a very large breakfast with loads of buttered toast and tea and was feeling rather sleepy again. The thought of the icy bed kept me well motivated to continue with my day.

I reached the chairperson's house as the sun broke free from its cloud cover. The melting snow had turned to water and everything was looking fresh and sparkly. Despite my fears, the single-track road up to her croft was fairly clear of snow and the many potholes had a covering of ice that stopped me and the car rattling around too much. I hoped the down road would be as good. As we were leaving, I mentioned the lack of snow on the up road.

"I'm hoping this down road will be just as clear." I turned the car to the left.

"Well, we don't normally use this route during winter. We only use the up road. The snow and ice never last long there." There was a slight pause, and she finished with "Actually, we haven't used the down road for a couple of weeks as the ice just doesn't seem to lift from there once it has set in."

Why she waited until that moment to inform me, I'll never understand. Anxiety started to slide chillingly down my back, but by that time, it was too late, it being impossible to turn around on the track. We were committed whatever condition the surface was in. I turned to the chairperson, dragged up a smile and said, "Well, we'll see how we go."

Fast, would be the answer to that. Way faster than I would have liked and without any way to slow us down. As soon as the tyres hit the heavy-packed ice, we were off, like a bobsleigh whooshing down a toboggan run. Luge competitors would have been impressed. The baby certainly was, giggling and laughing as we surged forward and slightly to the left.

I turned the steering wheel – why? I have no idea – and used the brakes – once more, I have no idea why, as nothing was going to stop our race up and down and through the raised ramps of ice. A passing place loomed to our left, and I could see a few loose stones poking invitingly at us. Flying toward it, I braked and enthusiastically threw the car to the left, the back end caught hold of the stones and we glided to a stop, much to the baby's disappointment.

"Well, I see the road hasn't cleared yet then," the chairperson stated rather obviously.

I was still trying to catch my breath and was too uptight to reply. My boss would have killed me, if I had killed the local chairperson by sledging down a toboggan run … in a car! And worse still, shamelessly lost a child destined for the new school. On top of which, I would have had to come clean to both Ellen and Auntie Lottie that I had bashed the car yet again, this time by inadvertently partaking in a winter sport best left to the experts. Facing their numerous jokes at my expense was not at the top of my leader board.

Looking around, it became obvious that there was no way we could go back up the slope as it was, indeed, just one big frozen slide, covered in a depth of at least fifteen centimetres of solid ice. The only way was down toward the main road. Yes, a single-track main road but the major highway in the area and cars still sped along it.

Toward the bottom of the lower section were two corners, a big dip and then a straight run out to join the other car drivers. We had to time our run just right. No checking on wind speed and icy temperatures for the chance of gaining first place with the best run. Instead, I was checking on probability of other cars, speed of said cars and likelihood of crashing off the run and into the bracken.

Looking back, perhaps calling out mountain rescue with their lovely ice picks and ropes would have been the sensible thing, but we had a group session to attend, and nothing was going to hold us back. A silent agreement was reached, and we decided to be totally blasé about the whole thing.

"Are you ready?" I asked the chairperson at my side.

"Yep, we're all strapped in and raring to go," she cheerfully returned after first checking the straps on the baby seat.

I took my foot off the brakes and steered the car out onto the run again.

In spite of what had happened at the top of the road, the speed still took us by complete surprise, no build up, nothing. Just a terrifying drop at breakneck velocity as soon as the tyres hit the ice. We flew down the steepest part, whooshed around the first corner, raced through the dip with a slight decrease in speed which, for a breathtaking second, had us both worried that we were about to slide back the way we'd come again. Then with a stomach-turning lurch, we were evacuated onto the main road. The tyres gained their grip, and we were once more in the land of normality, or at least, what passes for normality in these parts.

Chapter 32

Finally, the new hall was ready. At last, for the first time in years, a wedding could take place in the actual village. The wedding we'd attended in the summer has been held in a church not far from Inbhirasgaidh. It had been one to remember but not for the right reasons. This wedding was going to be different; we could tell. No need for us locals to book into a hotel, arrange for pet care or a weekend away. We could go home to our own houses after the celebrations ... if nothing more exciting came along.

Weddings in the area were becoming a bit of a rarity. Partly due to fewer people getting married and partly due to our school-leavers going off to college, university and work and not coming back. This wedding, taking place in the depths of winter, could bring back some of the locals who had not been seen for years.

December is when the trees are mere silhouettes against the cobalt heavens. Big skies are seen most nights, and the weather is often clear, sharp and intense. Often is the important word here, as unlike places like Florida where you can set your watch by the rainfall, here we cannot offer that predictability.

A week before the big event, the skies were a sheer blue, the mornings frosty and clean, the hillside purple and orange, breathtaking as ever. Two days before the wedding, the skies were ink-blue, the morning as dark as the night, and you couldn't see the hillside for the debris flying past the window. The sea was roaring up the beach and being blown onto the road. White foam sailed around the village like strange alien creatures. Some houses were threatening to flood, either due to the rising sea level or the burn bursting its banks thanks to the heaving rainfall. Seaweed flew through the air as did washing lines, tin cans, leaves and anything else that wasn't nailed down. Rain slashed and cut into people, hillsides and tracks. Everything was dripping wet and torn apart. Roads were shut due to trees falling and the occasional landslip.

Unfortunately, one of these landslides was on the main road just before you got to the village turn-off. Lights had been flashing and flickering all day until they eventually went out altogether.

The bride, one of the few who was returning to live and work in the area, had always been one of those laid-back people who let nothing faze them. In her hurry to return, she had stuffed her bridal gown into a bag, expecting to be able to steam it in the village before use.

At least she was in the vicinity of where the wedding was to take place. Her groom-to-be, minister and half the guests were marooned on the other side of the landslip. The community bus, driven by the groom, and a host of cars had gone to pick up the visitors from various locations including the airport and the bus and train stations in Inverness. None had made it back so far.

As the day wore on, there was nothing anyone could do but batten down the hatches and hide from the elements. A dress rehearsal was scheduled for the following day, but as yet, not enough of the bridal party had made it back safely for this to take place. Unlike many a bride, Susan appeared relaxed and fairly content with proceedings.

"Ach, it will all blow over by the morning. No point in getting in a fuss; nothing we can do anyway." True, but at the very least, the ceremony required the groom to be present.

I awoke the next morning. Something was wrong or at least missing. It took a while before I realised what it was. No sound, not a whimper, just eerie silence, even the seagulls had lost their voices. The deafening wind had vanished. The same couldn't be said for the debris scattered around the area or the water that still engulfed most of the community. The calm after the storm was way more unsettling than the roar of the wind.

"You heard the minister has made it then. No groom as yet. Some of the guests have been delayed at other airports. One poor bugger had been wandering around an airport all day on his own. He got the last plane in and had to wait on another one up to Inverness that was sitting on a runway somewhere. Unable to fly with the storm so bad." Maureen was busy keeping us all up to date with proceedings.

No electricity had been restored, but at least, some more roads were open. The floods began receding during the day, and more and more guests drifted in. Clear-up work had started. There was no point in staying inside; it was colder and darker than outside anyway.

Once their own little corners had been cleared, villagers set about clearing a path between the cottage where the bride was staying, the church and the village hall.

A wedding rehearsal was scheduled for 5 p.m. in the hope that the groom would have made it back by then. Unfortunately, at the appointed time, there was still no sign of him or the other missing guests. The best man had to stand in with the bride's younger brother filling in for the best man.

"You'll be keeping him right tomorrow now, won't you, Iain?" Susan smiled mischievously up at Iain. Considering he was only standing in for his best friend, Iain looked as nervous as any groom on his big day. His face matched the red of his hair.

"Aye, aye, he'll be back in plenty time."

Eventually, at 10.30 that evening, the groom finally made it home with the rest of the missing guests, having shifted some of the rubble from the road to get through.

Electricity had still not returned to the area, and it looked likely that it wouldn't be around in time for the wedding. An ad hoc meeting between the bride, the families and anyone else who could make it to the hall had been called, and a contingency plan had been agreed.

Those with ranges, who still therefore had access to a form of heating and cooking, were commandeered to cook food for the wedding day. Large pots of soup were to be kept on the heat for those who had no method of heating up food. Those who had extra room, camping stoves, barbeques or anything that could heat water or food would take care of coffee, teas and snacks throughout the day.

A call had been sent out for extra candles, torches and other forms of non-electrical lights. The smell of tilley lamps filled the air in the houses of the most ancient in the village. Open fires were kept alight and those in totally electric homes were moved in with those who had space, heat and light. Both the wedding party and the community at large would be taken care of.

The wedding-day sky was once more a cobalt blue with tiny wisps of white clouds. A slight frost edged the countryside, the scenery was breathtaking. As the day wore on, the temperature rose along with everyone's spirits. The church without heating was no colder than it would have been at the height of summer. The sun was shining through its stained-glass windows which kept the atmosphere elegant, warm and bright.

No formal request had been sent out by the bride and groom, but they had managed to pull off a fashion coup that other brides and grooms would have struggled to enforce. A wedding theme had emerged naturally and was adhered to by all the guests. Everyone had either the same colour or design as the happy couple. The whole community of revellers was wearing wellies. Jill, however, had come up trumps. She had spent the night before under candlelight, gluing shiny sequins, buttons and nick-nacks to the bride's boots. The groom's wellies were not so dazzling but had been customised enough to make them special.

The parade to the village hall was led by a wellie-wearing, kilt-clad piper. Dresses and finery were lifted high to avoid puddles and debris. There was no point in stopping the children jumping in puddles, after all, they already had the right footwear.

Inside the hall, a magical effect had been created by the many assorted torches, and battery-operated spotlights and fairy lights. Tilley lamps wafted their distinct odour across the room and rows of lit candles were spread along the food tables. The wedding breakfast was unusual in that it wasn't what had been originally ordered, but given the situation, any food was a bonus.

Large pans of homemade soup were available, after all this was Scotland, and what celebration is worth anything if hearty homemade soup is not on offer. This was followed by a big pot of stovies, and there were sandwiches or egg salad for non-meat eaters. Pudding was a variety of what was available in people's fridges that needed to be eaten before it went off and any other pre-made food that didn't need any cooking. Packets of custard, tins of fruit, instant milk puddings and a mixture of fresh fruit was available. Biscuits and lots of cheese were also on offer. The cake had already been finished and delivered and didn't require electricity to enjoy.

Thankfully the entertainment was a cèilidh band who could play anywhere and almost anything. Musicians, as always, once fed, just picked up their instruments and set off at a rocket pace. The music and dancers got wilder as the weather and night got calmer. People swirled around the hall to loud, pacing, old and new Scottish tunes. Ancient and young, hooting and cheering the hours away. More cold food and snacks arrived as the night danced on.

Eventually, just as dawn was breaking, the lights came on. Feet began to complain, and eyes started to grow tired. The electricity was back and sparked the return to normal modern life. It was generally agreed that this was the best start the new village hall could have had.

Chapter 33

Snow, when you don't have to drive in it, can be a beautiful thing. Large, soft flakes floated down, tinged with pink. A peaceful silence settled over the village. There was no point in rushing as there was nowhere anyone could go.

Everything was covered. The muddy fields and puddles disappeared, and the litter and rusting objects became invisible under the thick, fleecy blanket of white. Voices became hushed as the snow continued to fall. Our burgh was cocooned and cut off from the rest of the world. A dream-like quality existed.

It stopped snowing. Voices could be heard echoing around the neighbourhood, children shouting and laughing in delight. People dressed in woolly hats, gloves and scarves started to creep out of doors with shovels and salt in hand. Snow was cleared, exposing rubbish that had been forgotten for a while.

It was not long before the children were running about, pulling sledges. Trays and plastic bags were grabbed if sledges from last year had been stored in forgotten places. Homemade soup was kept on the boil for frozen hands to clasp after the children returned exhausted from play.

No one could leave for paid work today, not with no way in or out. The festive atmosphere in the air was as real as the snow and just as fragile. Adults, finished with the snow-moving and already having eaten their share of soup and sandwiches, were now ready to join the children who had returned for the second session of play.

*

This is when the accidents happen. Almost without exception, it involves an adult, and most likely, it will be an adult who gets hurt. The children are used to throwing themselves about after spending a summer climbing rocks, dashing around in the sea and playing rough and tumble games together. The adults, on the other hand, haven't acclimatised themselves and have gone straight from indoor working to outdoor adventure. Running behind sledges and rolling around in snow takes its toll. As ever, it is on MacPharlin's Brae that any reckoning occurs.

Each year, when there's a large drop of snow, there it looms, a white Everest, waiting for its newest victim. The hill sweeps under a cliff and down toward the beach. During summer, cows and sheep graze on it, would-be mountain bikers darting in-between them, practising on the steep incline.

Unfortunately, a slight veer to the right is where a large amount of machinery is stored in the open for use on the land. Most of these appliances would not look out of place in a medieval torture chamber. That area obviously has to be avoided at all costs, otherwise someone could end up impaled on a spike or worse.

Here, you would think, is where the danger lies. But when snow falls, MacPharlin's Brae has the best and fastest run anywhere in the district. It is well worth the risk of impalement. Villagers, over the years, have turned a blind eye to the dangers. In any event, no one has ever come close to hurting themselves on the machinery. No, the real danger begins, without exception, when someone says, "Why don't we build a ramp with this?"

The answer should be, "Because any time we do, someone gets hurt." But the answer always is, "That's a great idea."

Ramps are built from the fallen snow. Someone brings along a shovel from the earlier snow-clearing. This is used to build, build and build. The end result is that most of the children have become bored and are off snowball fighting or sledging further away, enjoying themselves. The adults, however, are busy inspecting a course that would give the Winter Olympics a run for their money.

"Can you move that ramp a bit more to the left? Nope, nope, your other left. Yes, great, bit higher I'm thinking too." They never learn. As inevitable as spring following winter, heavy snowfall brings out the ramp course builders.

Once built, the test run takes place. Generally, a sedate pace, if possible, is set to steady the nerves. Every participant gets a test run, and if no one falls over, adjustments are made to take care of that the next time.

To hoots and screams of laughter, the adults take turns, gradually increasing their speed, whizzing down the track, flying off the ramps, through the air and into a soft snow bundle specially built to cushion any crashes.

Around about the fourth trip is normally the time of injury. Momentum has increased to a breathtaking degree, and competitors are beginning to get tired and wet. Someone goes over a ramp, gives a high-pitched scream and lands at a weird angle.

"It hurts. Ooh, it hurts."

"Ach, away man, that was nothing. Didn't you see Paul that last time? Not a scratch on him, and he landed way worse than you. Come on, get out the road."

"I can't; it hurts."

"Away with you. If you're going to play silly buggers we're all off for a wee nip to warm up." And off they go, leaving their unlucky companion in the snow. It's left to the children to notice the poor unfortunate still stuck there, sitting like a frozen turkey. After digging them out a little, thanks to the shovels that have been left from constructing the ramps, the children find that their patient's foot is at a rather inappropriate angle.

Thankfully, being high on the slope, someone normally has enough signal to contact an appropriate adult. That's an adult who has not previously taken part in the ramp-racing as they're all ensconced in the pub.

By the time MacPharlin's victim is taken to hospital, they're probably suffering from hypothermia. Often an operation will have to be undergone, followed by a possible eight weeks off work.

How will that affect the adults' behaviour the next time there's a heavy snowfall? Not by much really, only now, they will have something to cast up to the poor victim and laugh at their expense before zooming off down MacPharlin's Brae at ridiculous speeds again.

*

Christmas time was always special in the community, not because everyone was that religious, but because it was the time of homecoming. Men, mostly, who worked away from home, tried as much as possible to time their leave so they could be back in the village for the festivities. Students, who during the term had other more important people and places to go and see, never had anywhere more important than Blàs to come back to at that time of year. Even those who had left, living and working elsewhere, would try and make it.

"Ach, you know the festive season is on us – Grace has finally found the bus home." This had been the call now from

Paul of the Sheds for the last ten years. Grace, his daughter, was the third female in our girl team growing up. While Karen and I stayed put in the community, she had traversed the world on foot, bike, motorbike, and in a battered van, exhausting as many forms of transport as travelling companions. Financing her journeys was done by picking up work mostly in the hotel trade and occasionally as an au pair.

Regardless of where she was in the world, she always made it back, just in time. Grace was always the last to arrive back in the village and was now regarded as heralding in Christmas itself just as much as *Bodach na Nollaig*, or Father Christmas as he is better known.

As soon as the local children could understand about Father Christmas coming, their slightly older siblings would inform them that Grace came just before him. They could be heard asking Paul of the Sheds early on the twenty-fourth of December, "Is she on the bus yet? Has Grace arrived yet?"

Paul of the Sheds had long-ago accepted that his daughter would not arrive until the very last minute. If the last bus arrived at the crossroads and Grace didn't get off it, everyone knew that sometime during the night some stranger would drop Grace off or come with her and stay for the season. The bedtime story on Christmas Eve was not *The Night before Christmas* but The Night Grace Comes Home.

That year, I was bringing home the honoured visitor who proclaims the arrival of Christmas. I had a meeting in Inverness so picked her up from the train station on my way back. After we had caught up on what was happening in our lives, the Christmas question was asked, "Looking forward to Christmas then? I know everyone can't wait to see you."

"Ach, I'm so tired I'll probably just sleep most of the time, you know."

Actually, I didn't. Each year she would say this, and each year you would find her along with all the other unattached males and females celebrating in the local pub.

"So, we won't be meeting up later then?"

"Now, I didn't say that. I'll have to come out and catch the craic with a few friends. Looking forward to it."

We drove into the village. Bright lights sparkled and shone from most of the windows.

"Wow, that's new. I wasn't expecting to see lights already in the new housing. Are they all filled then?" Grace hadn't been home since the foundations were laid. The extra light that shimmered its way out of the buildings added to the magical feeling of the season. Frost outlined the rooftops, fences and cars. The community Christmas tree shone out in its own multi-coloured way. Another holiday, another breathtakingly beautiful scene lay before us. The brightest light, however, was coming from the pub.

"Just stop here; I'll have a quick pint before I head home."

"That's not going to happen. You know what we have to do."

"Oh, remind me why I have to do this again?"

"It's your own fault. If you hadn't insisted on doing this all those years ago in a drunken stupor, then the bairns wouldn't expect it now."

"But they're all grown up now. You know, one year I might not make it. Then what will you all do?"

"True, but they've told their younger brothers and sisters. Now you have new bairns listening out for you. It's traditional now. Are you ready?"

I turned up the volume on the music in the car so that Slade's 'Merry Christmas Everybody' boomed out. Grace leaned out of the car and yelled the song at the top of her voice. We stopped in front of some of the houses where we knew children would be waiting for just this before they went to bed, and we waved at them all. This was Grace's very own version of carol singing. Maybe not as musical, and definitely not as religious, but just as keenly anticipated.

Chapter 34

I couldn't' quite believe that my parents' generation had broken the tradition of cleaning the house from top to bottom on Hogmanay, the last day of the year, only to have the next generation in myself and Grace doing it all over again. Mark you, if it hadn't been for Mary, we would both have been in the pub.

Only, when I thought about it, would we? Grace, after her initial arrival, had kept a low profile. She had invited me, Iona, Ellen, Mary, Auntie Lottie and Maureen over for a meal on Boxing Day. But then stayed in with her dad, Paul of the Sheds, rather than coming out with Iona and myself to the pub afterward.

Karen and Jack had laid out a buffet on the twenty-seventh of December for everyone who wanted. The table was heaving as more and more guests turned up with leftover puddings from Christmas, snacks and crisps. The children all played and ran around together, exchanging news of new toys and goodies they'd received on Christmas Day. By night-time children and adults were flagging a bit, so most of us went home to our respective houses.

The twenty-eighth of December loomed, and I had to return Iona to Inverness to catch the train back to Edinburgh. We had tears and hugs and the usual promises of returning home soon, but we both knew it would be months before she would turn up again. I didn't mind; she was happy with the life she had in the city, and maybe one day, she would return to stay. Although deep down in my heart, I knew Blàs could never contain her, especially with Angus gone.

I finally got around to checking my e-mails on the twenty-ninth of December to find that an application to rent with a possible buy option on one of the semi-detached two-bedroom houses had been approved by the sales and rent committee of the Development Trust. I gave it scant attention as the doorbell went, and in walked Karen and Grace, along with yet more leftovers from the buffet and much-needed fresh salad for lunch. They knew I would be missing Iona and were here to rescue me from any brooding on my part.

"I have freedom from Fergus for a couple of hours. Jack has taken him sledging." She loosened the sleeping Lindsay's outdoor clothing and settled her down in her pram. "So finally, we get a chance to catch up before this one trots off again." Karen nodded in Grace's direction.

"Ach, maybe I'll hang around longer than you think. I've not made any plans to leave yet—"

"Aye, that'll be right," I interrupted. "You never make plans as we know. You'll just wake up one morning, and that will be you heading off, leaving poor Karen and me a duo again."

"And what's wrong with that? I quite like not having to share any goodies like this chocolate cake with more than one person," Karen replied. "Oh, before I forget, Ellen asked if you two could help Mary gut her house on the thirty-first. She is determined to do it alone, but Ellen is a bit worried it will be too much for her. She reckons she would accept help from you two but would wave away offers from her or Maureen. You know what she's like."

We did. Mary was very independent, and Ellen was right, there was no way she would accept help from Ellen, Auntie Lottie or Maureen. She'd be saying they had their own households to take care of. Grace and I were seen as free, young and able. No babies, children or partners to care for.

"Sounds alright with me," Grace said. "Shouldn't take us too long, and Mary is treating me, Dad and Ellen to homemade steak pie that night for tea. This way I can repay her for my dinner."

"Well, I have to be finished by three as I promised Auntie Lottie that I would pick her up and bring her home. She hitched a lift with me and Iona to Inverness yesterday to stay with Alice for a few days. I'm having my tea with them, but we'll be home to celebrate the bells with you all."

We spent the rest of the afternoon catching up on each other's lives. Grace confessed that the brief fling she had had in Brazil had meant more to her than she had admitted to us at the time in her e-mails. To be honest it didn't really surprise us. We had discussed it at the time and knew there had been more to it than Grace had been prepared to say. Grace who was normally so full of information and descriptions, especially with regards to any interesting males in her life had been pretty resistant when it came to mentioning anything about Marcos. All we'd go out of her was that she had met him at a lunch with friends. He hovered in the background of what she was willing to disclose about her life before she left Brazil abruptly, spending some time in Chile before heading back home to us.

"Anyway, I've got something to tell you both," Grace said just as Karen's phone pinged.

"Can it wait? I've got to go," said Karen. "Fergus has come off his sledge and has burst his lip, blood everywhere. I'll catch you later and let you know how he is." With that Karen ran out the door, struggling between manoeuvring the pram and trying to get into her coat.

"Okay then, spill the beans; what is it?" I smiled at Grace.

"Oh, it's nothing much. I'll catch up with you both hopefully before the year's out. I'd better get going too. I promised Dad I would meet up with him, and I'm already running late. See you later."

Only we didn't manage to all meet up together. I had to babysit for Jack and Karen while they took wee Fergus to the doctor to make sure his lip didn't need stitched. Thankfully, it didn't.

There was no sign of Grace on the thirtieth of December. I nipped round to Karen's to see how Fergus was bearing up and stayed for lunch. Then later on, I had tea and cake with Maureen and Mary at Ellen's.

Ellen's partner worked offshore and couldn't be home for any of the festive season that year as she had been home for it the year before, so we were all determined Ellen wouldn't feel lonely. I loved our quiet wee chat after all the festivities of that week. It was a pleasant little oasis after all the noise and partying. Maureen filled us all in with the gossip she had heard over the week. Lots of meeting ups, falling outs, breaking ups and patching ups that seemed to happen more frequently at around Christmastime.

*

The thirty-first of December arrived, and Grace and I had finished helping Mary with her cleaning.

"Thank you so much, girls. I've got a nice piece of fresh baking all set out in the kitchen for you. The tea is already in the pot. Come on through; you've earned it." Mary shuffled back to her kitchen. "Well, this is nice. I'm so glad I have the two of you all to myself. I don't often get the chance to have you young ones here on my own. Well now, so Grace, we haven't had a real chat since you came back. I had your dad in last night you know to fix one of my taps; it just wouldn't stop dripping. Such a lovely man is Paul. We had a fine old talk, so we did. Think he enjoyed having an older woman to talk to." Her eyes twinkled at Grace who, to my surprise, turned a deep shape of red and started squirming in her chair. I glanced between the two of them.

"Oh, nothing much to tell." Grace said unconvincingly. Mary said nothing just sipped her tea and silently offered me a slice of cake. I noticed Grace wasn't offered any. Mary obviously didn't want the distraction of eating cake to be a reason to stop Grace from talking.

Mary silently picked up Grace's hand and held it between her own, gently rubbing the back of it. "Aah, come on, lass. You have nothing to worry about. We are all your friends here." She lifted Grace's hand to her mouth and placed a fairy kiss on it. She kept hold of it and continued, "My Angus will be listening; he's always here and abouts next to me. I feel his presence all around Blàs, but here, here in my kitchen where he fed all you girls stories and cake, is where we felt the closest we would every get to being parents." Mary's eyes now shone with unshed tears. "This is the place, Grace; this is the place you can tell us everything. You're safe and loved beyond your wildest dreams. Come on, my love, it's time. Time to tell us now."

And so Grace did.

*

I was late arriving to have tea and pick up Auntie Lottie from Inverness. I couldn't have left Grace after she had told me what had happened in Brazil. Mary had eventually shooed us both out.

"Away with you both. I've a steak pie to get ready, and you, Stroma, haven't even defrosted your car. Lottie will be waiting for you." Mary shook her hand at us. "Go on now, hurry up. I want to see you both back in time for the bells at midnight."

Grace and I hugged and went our separate ways. She to make her way to Karen's to divulge her story. Me to finally start my journey to Inverness. First, however, I had to defrost my car. I turned the ignition and shivered as I watched the ice slowly melt down the windscreen like rivulets of tears.

Poor Grace. I wished she had felt able to confide in either me or Karen earlier. The need to get away from Brazil had taken priority over all her actions. I wondered how this new situation would affect our friendship.

I drove out of Blàs, my attention focused on the road. It had been gritted, but I could see it was still icy in parts. It wouldn't have taken much of a snowfall to make driving conditions difficult.

Alice and Auntie Lottie welcomed me with open arms. I think mainly because they were hungry and had waited long enough for my arrival. They sat me down at the table and filled my dish with the sort of warm, hearty food that sticks to your ribcage and lays down a barrier for all the alcohol that could be drunk on Hogmanay.

"Aye, get that down you, Stroma. Lottie was telling me you'll be out first-footing when you get back. I'm off to my neighbours' myself to see in the bells." Alice was ninety-four years old with the attitude and health of a much younger woman. She had buried her third husband and was well on the way to marrying number four. They had met at the local salsa class and were intending to dance their way down the aisle early in the new year. It was easy to see why she and Auntie Lottie got on so well, even given the forty-year age gap. They both radiated a love of life. As to first-footing, well, traditionally, Grace and I had always gone first-footing together around the village. We knocked on doors and were sometimes the first to enter homes since the bells had rung in the new year – hence the term: first-foot. We would wish everyone a Happy New Year, share a dram, then leave the householders with a wee gift of black bun (a sort of rich fruit cake), shortbread or a piece of coal for luck.

*

We bid Alice goodbye and *Bliadhna Mhath Ùr* when it came just as the first snow began to fall. Delicate flakes floated dreamily down as we made our way back to the car. Leaving Inverness, we entered the countryside proper, and the tranquil quality of the snow started to slip more toward the nightmare end of the scale. What could have been a merry drive home became a bit more threatening. The wind blew to gale force, and the snow flew past the windscreen horizontally.

"Well, are you going to tell me what's bothering you? You've hardly said a word since we left Inverness and don't even try to say it's the bad weather. I wasn't born yesterday, you know." I felt Auntie Lottie's stare, but with the worsening conditions, I couldn't take my eyes off the road. "Oh, for goodness sake, Stroma, it's hardly a secret; we all know it's something to do with Grace. For such a wild, lively girl she's spent way too much time being quiet this season. We've all noticed it, you know. Me, Old Tam, Maureen and Mary. Of course, Old Tam has her dead and buried from some tropical disease. We ladies are not so convinced of that. So come on, out with it – what on earth is going on?" Auntie Lottie started to smirk. "Actually, it has been sending Maureen up the wall not being able to find out what's happening. I suspect Ellen knows though; she has been so quiet on the subject of Grace. But we knew there was no point in asking her; she would just deny any knowledge."

"Well, it's not really my story to tell, but Grace *has* asked both me and Karen to let everybody know, so she doesn't have to explain herself over and over again. Oh, and Mary knows, she got it first-hand from Paul of the Sheds who was asking her advice."

"Crafty old soul that she is, don't tell me … Mary found an excuse to ask Paul around for help. Let me guess, help with a leaking roof or something, and then she produced the tea and sympathetic ear."

"Actually, it was a tap," I said.

Auntie Lottie was way more astute than I had ever given her credit for.

While the wind buffeted the car and the wipers fought with the snow, I told Auntie Lottie Grace's tale.

It was not an unusual one and as old as the snow-covered mountains that towered around us. Footloose Grace had finally fallen completely and utterly in love with the handsome Marcos. He had wined and dined her, taken her around the sites of Brazil and introduced her to his friends. He was rich, attentive and unmarried. He offered to buy her a better flat, so he could visit her in a nicer area. But Grace didn't want a better flat unless she could share it with Marcos full-time. He wasn't prepared to promise her that yet, so they had carried on as they were, until one day at work, she was called into the manager's office. He introduced an expensively dressed, middle-aged woman then left the room.

The woman was the mother of Marcos. Grace was warned in no uncertain terms to steer clear of her son. If not, Grace would lose her job and things could be made very difficult for her. Although shocked and hurt, she had no intention of obeying, until she was informed that Marcos was engaged to be married, and she was just his final fling before he settled down the following month.

Distressed and unwilling to believe that the Marcos she knew would deceive her like that, she left work and tracked him down to let him know how horrible his mother had been.

Only, instead of denying any of it, Marcos had offered pleas of undying love, much bluffing and, again, to buy a flat for her, this so he could visit her after he was married. Stunned and distressed, Grace stormed off, packed her bags and jumped on the first flight available out of Brazil.

She ended up in Chile, where she nursed her broken heart, threw up every morning and finally admitted to herself that the best course of action for the new life now growing in her was to head for home and Blàs, to the people who loved her the most.

"Aha, much as I thought then. Poor Grace! What a nasty man; she's a lot better off without him. Is she just going to stay with Paul … oh" — Auntie Lottie started to roar and laugh — "oh my, Grandad Paul, that won't look good for his womanising." And off she went into another bout of laughter.

"She's not going to be staying with Paul as it turns out," I said. "You were right, Ellen did know something. After Grace had her pregnancy confirmed, she Skyped her dad from Chile and asked him to look around for a possible home for her. He approached Ellen and asked her to keep it quiet that he wanted to put Grace's name down for a two-bedroom house for rent with an option to buy. It was only when Grace actually got home, and she saw the finished housing development that she knew in her heart that it was the answer she was looking for."

If only I had given more attention to that application that been approved on the twenty-ninth of December, I would have known something was up. Paul's name would have been all over it. The question as to why he needed to rent one of our housing development stock would have immediately grabbed my attention. As to not seeing Grace on the thirtieth of December, well, between picking up the keys to her new home and having her first baby scan, there hadn't been much time left for doing anything else that day.

"Just think, a new year, a new home and a new life – what better way to start the year for Grace. It will be lovely to have another new baby in the community," Auntie Lottie mused.

We drove out of the storm into the welcoming glow of Blàs. Fresh, soft snow reflected and sparkled our way home. Lights from the new housing development glittered out, sending their own bright messages of hope and encouragement. I looked forward to visiting Grace there when her own Christmas lights would be shining out along with the rest. *Oh God!* It dawned on me just then that Grace had no partner. Would she expect me to go with her to the birth? If so, I hoped she wouldn't transform in the way Karen had done during her labour.

We carried on through the village. Lights blazed from every home, creating a perfect festive scene. It was near midnight, and some revellers were gathering around the Christmas tree in the centre of Blàs. We had only minutes left to get to Mary's house. She threw open the door as we pulled up, and we ran inside.

A minute after midnight, Ellen, Auntie Lottie, Paul of the Sheds, Grace, Maureen, Old Tam with the ever-present Shep at his feet, Mary and I clinked our glasses together.

"What a year it's been. I still can't believe I'm home to stay." Auntie Lottie raised her golden whisky above her head. "To absent friends and health to everyone. *Bliadhna Mhath Ùr.*"

"Aye, *Bliadhna Mhath Ùr,*" echoed across the countryside.

A Little Taste of Gaelic and Scots

Scotland is lucky in that we have a few indigenous languages including English, Gaelic and Scots. The meanings of the Gaelic and Scots words from the story you can probably work out from the context, but here are a few translations for you.

Gaelic Words

Gaelic	Translation
air ais air adhart	backwards/forwards
blàs	warmth, kindness, affection
Bliadhna Mhath Ùr	Happy New Year
Bodach na Nollaig	Father Christmas
bùrach	untidy
cèilidh	visit/dance
craic	news
cròileagan	Gaelic pre-school group
fàilte	welcome
fear an taighe	compère (m)
greas ort	hurry up (sing.)
oidhche mhath	goodnight
Oidhche Shamhna	Halloween
robach	old/tatty
seann dùthaich	old country
thugainn	come along/come

Here are also some useful Gaelic websites.

Check out faclair.com if you want to look up the meaning of the odd word.

www.parant.org.uk for information on Gaelic Medium Education.

www.gaelic4parents.com has loads of information and audio for learners/parents.

www.ancomunn.co.uk for An Comunn Gàidhealach, the organisation that runs the Royal National Mod.

www.gaelicbooks.org for the Gaelic books council which supports Gaelic writing and publishing as well as selling books for learners to fluent speakers of all ages (including my Gaelic storybooks for young children)

There are many other Gaelic organisations that support music, culture, development and other things. Most can be found online if you simply key in 'Scottish Gaelic'.

Scots Words

Mostly the Scots words used are spoken by Old Tam.

Scots	Translation
ach	expression of impatience/but
afore	before
ain	own
anie	any
auld	old
awa	away
aye	yes
bairns	children
breeks	trousers

cannae	can't/cannot
cludgie	toilet
dae	do
didnae	didn't/did not
dour	gloomy
fae	from
hae	have
hame	home
hert	heart
ither	other
juist	just
mair	more
mun	man
nae	no/none/not
ony-whair	anywhere
oot	out
oure	our
oursel	ourself
peur	pair
richt	right
tak	take
takin	taking
tatties	potatoes
thar	there
wee	small/little
weel	well
wher	where
wi	with
yer	your
yin	one
yit	yet

For more words and meanings in Scots look up www.dsl.ac.uk to find the Dictionary of the Scots Language.

Some wonderful literary classics are also written in Scots, notably from writers such as Lewis Grassic Gibbon. Also check out Luath Press and other publishers for more up-to-date books. Children's books such as *Harry Potter* can be found along with other books in Scots at Itchy Coo and similar publishers.

Acknowledgements

Although this is a work of fiction, I would still like to thank the communities and the many hard-working volunteers who I have had the pleasure of working with over many years, throughout the Highlands.

Thanks also to my editor, Fran Lebowitz, who gave insightful help and advice. This piece of fiction developed into a much more cohesive and enjoyable story because of her comments. Also, thanks go to Sadie Rittman for her edit. To Kat Harvey at Athena Copy, a special thank you for your input, advice, help and proofread. Annemeike Leverenz, I know you are mentioned on the cover, but I still love it – thank you. Many thanks, or better still, *mòran taing*, to my first publisher Lisa Storey and the Gaelic Books Council. Your trust in me and guidance allowed me to carry on and write in English.

My writing buddies – both the once-a-month (mostly) children's writers and illustrators who meet in Eden Court and the occasional bashing-it-out writers online – thank you for keeping me motivated and on track. Special mention must go to Barbara Henderson for the encouragement, friendship and lovely quote. That's another coffee I owe you.

Special thanks go to my family who allowed me to steal the time away to finally finish something adults and the non-Gaelic speakers among you could read. In particular, I must mention

Malcolm who has supported me in so many ways. Lastly, Mum, your patience and guidance are boundless.

Mòran taing a h-uile duine/Many thanks everyone

Ceitidh x

About the Author

C C Hutton lives and works in the Highlands of Scotland. She also writes under the name of Ceitidh Hutton and is better known for her many Scottish Gaelic children's books. *Grumpa agus an Latha Fuaimneach* won Best Young Children's Gaelic Book of the Year 2019 at the Royal National Mod. She is registered with The Scottish Book Trust Live Literacy Programme.

Having spent many years dashing around the Highlands as a Gaelic Development Officer, she now divides her time between writing, book festivals and other events, workshops, school visits, Gaelic Bookbugs, and family and dog duties. She still helps to promote Gaelic when she can and finds it difficult to say no to a cup of tea. She can be contacted via Facebook or her website: cchuttonwriter.com

Ceitidh hopes you enjoyed meeting the community of Blàs.

Stroma and her friends will be out and about again in the next book due out in 2021.

If that is too long to wait, you can catch up with Ceitidh and the Blàs community on Facebook and at cchuttonwriter.com. She would love to hear from you.

Printed in Great Britain
by Amazon

62950151R00154